DEADLY DUEL

"Give 'em everything we got!" Justin Ross ordered his men as Sewell kept the chopper hovering directly in the path of the armor-plated black sedan.

The men behind him switched magazines again—the car was a half-block away now, gaining speed the whole time—as they unleashed another thirty round burst at the front of the speeding limousine.

"He ain't gonna pull off, Justin!" There was a tone of urgency in Brent Collins's voice.

"Steady!" Ross sounded confident as he smoothly replaced his fourth empty clip. Smoke drifted in front of the barrel until he pointed the weapon out the hatch again and sent flame out the muzzle in scattered, five round bursts at the blacktop in front of the car. "Steady . . ."

The car was almost on top of them. If one of them didn't chicken out, they all would die in a ball of fiery wreckage . . .

NIK-UHERNIK

WAR DOGS
#2
M-16 JURY

ZEBRA BOOKS
KENSINGTON PUBLISHING CORP.

ZEBRA BOOKS

are published by

Kensington Publishing Corp.
475 Park Avenue South
New York, NY 10016

First printing: March 1985

Printed in the United States of America

Dedication

This book is dedicated to the 2,594,000 who answered the call to duty and fought in Indochina, and the 57,704 who never came back . . . men and women who sacrificed their lives in hopes the people of Southeast Asia could live in freedom and tranquility.

But it is especially dedicated, with the utmost respect, to Army Captain H. Roque Versace and Army Master-Sgt. Kenneth Roabalk, the only American POWs to be publicly executed by the communists.

The Death Squads depicted in *M-16 Jury* were more phantom than fact. Many career soldiers and foreign policy analysts believe they were ultra-secret Army assassination teams unleashed during the Korean and Vietnam wars.

Some speculate the teams went "rabid" after the abandoning of Saigon to the communists in the spring of 1975, and that the government dispatched Special Forces and Agency spooks to mop up what was left of them. But others swear the military failed in its quest to wipe out any evidence of such covert, behind-the-lines operations, and that the teams exist to this day.

M-16 Jury is a novel, and as a product of the author's imagination, its characters are not patterned to resemble actual persons, living or dead. The villain in this Vietnam adventure never existed. To compare her with any public figures presently active in our democratic society, one would have to produce a traitorous woman capable of hypocritical political views and philosophies, libelous statements against America's war heroes and POWs, and treasonous acts she was never prosecuted for only because of a fluke in the judicial system she so vehemently denounced.

Nik-Uhernik
Beirut, Lebanon
February, 1984

There is no more bloodthirsty creature on the face of the earth than a well-educated young woman with liberal convictions.

—Daniel Ford

Man is a killer, a hunter, a conqueror, or, now that he has a brain—a technician. Man is what little boys play at being. What little boy ever played at being a poet or philosopher? The refinements—they were tricks of women to soften their men and keep them at home, thus ensuring female survival. And when you tamed a man—or any animal—you degraded him!

—Walter Sheldon

It may be that Vietnam will destroy all those who touch it.

—Henry Kissinger
October 10, 1969

The last soldier to die in the Vietnam War has not yet been born.

—Editorial
Paris newspaper
January 17, 1973

PART I

1

Bangkok . . .

Gray wisps of incense, floating out lazily from the temple, told Brent Collins the air was calm. He would not have to compensate for wind. The former policeman could feel the almost eerie shifting of humidity, though. And far down Witthayu Road, a wall of storm clouds was pushing sheets of rain through the neighborhood, accounting for the muggy change. But there was no wind. And quick as the monsoon tantrum had swept through downtown, it was gone, leaving only a faint rainbow as evidence of its passing. The wary sun had never even been threatened.

Collins tightened his grip on the M40 sniper rifle but let his eyes wander back to the sudden flurry of activity down in the temple. The gold-leafed structure rose like a lance four stories up through the blue Bangkok smog, and all around it, monks in bright orange robes were rushing about. Planning a diversion? Collins wondered, hardly worried as he adjusted the Redfield 3X9 scope.

Across the street, two U.S. marines were slowly

screening the ID cards of Thai employees returning to the embassy grounds from lunch. Open-air cafes lined the boulevards running out in all directions, and the sidewalks in front of the high compound walls were crowded with vendors and the odd assortment of western tourists.

The compound walls would not be a problem, he decided. Only eight feet high and topped with a few strands of barbed wire, the kill zone—four to seven feet above ground—was obstructed only by an iron grille network of narrow black posts. They had been erected more for decoration than security, and a good four inches separated the vertical bars. More than enough space for a few 7.62mm rifle slugs to squeeze through. At a mere 500 meters, it was a cinch.

Collins's left eye took in the round American seal above the archway leading to the consular office: it was the same likeness of a proud eagle, clenching thirteen arrows and thirteen oak leaves in its powerful talons, as could be found on the back of any one dollar bill. Above the eagle's beak were thirteen stars and the word: EMBASSY. Supporting the eagle: thirteen stripes and UNITED STATES GOVERNMENT. When Collins closed his left eye, blocking out all distractions, his right was focusing on a group of men just leaving the doors beneath the seal.

His target, a small Thai man in his early thirties and impeccably dressed, was smiling and reaching out to shake the deputy ambassador's hand. Collins brought the scope's cross-hairs to bear on the man's head. With the rounds he was using, he didn't anticipate a problem with distance, but any drop in the line of fire would still culminate with a chest hit.

Collins let his left eyelid flutter open again briefly: the five burly assistants Soomong Prasert had brought with him to the embassy were all reaching into their suit jackets now. Toward the bulges below their left breasts.

Collins took in a deep breath, exhaled, and let the left eyelid drop shut again. He slowly pulled in on the trigger now—the slight movement of his index finger and the sluggish beating of his heart being the only motion in his body just then.

And before the communist leader's bodyguards could draw their pistols, taking the deputy ambassador hostage, Collins's shoulder was being punched by the rifle stock, and the single discharge was echoing off tenements and storefronts all down along the block.

Suddenly decapitated, Soomong Prasert's rigid body made as if to move forward a few steps, arms outstretched now, but only toppled over onto its chest. Deputy Ambassador Andrews, mouth agape in horror, watched the man's spinning head bounce off across the embassy lawn. Flung with such velocity, no doubt, it was not going to stop until it slammed into the far wall, a pulpy, misshapen mess. Andrews watched, unable to move, yet, as a sentry's guard dog on the other side of the fenceline jumped against its leash, snarling and barking. Trying to get free. To pursue the rolling head that was leaving a spray of crimson behind with each new bounce across the grass.

Deputy Ambassador Andrews winced as the severed skull was about to strike the wall, but he did not see the actual collision between wire mesh and flesh.

Somebody had rammed him from behind . . . was all over him now, pressing him face-down into the sea of green, dew-drenched grass. Covering him up almost entirely.

Serves you right, Collins grinned inwardly at the ambassador's predicament. That's what you get when you mess around with secret, glory-hunting negotiations with the insurgency movement. Maybe next time you'll confer with your security chief first. Collins slammed a fresh cartridge into the chamber and moved his sights to the left slightly—onto the first bodyguard to produce a pistol. But before he could squeeze in on the trigger, a blur of a form was flying down off the visa building, and the burly Thai had lost not only his weapon, but several teeth and consciousness.

After that, Collins sat back on his fourth floor rooftop to watch the show: the rest of his team members had gone to work.

After taking out the first bodyguard, team leader Justin Ross lashed into the closest man, while Cory and Amy eliminated the remaining three with bursts from their snub-nosed, stockless AKs. Big Chad Chandler lay across the deputy ambassador, covering them with his pistol, while he protected the embassy official from any stray rounds.

Hardly had the gunplay begun when it was over. Five hoods lay gut-shot or otherwise incapacitated—all before the weapons clatter had ceased sending thunderous echoes bouncing down Witthayu Boulevard. And the leader of the Communist Party of Thailand, Soomong Prasert, would concoct no more raids into border villages, kidnapping young maidens just to keep his frontline jungle warriors happy. He would spend no more idle time intercepting the poppy caravans from the north . . . stealing the raw opium to finance his insurgency force, and selling what was left to Bangkok merchants who would see to it the death drug found its way to the schoolyards and playgrounds of distant America.

The man who had agreed to meet with the deputy ambassador to discuss limiting his movement's operations so that everyone would benefit now lay dead . . . beheaded. And with his head gone, as most Orientals believed, his ghost was destined to wander the scene of his death for eternity, in circles, bewildered.

The Thai government had never been consulted about the secret meetings. They had too much to lose, financially, should negotiations with the guerrillas begin and hostilities in the northern regions of the kingdom of Siam cease. The Americans had enticed Soomong from his rain forest sanctuary with promises of medical aid and a temporary truce, but the shifty renegade had arrived all smiles, and with a secret mission of his own in mind. . . . What better way to strike at the heart of the imperialist war monster than to capture and slay one of its many heads—the embassy in Bangkok?

But a turncoat in Soomong's own legion had, for a price of course, betrayed his plans to an operative in Nong Khai. When that agent turned out to be one of Mr. Y's people, instead of CIA, Ross's team was alerted to the mission and told to handle it. *With extreme prejudice*. . . . The embassy itself would not be alerted. If their intelligence wasn't up to par—well . . . after all, *they* were the ones to first approach

Soomong. It then became *their* problem.

Amy was rushing from body to body now, plunging the dagger from her calf sheath into hearts or throats. Just practicing. Fine-tuning her "cold steel skills," as Collins called them. Old Man "Y" back at the Pentagon had told them this mission might not even come off. Their snitch was a low-echelon runner. Untested. A turncoat of the lowest order. The positive turn of events had made Amy's day.

Since the team was between missions, what better way to keep them in shape? the elusive director of the teams, back in The World chuckled to his anonymous associates. And Mr. Y enjoyed keeping the military brotherhood in Washington—most of whom didn't even know he existed—guessing about his people's whereabouts. They'd really be mystified over *this* unannounced rescue.

In fact, it was coming off so quickly it was doubtful the press would ever get wind of the true circumstances. As long as the marines at the gates sealed everyone out—as they were doing now—until the carnage could be sorted out and a believable story fabricated. Hopefully they'd manage to lose Soomong's head in all the confusion, too, Collins mused as he watched all the action below. Now *that* would be jungle justice!

The slapping of chopper blades against the thick, muggy air was overhead now. As Amy slit the throat of the last communist gunman, Matt Sewell was setting the sleek Huey down into the courtyard forty meters away. The sloping hill was covered with grass, tang vines and flowerbushes—there was little dust kicked up by the rotor's powerful downblast.

The marines at the gates were glancing back wide-eyed at the black chopper as they fought to keep the curious spectators and visa-hungry, would-be immigrants behind the gates. They could not abandon their posts to investigate, and the sentries on the main embassy rooftop were refusing to fire on the white faces.

A squad of shock troops in a lorry was rolling up now, from the marine barracks, but already the commandos in black were racing across the courtyard, leaping into the gunship.

"All right! Let's move it! Move it! Move it!" Collins could hear Ross yelling through the clouds of teargas and multi-colored smoke Sewell had jettisoned from a skid pod.

Chandler holstered his Russian-made Tokarev revolver and patted the stunned deputy ambassador on the shoulder roughly as he jumped to his feet. "Keep up the good work, Andy!" he called out as he ran for the helicopter. It was already lifting off, but the lanky American sprang up and grabbed hold of the skids, and the others scrambled to pull him aboard as the craft rapidly ascended, heading directly into the approaching stormfront.

Seventeen-year-old Cory MacArthur tilted his head slightly as he surveyed the man sitting across from him. He was wondering what Brent Collins thought about when he saw a target's head pop off through his telescopic sights after his sniper rifle discharged. A few yards from the table of six Americans, beautiful Asian women were dancing atop a stage with slow,

19

hesitating movements. Dressed in glittering palace attire, with spired crowns and long colorful fingernails, they were acting out a love story with traditional Thai dance, barefooted. The other tables in the Grand Prix bar on Patpong Road had grown silent, attentively watching, as gongs and chimes emanated from the huge stereo speakers in the corners of the establishment. It was quite a contrast from the usual hard rock.

"I wish they'd put the go go girls back on," Chandler whispered over to Ross after taking a long swig from his mug of golden *Singha*.

"So what are *you* staring at?" Brent Collins reached out over the platters of *khao pawd* and made as if to latch onto young Cory's collar.

MacArthur slid back in his seat and almost tipped over. "So here we are in Bangkok!" the kid said defensively. "And you still haven't got me laid by one of these 'most beautiful women in the world.' "

"Jesus, youz guys," Amy all but choked on her Singapore sling. "Can't you just enjoy the show?"

"Yah," agreed Sewell good-naturedly. "All you clowns ever talk about is s . . . e . . . x. . . . "

But the show was over, the Thai dancers were scampering off, the stage lights dimmed, and a jukebox began clicking away. The bar was soon alive with Herb Alpert and his Tijuana Brass playing, *A Taste of Honey.*

Justin Ross, clad in a dull white safari suit, grinned but did not laugh with the rest. He brought his beer to his lips. The others were still in their swimming suits, fresh up from the pool, except Amy. She had spent the evening browsing the shops outside *Wat Phra Keo* and was looking her seductive best in a light, flowered sarong.

Brent stared silently at his teen-aged associate across the table. He could easily remember back to when *he* was that age . . . all those crazy, illogical thoughts. Collins, who had always been so meticulous and cautious about everything he did, especially on the street as a cop . . . Collins, who had only screwed up once in his life, (the consequences of that error had been a "life sentence" with Ross's team), never liked working with such a young soldier. Kids could be so unpredictable. But hadn't he proved himself, under fire, several times already?

Collins thought about a recent mission: the assassination of a terrorist squad leader in Tokyo who was planning to disrupt the 1964 Summer Olympic Games by taking members of the American delegation to Japan hostage. The political radical was, beyond any doubt, criminally insane, but such an aura of almost folk hero-worship by the man's fellow countrymen in Canada made it difficult, if not impossible, to publicly chastise him and discredit his international activities. The team had finally been sent in, and Collins could still clearly remember how MacArthur had spotted the target, despite his elaborate disguise. Moments before the terrorists were to make their move, the seventeen-year-old had caught them in a deserted corner of a marathon arena and maneuvered them down into an underground access tunnel, where the team finished them off. The location of the bodies was later tipped off to security officials, and word of the hit had never reached the newspapers.

Before that, the team had been in Saigon. In

November 1963. And before they left, South Vietnamese President Diem and Secret Police Chief Nhu had perished under a hail of bullets in Cholon. Young Cory had been one of the triggermen. With all he had seen and done, Collins marveled how the youth could still joke about virginity and losing his cherry to a Thai whore. . . .

In the background, the Latino drumbeat—out of place yet soothing in the dark nightclub—was fading out. Clouds of cigarette smoke were billowing across the space between the two Americans. Four slender women in haunch-hugging bikini bottoms and tinseltops were climbing onto the stage.

"Don't worry, young-blood," Collins laughed finally. "We'll line you up with a real cherrygirl before the night's over."

The female bartender, a buxomy Thai in her late thirties wearing a miniskirt, had glided over to the electric-blue jukebox and slipped in a handful of precut slugs.

"Nothing in the *Bangkok Post*," Sewell glanced over at Ross from behind his English-speaking paper. "Just a small five-liner on page ten about the marines at the embassy being 'reprimanded' for over-doing the fireworks celebration yesterday. . . ."

"Lucky the whole thing went down on Independence Day," muttered Chandler, clapping now as the speakers came alive with a medley of high-pitched hits from the Four Seasons.

"No mention about the chopper?" Ross's eyebrow cocked back slightly, waiting for an answer.

"Nothing."

"I wonder how they explained all the Thai bodies,"

said Amy. "Even if the embassy managed to clamp a lid on it all, surely the guerrilla leaders back in Nong Khai will blow this up into an international incident."

"If it's to their advantage," said Ross. "It's only been twenty-four hours. They're probably still trying to sort everything out."

"Both the commies *and* the embassy," added Chad. "I'll never forget the look on those leathernecks' faces when Matt's Huey made its appearance. Talk about a dramatic entrance!"

"Yah, them jarheads'll be talking about *that* one for a few months to come," Sewell smiled.

"I'm just surprised we didn't get shot out of the sky," Amy took a sip from her tall, frosted glass.

"I doubt the marines even had loaded weapons," Chad wanted to chuckle. "Poor guys get plopped down in the middle of no man's land, told to secure and protect a piece of the American rock . . . next thing they know, a jet-black Huey full of round-eyes is intruding upon their 'space.' What could they do? I doubt they were ever drilled to repel aerial assaults."

"Don't assume so much." Ross filled his mug from the pitcher in the center of the table. Collins carefully watched his team leader—he rarely saw Justin drink liquor—but there was no visible vibration to the thick forearms. Steady and sure . . . as usual.

Don't assume anything, Collins thought back to their training at LZ London. How Ross had caught him off-guard on a simulated jungle patrol, and disarmed him. How he had remarked he "assumed" the instructors were neutral and could be trusted—were not members of the opposing, mock-assault team. How Ross had marched him back into the field class-

23

room and written the word ASSUME in bold letters on the chalkboard. Put vertical slashes down either side of the letter "U," separating the word into three parts. He could still hear him clearly, even now. "In this game, Brent buddy, when you *assume* anything, you make an 'ass' out of 'u' and 'me. . . .'" Collins would never *assume* anything ever again.

The Korean War veteran glanced back at young Cory again. They were separated in age by only twelve years, and the time seemed even less when one compared faces. Expressions around the table, except for Amy, were identical as MacArthur, youngest member of the team, gawked at the near-naked women dancing frantically to the beat of the Four Seasons singing *Dawn Go Away*.

The tallest girl, perhaps an inch above five feet, with high cheekbones and sleek thighs, had discarded her top now, and as her breasts sprang forth, Cory's eyes lit up.

So much death, Collins mused, as the girl ran her fingers along the inside elastic band of her bikini, teasing the audience but refusing to surrender the sheer garment. *The kid's seen . . . inflicted so much death, yet he hasn't seen a single sunrise beside one of these Thai beauties. . . .*

Or so Collins *assumed*. He smiled at his own jumbled thoughts and self-reprimand.

"Another story here about that goddamned Wanda bitch," Chandler hacked up a throat-load of smog, and spit it out into a flowerpot against the wall. "Looks like she's going ahead with her latest jaunt to North Vietnam after all . . ."

Collins's eyes shifted from Cory to the amber

24

shades of women dancing wildly on the stage, but his mind was seeing his collection of June Wanda records back in The World. The different album covers of the rising rock star were rushing past him in a colorful blur, and he wondered who had the recordings now. . . . Now that he was roaming the globe with "the team" and hadn't been home in over a year.

June Wanda. Young, pretty, wavy blonde hair like Marilyn Monroe. Three of her tunes had already hit the Top Ten chart, and now some Hollywood producer had signed her to a movie contract. Something to do with the motion picture adaptation of a play called "Short Stories."

Collins had never paid much attention to her politics. He had heard she was an outspoken communist sympathizer . . . was publicly chastising the U.S. government for its escalating role in Southeast Asia . . . and now—so the gossip went—was venturing to Hanoi and Vientiane to stir up more publicity for herself and, they all *assumed*, her soon-to-be-released motion picture.

There was that word again. Collins grinned as the closest woman in the floor show tossed her bikini bottom at him. *Assume*. He not only wanted to avoid assuming anything about Wanda's intentions in Indochina, he also wanted to avoid all talk of politics. There were too many contradictions and hypocrites involved. All he knew was he liked the woman's music. And she *did* have a rather shapely body, for a bleached blonde. Maybe she'd do a poster someday. . . . But then again, as bleached blondes were false, so too could be her—

"Another round of *Singha*?" The grim-looking bartender had drifted up to their table. It was obvious to everyone in Ross's team that the man had a snub-nosed revolver tucked inside his belt behind the apron. Probably a Thai policeman. Off duty.

Collins glanced around for the female bartender he had seen earlier, but she was gone—probably the end of her shift. Her replacement was a depressant in an already dreary and smoke-clogged atmosphere. Collins' knew the owner of the bar was American. And that he was away for the week—in Hong Kong on business. There was no way the girls would be shedding their bikinis if he was around. The Thai government would close the joint down. But now an assistant was in charge, and Bangkok's Finest were not only "compensated for" but moonlighting as bouncers. There would be no interference from the law. The place was packed.

"Fill 'er up." He passed three 20 Baht notes to the off-duty officer. The man smiled for the first time, pocketed the bills, and headed for the bar. Neither of them felt any emotions about the transfer of money . . . how could you fault a policeman for scraping up funds any way he could when one day he might be fighting terrorists in the jungle, and the next side-stepping eight lanes of kamikaze traffic atop a little TCP box downtown—and all for a measly 25 bucks a month. His demeanor made the ex-cop think about the differences between Western and Eastern police-men, and yet they were really so alike. . . . Perhaps it was the cynical look in the bartender's narrow, blood-shot eyes.

Collins's own remark, "fill 'er up," sent him remembering all the pre-dawn lines he had waited in at the police gas pumps back in that steel mill town in the Rocky Mountains. Before they had stripped him of his badge and service revolver. Before they had spared him "state time" in the Canon City pen and handed him over to Justin Ross.

He had worked the graveyard shift for three years, and the worst part about end-of-watch was not all the paperwork awaiting him, but filling up that patrol car gas tank. Especially during the bitter winter's cold. His partner had been a senior officer. A nice-enough guy, but tempered with tradition. The other units were made up of cops who traded off topping the tanks each morning, but not *his* partner. It was always "fill 'er up," and Collins would always bite his lower lip and hum a Wanda tune until the twenty gallons were pumped into the hungry Plymouth.

A Wanda tune. *That* was why they got along so well, now that he thought back on it, he and his partner. For all they *didn't* have in common, the old geezer collected her albums too. Ignored her politics as much as Brent, which was unusual for small-town cops. On their days off, Collins had even been invited over a couple times for fries and hamburgers. A Wanda record was always on the turntable, and they would later critique the music more than her words.

Her words. He had to admit now, as he listened to another Four Seasons song blaring from the jukebox, he didn't know that much about the woman. Had there been subliminal messages hidden deep in her recordings that had been working on his brain all these years?

Born in the late thirties to a traveling circus family in Los Angeles, she had been moved to New York a month later. Expelled from school after school for telling dirty jokes to her classmates, most of Wanda's early education was given by her mother. Her father hung himself from a trapeze rafter when June was only thirteen, leaving no suicide notes behind to explain his actions. His daughter blamed the men who were constantly flirting with June's mother, an attractive gymnast with the big show, who was rumored to be involved in a new affair at each succeeding town they travelled to. At fourteen, she was given probation for attempting to kill one of her mother's lovers with a derringer. The bullet missed the man's head by inches, killing an elephant performing in the center ring when the tiny round punctured an eye and lodged in its brain.

She ran away from "home" several times, but where could she really go—the circus? A troupe of clowns always tracked her down and brought her back.

Her late teens were spent in relative tranquility, though she went over two years without speaking to her mother. Filling in for an ailing comedian who emceed an animal act at the circus, she was spotted by a talent agent who got Wanda her first taste of television: three minutes on the Jack Benny show, where she ran a trio of dobermans through hilarious antics.

After winning a New York State lottery, her mother sent her to Europe for several years of prep school. Wanda swallowed her pride and took the trip—she needed the fresh air away from the family: her older brother was heavily into drugs, and her younger sister had run away with a motorcycle gang, driving mama into lengthy bouts with depression. Then there were times when windows and furniture were broken to ease the pain, and Wanda herself showed up for work under the big top sporting a black eye more than once.

Upon returning from Italy, Wanda discovered a field which would later become her life's work: music. She spent a year as a beatnik band's groupie, and after a much publicized incident in which the group's drummer committed suicide in her apartment, she made the front pages of the gossip rags and received an audition at a Los Angeles recording studio. The tapes were flops, but the following month she appeared nude in a porno magazine, and her music received widespread air time. She became an instant celebrity, especially among the younger set.

And now they were offering her immortality on the screen. . . .

"Some *Singha*." The bartender had sent a young, top-heavy waitress back to the table with the second pitcher of beer and a free round of drinks on the house. Collins stared at the rich swells of flesh straining against the edges of the low-cut blouse as he handed her a satang coin. He wondered how so many of these women managed to display such healthy chests when milk spoiled so easily in Southeast Asia and was always in short supply and sharp demand. And come to think of it, he never knew a Thai woman who cared to drink milk when it *was* available. Maybe it has something to do with their glands, he thought. At the same time he was saying, "Punch a Wanda record into the jukebox there for me honey, will ya?"

A startled look fell over the woman's slender face as she stared down at the coin, over at the jukebox, then back at Collins. "Oh! We no play *her* music here, mista," she said, insulted. "The customers would burn down the bar!"

Brent glanced around. There *did* appear to be a large number of American seamen at several tables nearby. Could he really have been so naive all these years?

"Dumb broad oughta be strung up and executed in a public square," Chandler muttered, his tone drenched with disgust. He roughly turned the page, then, on second thought, wadded up the entire newspaper and heaved it playfully at one of the dancers gyrating to the beat of the wall drums. The woman smiled at the challenge, rushed forward and caught the paper ball between her knees. She quickly whirled around, tossing the newspaper to the girl beside her, who caught it between her thighs and popped it off the stage, into the audience.

"Yes, these ladies got magic legs," Collins changed his train of thought and challenged Cory verbally.

"I'm ready whenever *you* are, short-stuff!" came the brave reply.

Amy blushed and hid her eyes behind long, slender fingers. Attractive extensions of smooth hands that belied the skills they possessed . . . the arsenal of weapons they had handled.

Ross checked all their expressions in turn. He could detect no hint of jealousy in Amy.

"My balls are draggin', it's been so long," Chad joined in.

"Yes, they say Thai women are the most beautiful in the world," Collins repeated. As an afterthought, he glanced over at Amy. "Present company excepted, of course."

"Of course," Sewell slurred his speech and directed

a limp-wristed wave at Brent. The table erupted in laughter.

"I want the one in the middle," Cory pointed at the tallest girl, feigning intoxication as though it were an excuse for his display of arrogance toward the dancers.

"I doubt any of these 'ladies of questionable virtue' are available to gents of our doubtful integrity," Ross argued mildly.

"I know of a reputable bordello a few blocks down the street," grinned Chandler.

Cory's eyes were glued to the woman on the stage twenty feet away. Her eyes were locked on his, and her hands rested on wildly swaying hips that jerked back and forth now and then with the shifting drumbeats, but the team's teenager was watching her firm, youthful breasts bouncing up and down. He couldn't believe there'd be women more beautiful than her "down the street."

"I want *her*!" he insisted, upending the table now as he charged the stage. The girls instinctively covered their bare G-strings with fanned fingers, but Chandler and Collins managed to catch young Cory by the arms.

With Sewell directing traffic through the bar patrons with robot-like, waving arms, the team dragged the kid outside into the clamor of bumper-to-bumper taxis, and headed for a sparkle of red and pink neon lights down the block.

2

*At the Hanoi Hilton, an American POW center
in North Vietnam. . . .*

Colonel Southe drew his chin in, attempting to
shield his teeth from the guard's boot, but the North
Vietnamese sergeant merely corrected his aim so that
the thick heel glanced off the side of the American's
head, martial-arts style. The impact of hard rubber
against his temple drove Col. Southe toward the black
pit of unconsciousness again, but the camp guard was
good: he would allow no such relief. The stocky Asian
reached toward the cell door, picked up a wooden
bucket, and splashed the airman's face with it.

The force with which the water was hurled at him
made the colonel swing about slightly, for he was suspended from the ceiling by wires, nearly upside-down
now. And when his head came back to face the NVA
sergeant, another heel blow slammed against his ear.
Waves of intense pain racked the man. From the
short, sparse hairs on his head, down along his shoulders and ribcage. Bolts of light and multicolored stars
flashed behind his closed eyelids. He could feel an-

other kick coming toward him, slicing through the oppressive heat in the cell, but it merely glanced off his forehead this time. At least the sonofabitch is ignoring my teeth, Col. Southe thought, his own words fighting to be seen in his mind's eye, each syllable a stab of pain, competing with all the brilliant stars. At least the bastard is not trying to kick out my teeth like he did Subowski's.

Col. Southe knew nearly all his teeth were abscessed. Some nights he'd wake up gagging on the flow of pus into his stomach. The guards would toss cruel insults at him in lieu of medication—never once had they summoned a doctor—and he was sure it would be only a matter of months before he was totally gums. He would throw up in the corner of his cell, and they would make him live with the stench for days before directing him to clean out the mess himself. Mornings he would awake with the taste of blood in his mouth, from the soft gums. One could only survive on pumpkin soup for so long. . . .

The guard gently placed his hands on the American's head to steady him. There was nothing the colonel could do to either cooperate or not cooperate . . . only keep his mouth shut and try to dodge the blows. His ankles were bound with leather manacles that hadn't been off in two weeks now. His wrists were tied behind his back with chicken-wire so tightly that the strands were cutting through the flesh. Rivulets of blood trickled down onto the small of his back. The guards had, after tying him up like cattle bound for slaughter, looped thick ropes that fell from a pulley in the ceiling up, under, and around his emaciated biceps, and jerked him off the ground. The shoulders

33

were forced taut, arms nearly plucked from their sockets. Carefully calculated, excruciating pain that refused to subside was the result.

After the sergeant steadied Col. Southe, he smiled broadly and whispered into the pilot's ear. "You cooperate now, Colonel?" The man ran a rag along the line of sweat on the American's forehead. "Just a little visit with our guests. Just a little show to prove to the world how well we North Vietnamese treat our prisoners of war. . . ."

Were it not for the pain lancing through his upper torso, Southe would have grinned back: the bastards were clever. Torture his airman ass to the limit, but leave his face unmarked. Nice and pretty for the cameras. Unabused, for the press that must be waiting in a pleasantly furnished room somewhere on the other side of the prison compound.

"I am a prisoner of war . . ." Col. Southe began the usual boring response. He was not about to cooperate with the enemy or any naive Cong sympathizer they had flown over from Berkeley. The gears in his mind meshed in protest, *I don't need all this grief . . . why me? . . .* while all the time he was continuing his conditioned reply, "And under the rules of the Geneva Convention—"

The sergeant's knee came up like a bouncing-betty landmine . . . suddenly, without warning. Exploding into his chest.

The assault sent him spinning around again, and the movement caused the wires and ropes to tighten up, sending fresh bolts of pain down through his limbs.

"I am a prisoner of—" he tried again, well aware

34

that if the guard gave up on him, he just might lose his teeth after all. The sergeant whirled around, almost casually, like he was working out in a gym, and caught Col. Southe's cheek with a fierce, open-handed slap.

Blood splashed into his eyes. He did not need any of this. Why didn't he just cooperate. . . . Blakerz had cooperated just last month, and they had treated him to fish heads and seafood instead of that watery pumpkin soup, but now Blakerz was gone, and nobody knew where they had taken him.

"The Geneva Convention guarantees me—" but another kick landed against his ribs and Col. Southe began to gag and cough like he was about to vomit. He wanted to laugh past the tears: they had torn his laminated Geneva Convention card up in front of him just . . . last year, was it?

"You need only agree to pose for a few photos," the Weasel snickered. Southe and the other POWs, through their intricate cell-to-cell conversation codes of thumps and taps, coughs and wheezes, had nick-named the NVA sergeant "the Weasel" because he walked with a suspicious stoop and had beady, probing eyes only a weasel would have—though Southe had to admit he couldn't remember the last time he had seen a genuine weasel face to face. "Just a five minute session so you can say hello to the folks back home, eh?" the Weasel's rank breath, heavy with the stench of *nuoc-mam* and so close to his face again, sent a nauseating shudder through the colonel—he could not back away from the intrusion of space and thought. And the Asian's precise English only served to add to the frustration Southe was experiencing just then.˘

"Cram it where the sun don't shine!" the American shot back as he swung helplessly from the ceiling, vulnerable to more unprovoked assaults. A squadron of ants seemed to be sliding down the wires holding him off the ground just so they could bite into his wrists . . . or was it just the chicken-wire?

The Airman's Code of Honor was flashing down at him, the words pulsing, lit in bright blue neon . . . he could see visions of his co-pilot smiling proudly over the heavenly display, face floating in the clouds. But Col. Southe also knew there were only bricks and a cement ceiling above his head, and the hallucinations faded.

Again, a heavy boot glanced off his side, sending him twirling beneath the wires and ropes.

"*Du roi!*" a voice from the shadows interrupted the attitude adjustment session. *Enough!*

The voice sounded to Southe like one of the camp officers, but the bolts of pain racking the space between his ears was affecting his hearing now. The ever-present dull aches he had experienced since being shot out of the sky over Haiphong Harbor were now bursting into secondary explosions that seemed to block out all other sound around him. The conversation in rapid Vietnamese between the two Asians was forced away, beyond the wall of hurt. Now he could hear only his heart pounding and his skin stretching against the wires, tearing . . . the roots of his hair alive, screaming in protest, but he didn't care anymore. The pain was numbing, all-encompassing, and soon it felt like his mind was almost separate from his body; not looking down on it, but in a different dimension entirely.

And then, though he knew he was still conscious . . . still enduring, the pain grew so intense that the mind blocked it out, and he was just hanging there, suspended in space, eyes tightly shut, watching the falling stars.

Col. Southe did not feel it when Sgt. Weasel released the ropes and he crashed to the cement floor. There was a vague sensation from the cool concrete against his face, and then they were dragging him back to his cell.

After he was deposited roughly beside his sleeping mat, the Weasel muttered something about *round-eyed D-ua*—"fool!"—and the iron door slammed shut.

Visions of his RF-4C Phantom being struck by flak and crashing like a billowing fireball into the harbor were flashing through Col. Southe's mind now as the pain started to roll back over him. Like a projector showing some worn, multi-spliced black-and-white newsreel, he was seeing a mob of North Vietnamese civilians pummeling his co-pilot with rakes and hoes after the fishing boat had dragged them to shore. He could hear his own voice screaming that their flight had only been an unarmed recon mission, but the villagers were yelling louder, uncaring, smashing shovels and machetes against the young lieutenant now. Until he was dead. Dead as the school of fish floating to the surface of the oil-slick waters along the bank, a swirl of bubbles still rising from the wreckage.

Southe had sustained a compound fracture of the left leg when his ejector malfunctioned, but despite the grisly chunks of brilliant white bone protruding from just below his knee, they dragged him harshly through the dirt, and would have killed him then and there had the lorry full of screaming soldiers not driven up in time to save him.

Save him for the camps.

He was seeing his wife's face now. Poor Therese. He could see her surrounded by family and friends those first few days, chin up, proud, terrified. Persevering. Trying to comfort the daughter in high school who had to endure the waves of anti-war sentiment from her peers.

Southe spent the next twelve hours lying in silence. And darkness. Healing. Recuperating from the constant stabs of pain. They were still there, but had lessened considerably. Now that he was back on home turf, in his private little fortress of solitude.

There was no way to gauge the time of day. For the last six months, he had been incarcerated in that wing of the compound reserved for "uncooperative prisoners." The windows were bricked shut, and light bulbs burned 24 hours a day. Sleep was not a relief, or escape, but a task—something difficult to achieve at times. But they had uncharacteristically extinguished the bulb in his cubicle. The cells on either side were lit up, though, chasing away total darkness, but at least his eyes were not subjected to the usual, perpetual assault of soul-probing light.

After the guards' footsteps faded down the hallway and a distant door slammed shut, there came a soft tapping . . . and a dull ringing in the bar that ran along the floor, connecting all the cell doorframes together.

Morse code.

Are you okay?

Southe ignored the American in the adjacent cell. He was too weak to move. Too sore to respond, except to smile back with his thoughts in appreciation. His rasped, uneven breathing against the muggy, humid air in the narrow, one story structure was his only response. The pilot next door would understand.

A few hours later, Southe had summoned the energy to roll over onto his side. Moments after that, he was sitting up. He vaguely remembered noises in the back of his mind . . . doors grating open, prisoners being hustled out onto the work details. And the noise made when his meager bowl of pumpkin soup was slid under his cell door.

He glanced down to his right. Weasel had pushed a platter of uncooked rice—maybe fifty grains at most—into his cell. Variety: the spice of life. Or Weasel's black sense of humor. Obviously, he was being punished. No soup today.

He lifted the bowl to his nose and sniffed. One of the guards had urinated on it. The odor made him wonder how often they relieved themselves in the big vat of pumpkin soup.

There came a slight squeaking from the shadows at his feet, and Southe smiled, moving his legs aside painfully so the dim shafts of light from outside his cell could lance in.

"Why Little Joe. . . ." His expression perked up, though he did not smile. "I was beginning to wonder about you. . . . Where you been, young man? Out romancing the ladies?"

A foot-long gray rat scampered out toward the airman, pausing a respectable distance in front of him.

Southe slowly slid the platter of rice out to it, and the rodent sniffed at the gift a few times, puckered its snout as if offended, then quickly snatched up some morsels and rocked back on its haunches, staring back at the big American as it chewed away, suddenly content and unworried.

Slowly, so not to startle his "guest," Southe reached over and slid a portion of the bamboo frame from the wall where it met the floor. He pulled out a small roll of cloth which, when unfurled, became a tiny American flag the size of a matchbook, attached to a toothpick. He had painstakingly constructed it over the months, from bits of thread and cloth.

He tried to massage his upper arms, but merely touching them sent fresh bolts of pain coursing through him.

He began to wonder if it was all worth it. If spending years in an Asian torture chamber—not even knowing the length of your sentence—was worth the lousy thousand-a-month.

But each time he stared at the red, white and blue flag, the sight of the stars sent a tingle through him, and he thought about his daughter back in The World and how she was probably saying the Pledge of Allegiance right then.

Col. Southe began humming *God Bless America* under his breath, and as the tears of loneliness and abandonment and desperation slid down his cheeks, Little Joe stared back at him unblinking, balanced on his haunches, silently munching away at the soiled rice. Uncaring, but never taking his wary little eyes off the man.

Bangkok. . . .

Cory MacArthur's right eye popped open and he felt a sudden spurt of weak adrenaline course through his gut, but it didn't make it past the pit of his stomach. His body ached. He was exhausted. His head was throbbing. And he was face-down on the floor.

There was a strange pinging noise assaulting his ears . . . *Snipers?*

He tried to open his left eye. The shag carpet kept it shut, though he didn't realize this yet. There was still no feeling in his face. His whole head was numb, like a steamroller had bounced over it.

He commanded his right eye to scan out to the side: it was daylight, but there were no shafts of sunlight filtering in through the bamboo drapes along the far wall. Twenty feet away, but it seemed like light years.

A short distance from his face, a woman's pantyhose lay in a light, fluffy pile on the floor, beside a pair of high heels—one standing up, one on its side. He forced his eye to the edge of its socket, taking in the blurred object beside him: a flowered miniskirt hanging from a brass bedpost.

There came a sleepy groan from behind him somewhere—a woman's voice, laced with fatigue. Just now waking.

Visions of a crowded bar rushed back at him now as he tried to match a face to the sound. A dozen girls in white dresses, lined up behind a glass menagerie. . . .

He vaguely remembered following Chandler and

41

Sewell back to their hotel room with three beautiful Thai women. Prostitutes, none of them would deny it, but gorgeous all the same. Worn, but still sophisticated.

But damn: *what was he doing on the floor?*

He felt his arm moving beneath him—though he couldn't recall sending the mental signal—and then he was pushing himself up off the carpet.

He was lying between two beds. And what suddenly bothered Cory MacArthur was that his pants were still on. As well as his boots.

"What the fuck?" He rose to his knees and glanced around, suddenly dizzy. Like somebody just smacked him in the head with a baseball bat, but when he looked, there was nobody back there. Sheets of rain were beating against the bugwire across the window. There was no glass. A ceiling fan twirled lazily overhead. The relentless waves of monsoon downpour against the tin roof above accounted for the pinging sensation in his ears.

A man's foot was protruding from the bedsheets next to him. God, I *hope* that ugly thing belongs to a man! he thought. Otherwise we really struck out at the meat market last night! He grabbed onto it for support as he pulled himself to his feet. Matt Sewell sat up groggily as his ankle was twisted about.

"Hey, mo-fuck!" he growled in protest.

"Where's Collins?" Cory demanded, checking his forearm, but the wristwatch was gone.

Sewell frowned and shifted to his stomach, draping an arm around the naked goddess sprawled out beside him, upturned breasts like jagged peaks beneath the white sheet. Beckoning anyone man enough to climb her.

"Wrong hotel," muttered Sewell.

Cory shook his head, bewildered. Where had the night gone? The motion set his temples to throbbing again. He could remember the four of them leaving the whorehouse, together, arm in arm, the evening's delight between them. Collins and Amy had disappeared somewhere, and the rest of the night was a blank. They had had a *Singha* drinking contest with the girls and *he* had lost.

Had he passed out before he even had the chance to wipe the smirk off the long-haired, almond-eyed, enchantress Ross had hand-picked for him?

And where the hell was that goofy Justin anyway?

Cory staggered over to the other bed and ripped the sheet off.

Chad Chandler lay between the remaining two women, dead to the world, snoring loudly. Long, sleek, golden thighs were tangled all over him, and both girls gave Cory only a passing glance before laying their heads back across the hairy chest.

"Well don't this suck?" Cory muttered. He stumbled over toward the window. A sudden thought made him check a rear pocket, but the wallet was gone. "Well, shee-it . . ." He leaned against the windowsill, too weak to do any more complaining for a few minutes. ". . . And I don't even get laid for all my trouble . . ." At least he couldn't remember if he had, and *that* was the worst part about it.

Cory glanced out the window, to the streets four stories below. Baht buses and brightly decorated lorries clogged the six lane boulevard, and a raised median, covered with flowers, extended down the middle, rainbow-like, as far as the eye could see. Countless sheets of rain were sweeping over the crowds on the side-walk—some stood unaffected before fruit vendors, protected by pink or purple umbrellas. Others dashed through the streets for cover, newspapers over their heads, ignoring the skidding traffic and protesting horns—and though the clouds loomed ominously low overhead as they swirled past, rainbow arcs shot down here and there. A white disc was fighting to shine through the overcast. Cory guessed it to be about mid-afternoon.

From this vantage-point, he could look past the rooftops across the street, to the line of palm trees that appeared more like controlled landscaping than in-truding jungle. Off to the right, rice paddies extended to the horizon, like a grid network of vast green step-ping stones—each a different shade of lush flora. Cory could see a farmer guiding a wooden plow that was being pulled by a huge, powerful, water buffalo. The animal, pausing now and then to submerge its snout in the flooded field to snack on rice stalks, seemed bored. Beyond the dark old cursing man in baggy shorts were two more water buffalos, submerged to their bellies in muck, waving their horns back and forth at clouds of mosquitoes as little children walked on their backs.

"Stupid kids gonna get their necks broken," he muttered, but the water buffalos appeared to be ignor-ing the children. One naked boy slid off, disappearing into the muck, but he was soon climbing back up—using the animal's tail as a rope—smiling, embar-rassed, as the others made fun of him and resumed their horseplay.

44

"Huh? What . . ." Sewell was sitting up again.

"Aw, nothin'," Cory sounded as disappointed as he could. "I was just talkin' to myself."

"Why don't you go get us all something to eat," Sewell suggested.

Chandler was stirring now too, at the prospect of food after so many hours of lovemaking, drinking, and more lovemaking. "Yah," he agreed, taunting the youngest member of the team. "Breakfast in bed would be nice . . ."

"Why don't you two just chow-down on those beavers ya got there!" he said sarcastically on his way out the door. It slammed shut behind him.

Cory had no idea where to go from there. Or where he was, for that matter. The room he had just left was located at the end of a narrow hallway. His eyes scanned the corridor to his left: brown teakwood with panelled walls. Small green fans in the ceiling that were turned off. Two women a hundred feet away, at the end of the hallway. Beside the elevator. In peasant garb, ironing some clothes. Maids.

He took in a deep breath and started toward them, reminding himself this was not Vietnam. Ignore the black pajama bottoms. This is Thailand. The house-girls wouldn't be communist here.

One of the women turned to look at him as he got halfway down the hallway, but she just as quickly turned away and hid her face in her work.

Not even a giggle, he was amazed. "Do you know Ross?" he asked. "Mister Ross? Do you know which room he is in?"

The woman who had looked at him earlier turned again. She avoided his eyes, staring at his lips—or his

45

chin?—as she smiled tightly and shook her head no.

Cory decided she must be in her late teens: eighteen or nineteen. Older than himself, but not by much. High cheekbones. Maybe Hmong. He could tell her hair was very long, but right now it was tied up in a bun that rested haphazardly across her neck in the back, between the shoulderblades. Her fingers were long and delicate as she continued ironing dull, khaki shirts. The top few buttons of her blouse were open and he could see she had more than an ample supply of chest compared to the other Thais he had seen on the street. The bottoms of her feet looked rough as sandpaper. *Farmer's daughter*, he laughed to himself.

The woman beside her was older, perhaps middle forties. All business, no smile. Perhaps she couldn't smile: it looked like she had been the victim of an accident in her youth. A long, jagged scar disfigured her face from behind the left eye to her throat. She continued sprinkling the shirts with water from what had once been a bottle of window cleaner, ignoring him totally, and the younger girl would then iron over the sprayed area. The iron was an old one with no capacity to hold water in it.

"No Mister Ross?" he mimicked a large, broadshouldered man.

The younger woman giggled and rushed her hand up to cover her mouth in that peculiar Oriental reflex, but the older one snapped back at him, "You go check downstairs with receptionist, sir." She never once looked up at him, and her fluency took Cory by surprise.

The elevator, shaking and clanking, finally arrived, and as he stepped into it, he noticed the younger girl was staring at him now. He made a V with his fingers and brought it to his lips, ran his tongue through it as sensuously as he could, and grinned back at her, but the girl's smile instantly faded. As the elevator doors slid shut, she frowned at him and stared back down at her ironing.

"No sense of humor," he mumbled as the noisy elevator wheezed and vibrated menacingly on its descent to the lobby. But he wasn't worried. "Can't be as bad as the way Sewell flies his fucking whirlybird."

There was considerable activity in the hotel lobby. Thai police uniforms were everywhere, and Cory swallowed hard at the sight of the tough-looking brown hats: almost every *dtahm-roout* in Bangkok carefully bent the end flaps down so they gave the officer a menacing, almost evil, storm-trooper look. Cory loved it, but he was worried about all the uniforms. Ross would have been careful to pick an out-of-the-way, quiet hotel—one thing the team didn't need was attention.

Had they been identified—their cover, weak as it was, blown?

One of the policemen was staring at him. Cory nodded his head slightly, after their eyes met, and moved straight over toward the check-in desk, a long teakwood counter decorated with carved dragons. He didn't realize both men were measuring each other up, or that the thought had shot through his mind: *How many, if any, guys have you killed, buster? Fancy American-made firearm aside.* The officer remained where he was—leaning against the doors at the lobby entrance—carefully monitoring all who left and entered.

"Do you have a Mr. Ross registered here?" Cory asked the woman standing in front of the thick mahogany keyboard. She was pretty, but short hair and large round glasses hid what Cory felt was a potential beauty: the narrow chin, high cheekbones and intense eyes were all there.

At the mention of the name, those intense eyes went wide briefly and darted about at the policemen, then returned to his. Her expression exuded compassion, as if they were all expected to deceive the authorities when circumstances warranted it. "Room 12," she whispered, motioning down the nearest corridor.

That was where the crowd of investigators seemed thickest.

Cory got a strange feeling in his gut. *Ground floor.* That was not like Ross. But maybe the hotel had been full-up last night, when the group checked in. It *had* been rather late.

He started down the hallway, trying to appear innocent of any wrongdoing, like he was just looking for a restroom or something. *Excuse me, excuse me . . .* brushing past policemen a foot shorter than he, their revolver butts snagging him like weeds grabbing at a log rushing clumsily down a river . . . painfully aware he was unarmed—his weapon hidden in a safe house Ross had chosen somewhere on the other side of the city.

When he reached Room 12, he was not prepared for what he found: Justin Ross was sitting on a chair in the corner, calmly answering an investigator's questions. On the bed, a beautiful woman, half nude, lay face down in a pool of blood, dead.

Pop singer and rising starlet June Wanda balanced the small makeup case in her palm as she checked her reflection in the mirror. She ran the bar of strawberry lipstick along her lips, blew a kiss at herself, then went about brushing her shoulder-length bleach-blonde hair. Two North Vietnamese soldiers standing behind her smiled at each other and shook their heads: you'd think the crazy woman was preparing to appear in front of TV cameras instead of a radio microphone.

A short female cadre with wirerim glasses, who was 25 this week yet who had never used makeup, patiently waited until the American was finished, then handed her a long piece of paper, and pushed the French-manufactured mike closer.

"Ten second, Miss Wanda." She left the "s" off seconds on purpose, unsmiling.

Without acknowledging the woman, Wanda set down her makeup case, reached down by her feet and picked up a brown pith helmet. She made a production of balancing it atop her head without mussing her hairstyle, then picked up the paper and shook it in the air, as if to rid it of dust.

She was still focusing her bloodshot eyes on the light type when the radio announcer finished his introduction in Vietnamese and pointed to her through a glass partition.

"My brother Americans, listen to me," she spoke in English, her tone urgent. "I beg you to think about what it is you are doing! You men on the Seventh Fleet, I'm talking to you! You mechanics repairing the jets, you soldiers loading the planes, and you pi-

49

lots flying the bombers . . . are the Vietnamese really your enemies? Do you honestly realize what you are doing?

"My God, what will you tell your sons and daughters as they grow up . . . years from now, when, bewildered and ashamed, they demand to know why you participated in this insane action? What lies will you conjure up to appease them? There are no excuses for what you are doing today . . . now . . . this very minute you listen to my voice!

"Did you know that war criminals in past wars were eventually tried and executed? Did you know that your commanders—the men telling you what to do right now . . . the lifers giving the orders—are, by definition of international law, the same as Hitler and his legion: *war criminals!*

"Why, my brothers? Why do you obey orders that instruct you to bomb hospitals and kill children who are doing nothing more criminal than attending classes in school? Why do you do this?"

Wanda paused a moment to catch her breath. She was not used to talking "live" this way. The week before, she had recorded a dozen five-minute spots for Radio Hanoi, but those would be re-edited. Mistakes, heavy breathing, a wheeze could be corrected. This was not like the movie or recording studio where she could take her time. "I would think you would have more compassion . . . more self-respect than this. Some of you," she suddenly pushed aside the script. The woman at her side moved as if to turn off a switch, but the program manager behind the window waved her off. "Some of you have seen my movie . . . you have listened to my records. I speak of love among

50

brothers . . . cooperation among the masses. You know I wouldn't lie to you, that I wouldn't exploit the conditions here in Vietnam. Some of you probably have a copy of the *Stars and Stripes* in front of you at this very moment . . . you are shaking your head at the sound of my voice right now, muttering, 'Lousy commie bitch. . . .'

"Am I right? Well let me take this opportunity to tell you I *am* a Socialist, my brothers on the South China Sea! And I feel we should improve upon American society by turning the country communist. . . . Don't laugh . . . don't snicker, my brothers! I know that if you really understood what communism was all about, you would fall to your hands and knees and *pray* the United States would someday become communist!

"Listen to me, black brothers, brown brothers, white brothers . . . unite with our yellow brothers. . . ." She did not notice the woman at her side frown and roll her eyeballs toward the ceiling. ". . . tonight when you are in your bunk, alone with no one but your conscience, ask yourself: 'Why am I doing this? Why am I helping to kill these innocent women and children?'

"Accept none of the reasons brainwashed into you by some lifer in boot camp . . . but think in terms of human beings, not robots with a bayonet. Think about what you are doing! Why is it you continue to fly these missions of the death merchants? The Vietnamese people have done us no harm. . . ."

"Fifteen second, Miss Wanda," the female cadre, out of range of the microphone, spoke softly.

Wanda continued as if she were irritated by the interruption. "If you must refuse to fight, then so be it! If you must jump ship to avoid participating in these war crimes, then more *power* to you, brothers!"

"Five second, Miss Wanda. . . ."

"We must unite, my brothers in uniform. We must unite to make America a Socialist country! We must join in spirit and actions with our communist friends in Vietnam. They are brothers with the South . . . they are one people. We, the workers, are *all* one people. Follow me, brothers. Live by my example: to hell with tinsel town, and 'art,' and that phony, plastic society back in 'The World.' So long as The Cause requires funds, I will rip off all I can from Hollywood and the clowns at the box office. Soldiers of the political left should snatch every red cent they can get from the wealthy liberals. . . ."

The program manager waved his hand slowly, as if bored, and the red light over the door went out.

"Some of you have taken it upon yourself to seek justice in the jungles." Wanda ignored everything around her as she clutched the microphone with both hands now. "Some of you have 'fragged' the bloodthirsty officers among you who have—"

"We are off the air now, Miss Wanda." The female cadre laid a fresh script in front of the starlet. She waved toward the man behind the glass partition—he was busy reading into his own mike now; had taken over the broadcast and was translating Wanda's speech into rapid Vietnamese. They could not hear her voice. ". . . And switching to another frequency. We will broadcast a different program now, thank you. . . ."

"This will be going out to the bastards on the

52

ships?" she asked, focusing on the new script.

"No, the citizens of Hanoi and surrounding area," the cadre said politely, lips smiling but eyes like ice.

"Live?" Wanda made it sound like that was important to her ego. Or reputation.

"Yes, live, Miss Wanda. The listeners have already been told who you are, and why you are here."

Wanda glanced up at the other woman, her own eyes narrowing now. It was unclear whether she was more irritated at the sarcasm in the second sentence, or the possibility a whole nation had never heard of June Wanda.

"Ten seconds," the station manager was holding his ten fingers up against the glass and smiling. *Damn dinks*, Wanda gritted her teeth as she flexed her upper body for the performance. *Always smiling.*

When the woman beside the actress tapped her shoulder lightly, the heroine to so many naive American teenagers an ocean away—children who listened closely to the words on her records but rarely ever picked up a newspaper—began reading in French from the script in front of her.

"My friends . . . people of North Vietnam . . . we both have a common enemy we must defeat: American imperialism. In my home, the United States, the people are not happy. They have no desire to live . . . no reason to prosper. They feel betrayed . . . afraid of each other . . . uncomfortable at work, alienated from history and culture . . .

"We are confident that, very soon, you and I, with the aid of each other, can rid Vietnam of the American cancer, so that the miserable existence that has befallen the people of the United States . . . the sickness that has infected their souls, deep to their hearts, will not happen to the brave people of Vietnam. . . .

"When the bombs fall on your homeland, my brothers and sisters, rest assured that there are those of us who are fighting the imperialist running dogs from America in your defense, in our own way. . . ."

"We are out of time, Miss Wanda," the political cadre said, after the American celebrity had finished the script.

"But I have so much more to say." Wanda sounded like she was threatening a tantrum.

"There will be plenty of time for that, Miss Wanda. Plenty of time. The war has gone on for a thousand years," she said half-heartedly. "There is no hurry. . . ."

Wanda wanted to say there *was* a hurry. That her time was valuable, and she wasn't about to spend another night in the rat dump hotel they had put her up in, but she bit her lip instead.

Occidental faces were filing into an adjacent cubicle. Europeans. One man had a video-tape camera mounted atop his shoulder. Most of them were smiling admiringly through the glass at the woman in the bright green mini-skirt and tight sweater. It was not often they were treated to such bosomy displays so far north of the DMZ.

Wanda smiled back, though there was an annoyed twitch along the edge of her lips. She hated reporters, despite the success she had had manipulating them to this point in her career.

"A documentary?" she asked, eyes twinkling.

"The installation commander has given his approval for a meeting between you and some of the

American airmen," the short Vietnamese woman replied.

"I would like to talk with them alone first," she decided, feeling crafty. "Without the cameras."

"That could be arranged," the cadre tried to match Wanda's gleam, but it was difficult. She never knew quite what the woman was thinking, and how was one to figure out these temperamental round-eyes anyway?

A few minutes later she was sitting across the table from Captain Sean McKane. Clothed in blue-gray rags with dull red stripes the short, stocky airman stared across at her like a viper, waiting for the opportunity to strike. McKane felt nothing but revulsion and contempt for the woman.

"And how are we doing this afternoon, Capt. Baby-Killer?" Wanda bounced back with a defiant glare.

"Cram it up your kazoo and break it off, traitor!" The Air Force officer wanted to bend forward and spit in her face, but he knew any offensive moves would be met with a rifle buttstoke. He had been warned.

"He states he does not wish to participate in the discussion," the female cadre explained. She seemed almost childlike, compared to the actress, who stood nearly five feet eight inches tall.

"They could twist my nuts off with a pair of vise-grips," McKane expounded, "and I still wouldn't co-operate with jungle rot the likes of you, Miss VC Queen!" He rushed to pull up his shirt sleeves before the guards could restrain him. Cigarette burns and wire scars all along both wrists quickly came into view, but Wanda did not seem either shocked or dispirited. "Even if they squeeze me into their little torture chamber of horrors again," the captain went on,

"I wouldn't give in to a scumbucket like you!"

Two soldiers were quickly upon the officer however, each grabbing an arm and twisting it back as far as it would go.

"We only want you to admit the truth." Wanda stood up, surprisingly losing some of her own venom. "To apologize for your war crimes and beg forgiveness from the people of Vietnam—"

"You should be strung up in front of the Washington Monument and hung in a public execution!" McKane interrupted loudly. Wanda's face froze in shock now, moving back a couple inches as a strange new fear crept into her. "Or shot by a firing squad composed of Vietnam veterans!"

"You are a fool!" she shook her finger at him, springing forth from the numbing emotions that seemed to make the hot air in the tiny cubicle even thicker.

June Wanda stormed out of the room, slamming the door behind her.

It was going to be difficult finding a P.O.W. today who was willing to join her in a public statement.

Captain Sean McKane relaxed his muscles, allowing his rage to subside. It was over, done for the time being. Until the next peacenik graced his humble Hanoi abode. But the guards were not easing off at all. If anything, they were tightening their grip, gaining leverage on his biceps . . . twisting his upper arms back against the shoulders.

The woman cadre started out the door behind Wanda but hesitated. She turned to face the guards and nodded, blinking an eye slightly.

Captain McKane's arms were then forced back

until they both snapped in several places.

Jane Wanda did not bother to ask what the muffled cry in the room she had just left was all about. She wanted, instead, to make her way back to the cameramen and assure them a conference between film heroine and war criminal was imminent.

"Surely you have someone in this building who is willing—" she started in on the aide at her side, but there came a sudden whining noise overhead and a trembling in the air.

The building shook on its foundations, then several explosions sounded outside, and the lights dimmed. The whining escalated into an all-encompassing roar from above, and then the air was alive with bombs screaming as they fell and air raid sirens beginning their slow, mourning cry across the city.

June Wanda scampered under a metal table and began screaming. Kicking, she had to be dragged out and coaxed toward a stairwell that led to an underground bomb shelter.

Beyond several brick walls to the north, Col. Kenneth Southe hastily rolled up the tiny American flag as the walls began to tremble. He secreted it into its hiding place and fastened the strip of bamboo across the hole just before the guards appeared, dragging a bruised and battered form down the corridor.

The ceiling was shaking up and down now as explosions rocked the warehouses all around, and after the prisoner they had been dragging was hastily thrown into the cell next to Southe's, the guards sprinted off toward the nearest bomb shelter.

Southe listened to the airman in the next cell groan in agony as he tumbled across the cement floor. As soon as the sound of the guards' footsteps faded away, he stood up and grasped the bars of his own cubicle, trying to see out. Because of the clamor of crashing metal and exploding fuel tanks outside, he bypassed the usual formalities of tapping codes and "morse" coughs.

"Is that you, McKane?" he called out. "You okay, son?"

There came another groan, coughs soaked with blood and mucus, then a faint reply, "They broke my arms, Kenny. Broke both my damn arms 'cause I wouldn't cooperate with that Wanda bitch . . ."

"Can you hear it?" Southe's eyes slowly went wide as the bombing run increased in its intensity. "Can you hear it, son? Arc-light."

". . . Broke both my damn arms, Kenny . . ."

"Sounds damn good, don't it, son? All them angelic B-52s up there, droppin' their load on Charlie? Can ya hear it?"

". . . Just 'cause I wouldn't cooperate . . ."

"Give 'em hell, Air Force!" Southe was yelling at the top of his lungs now and shaking his fist out the bars as his eyes stared at the ceiling. "Blow this lousy town to kingdom come!" A chorus of deafening explosions, in a fiery ring all around them, seemed to answer him. The wall shuddered but held.

". . . I think my jaw might be broken too, Kenny . . ."

"Can ya hear it?" Southe's eyes were lighting up, as if he could see the monstrous stratofortresses gliding through the storm-clouds above. Other men in cells throughout the building were cheering along with him now.

"Yah . . . I . . . hear . . . it . . . too . . ." McKane rolled onto his back, trying to keep the untreated compound fractures out of the dust. His voice was that of an exhausted man, searching for something—anything to give him strength.

Wave after wave of B-52s roared overhead, their falling cargo making the earth shudder and shift about.

"It's like medicine." Southe had calmed down a bit now as the last squadron passed by and the bombing run shifted into the distance. "Oughta sound so good to ya them arms'll heal right up, son . . . heal right up . . ."

"I can hear it now, Kenny . . ." McKane said, unable to hold his arms out. They finally flopped down painfully into the dirt, but he fought to keep from crying out.

"Can ya hear it, son?"

"I can hear it, Colonel . . ."

"Beautiful sound, son . . . damned beautiful . . ."

"Beautiful," the faint, strained voice replied from the next cell, "Beautiful. . . ."

3

Bangkok. . . .

Blue and silver smoke swirled thick between the
tables, nearly hiding the people on the dance floor in
a music-laced, surrealistic mist, but he could clearly
see the woman dancing alone on the stage. Was she
really wearing VC guerrilla garb, or was it his imagination? The couples on the dance floor—grim American GIs and smiling Saigon bargirls—seemed to be
moving in confusing slow motion, and each note of
the music was now drawn out to last the length of his
frames of thought. He vaguely saw his hand reaching
to pick up his drink, but he couldn't remember his
mind ordering the motor reflex. A thin, camouflage
blouse fluttered through the air, landing across his
wrist, and he looked up to find the woman on stage
had abandoned her uniform—was now tossing the
black satin pantaloons out to a table of rowdy marines
in jungle utilities.

The rock music was fading away suddenly, to be replaced by a shrill chorus of brass upon brass. Castanets? He forced his eyes from the gossamer-thin

blouse across his arm and glanced up at the woman. She was now semi-nude, a string of little brass sea-shells around her waist hanging down across her crotch. Similar brass ornaments concealed her nipples—like pasties some barbarian warrior-woman at an ancient campfire orgy would wear. And her hands were above her head as she swirled around in her little dance . . . tiny brass cymbals attached to finger straps. Making music with metal. He stared at her, praying their eyes would meet—he could never remember wanting a woman so much. But she would only look down on the other soldiers in the room, her eyes smiling at them while her lips remained line-thin, uncommitting. She never once looked down at *him*.

Until she produced the rifle. Magically. As if from thin air. *Then* she was staring straight at him. Into him . . . Through him. Firing off a burst of glowing crimson tracers suddenly. And the whole time those damn Cong castanets kept clanging away!

Brent Collins felt the red-hot tracers—a dozen of them—sizzle through his chest and punch holes through his ribs on their way out the flesh of his back. At the same time, he seemed to be coughing, and someone was shaking his arm . . . pulling him out of danger: to safety.

Jerking him awake.

"Brent . . ." The whisper was harsh. Amy's.

The air was still alive with the damn castanets, too.

"Brent! . . . At the door," came the groggy yet arousing voice again. "Someone's trying to get in. . . ."

He was face down in his pillow, the scent of her still heavy on the sheets. He forced himself up onto his

61

palms and glanced around.

A hotel maid was peeking through the door, wide-eyed, startled by the makeshift alarm he had rigged the night before. Frightened by all the racket.

"Come back later!" he growled, letting his head fall back into the pillow. And after all the trouble he went to to rig the intrusion alarm—neither of them, after last night, had the energy to even react accordingly. Collins was already in heaven: some fool wanted to break in and terminate him, for whatever reason, more power to him.

The maid giggled and said, "Check-out time, sir . . ."

"We're up now," Amy said in Thai. "Give us a few more minutes."

"Very well, madame," and the door quietly closed.

The boobytrap alarm clock continued to clank away, but the spring finally wound down.

The team members had been rigging the alarms, as a precaution, ever since the incident at the embassy. There were still no damaging revelations in the newspapers, but twice Ross had spotted suspicious-looking characters turning up at their regular haunts, and he didn't want any surprises or unexpected trouble.

Though in this business, Collins was quickly learning, *all* trouble was anticipated. Surprises could mean delays, even a one way pass to never-never land, and would not be tolerated.

Collins chuckled to his pillow: if the intruder had been bad news instead of just some maid, he and the succulent piece of flesh beside him would now be just slabs of dead meat.

"What's so funny?" Amy rolled over and forced

one of her breasts against his face.

"Oh nothing . . . just thinking . . ." He started re-calling the woman in his dream. The VC guerrilla. With the wide, jutting breasts and the castanet pasties.

He laughed again.

Amy pulled him over on top of her, allowing his weight to move her thighs apart. "Christ, you're all wet!" She nearly screamed at the coolness of it against her flesh as she pushed him back onto his side.

"Make up your mind!" he snapped back playfully, reaching out to grab her hips. He roughly forced her onto her stomach and mounted her from behind.

"Get off me, you pervert!" she laughed. "I'm not a goddamned no-nonsense inflatable love doll, you know!"

"Oh yes you are!" He was laughing harder now as he held both her wrists above her head with one hand and tried grabbing hold of her flat stomach with the other. When she laughed, he turned it into a gasp, plunging into her suddenly. Deep.

"Brent!"

"Enjoy it, honey." He was whispering into her ear now, as he ran his fingers against her breasts under-neath and their pelvises fell into a smooth rhythm.

"You're . . . an . . . animal. . . . You . . . know . . . that?" she was already out of breath. "All last night . . . and . . . now this? And you . . . apparently . . . got your rocks off . . . lying right next to me . . . a few minutes ago. . . . Who were you . . . fucking . . . in your dream?"

"Shut up and enjoy it." He forced her thighs apart

wider with his knees and slammed harder. "You wouldn't believe it if I told you. . . ."

He almost wanted to hurt her—make her gasp again, but in pain this time. But he knew he couldn't. She was too experienced. Had had too many men between her legs—sometime in her past. Somewhere she never talked about.

Almost like a snooze alarm, the maid was knocking again thirty minutes later. Brent and Amy ignored her and the sound of the passkey being inserted into the lock. When the door creaked open an inch, the urgent sound of protesting mattress springs sent her scurrying away—two maids this time. Both giggling loudly as they disappeared down the hallway.

Later, as he lay against her shoulder, tracing his finger along the sweat line between her breasts, Brent brought up the subject for the first time. "How did it happen?" He moved his finger back and forth against the jagged scar across her chest, as if trying to erase it.

Her breathing suddenly lost its regularity and her voice was a forced rasp when she said, "Let's not worry about it, okay lover?"

"I'm sorry, Amy, but I was just curious." He rose up on one elbow, resting his ear against an open palm. "You don't get a scar like that unless you've come very close to death. . . ."

"Don't press it, buster." She said the words like a friend.

"But it's not the kind of scar you get on an operating table somewhere."

"Just back off, Brent, okay?" her eyes remained closed as she lay on her back, mind staring at a blank ceiling.

"It's the kind of scar you get in the street . . . at the end of a blade, baby. Cold steel. So confide in your *lover*, lover."

"You're touching on sensitive territory. . . . I'm just not ready to talk about it, okay? I have to look at it in the mirror everyday, you know. I'm not ready to *confide* in anybody."

"Not even with me?" he said. "After all the beds we've shared together since the Diem hit?" His own question almost made him shudder. Not from remembering what the team had gone through in Saigon. But from worrying how angry Ross might get if he found out the two of them had gotten so . . . intimate. It was a cardinal sin among squad members. But so was simple friendship, and look how many bottles of "33" and *Singha* they had all shared over the last several weeks. Men just didn't tell and re-tell that many war stories without growing close. And when you lived through the adventures together . . . well, lifelong bonds were formed from that kind of relationship.

"It's none of your business," she said, moving onto her side and turning her back to him. "You got what you wanted, now leave me alone."

"Oh." He got defensive, almost forgetting what they had argued about. "*You* didn't enjoy it too? It wasn't mutually rewarding? That final, all-out groan was faked?" He dug two fingers into her side, tickling, but she refused to budge. It was like trying to get a response from a corpse.

"Sir," the door was opening again. "I'm afraid we *must* ask that you vacate this room." It was the hotel manager. "We have a platoon of Americans fresh in from the Veeyet-Nam, and accommodations are sorely needed."

It was a welcome excuse to roll off the bed.

A few minutes later, Collins was sauntering down the crowded hallway, on his way to the lobby and the restaurant beyond. A platter of *kau-pawd* would more than hit the spot right then.

The large number of Thai police uniforms was eye-catching, but not alarming to him: probably just a raid on prostitutes. Or maybe a drug bust. No big deal.

Better check on Roscoe's room anyway, he decided.

Was that the back of Cory's head in his doorway?

Collins was suddenly rushing down the corridor, brushing past the brown uniforms. When he reached Ross's room, he was treated to the same sight Cory MacArthur had originally seen: their leader sitting on a chair, calm, stone-faced, answering an investigator's questions. And a beautiful woman lying dead across the room. On the bed, face down, in a pool of blood.

Collins's eyes flashed to Ross's wrists. They were not handcuffed—a good sign. Then he saw an old, bent-over pension-next-year policeman brushing fingerprint dust along the open windowsill. And there was Cory's face: innocent, smiling. No sign of alarm.

"You all right, Justin?" The words had barely left his lips when the investigator sitting across from Ross rose to his feet and gently grabbed Cory's arm.

"Okay . . . okay, gentlemen . . . I'm afraid you'll have to wait outside." His English appeared flawless. "We seem to be running out of air to breathe in here."

Without resisting, both Americans glanced back at Ross, and when he answered with a slight nod, they backed out into the hallway.

After the door was closed, Collins took Cory over to a corner at the hallway's end and asked, "What the hell happened in there?"

MacArthur chuckled. His eyes were appraising the unflattering tunic of a tiny policewoman who was writing something in a pocket notebook. Thirty feet away, she was the closest officer to them. "You're not gonna believe this." Cory was still grinning. "But you know that fox Justin left the whorehouse with last night?"

"I don't really remember a whole hell of a lot about last night," Collins admitted as he draped a thick forearm around the kid's shoulder.

"Yah—Amy *did* have to carry your worthless ass back to the hotel."

"So anyway."

"So anyway, the young lady-of-the-evening Justin latched up with turned out to be a katoy!" and he burst out laughing again, doubling over this time.

"A female impersonator?" Collins's eyes went wide with disbelief.

"Yep!"

"But I thought I remember seeing quite a set of jugs on her, and—"

"Can you imagine the surprise on Justin's face last night when he slid off 'her' panties and came face-to-face with an Asian erection?"

Collins was holding his stomach now too. "But—"

"Butt!"

"But—"

"Can you believe it?" Cory was on his knees, well aware the laughter was probably drifting into the room with Ross now.

"Now that kind of luck sucks to high heaven!" Collins tried to put himself in Ross's place.

"Poor guy," Cory said sarcastically.

"But what about the body?" Collins's mouth dropped again as his mind flashed back to the set of brown haunches rising from the pool of blood in the bedroom. "They're gonna hang his ass! You can't go around offing katoys just 'cause they suddenly dangle their dick at you instead of a—"

Cory did not look worried. "It seems our little katoy was not working alone," he explained further. "Just as Justin made his discovery, another Thai was climbing in through the bedroom window from the ground floor outside."

"They were going to rob him," Collins said matter-of-factly.

"Right. But Roscoe commenced to kick ass, and the katoy caught a slug from her—"

"*His*," Collins smiled.

"His."

"*Hers*," the ex-cop laughed.

"Hers . . . his! The katoy's partner wrestled with Ross for like the blink of an eyeball—no contest. And the cowboy's gun went off and cancelled the katoy's ticket."

Collins moved closer and whispered. "They didn't find any weapons on Justin, did they? Nothing in the room?" Firearms possession in Thailand could mean a stiff jail sentence, and in some cases, the death penalty.

"Naw . . . everything's at the safe house."

"What about—" But the door was opening, and Army Lt. Justin Ross, wearing his usual safari suit in lieu of a military uniform, was stepping out, AWOL bag in hand, all smiles.

"Gentlemen, we are free to go," he said.

"Another beer, Justin?" Chad Chandler was bouncing a handful of bargirl on his knee.

"Bet you could use an entire brewery, after last night," laughed Matt Sewell. He was alone.

"I'll tell you boys," Ross squinted through the thick clouds of cigarette smoke in the hotel nightclub. "One thing the team doesn't need is attention like *that* . . . especially from the police. I'm still not sure some TNP agent isn't on to us—watching from some dark corner from behind a newspaper at this very moment." He could barely make out the go go girls dancing in slowly twirling, neon-laced "cages" suspended from thick rafters in the ceiling.

Cory and Collins both slid mugs of golden *Singha* in front of him. "I warned you to check for adams apples," Brent ribbed his team leader. "Serves ya right, Honcho . . . you shoulda checked for a damned adams apple. . . ."

"But you saw the set of jugs on her . . . *him*—Christ!"

"Poor Roscoe," Amy spoke in a low, throaty, drag-queen voice. She had her breasts cupped in her hands and was pushing them together and up until they were straining against the thin fabric of her Thai sarong. "Can't even tell the real thing from a cheap, back-alley silicone job."

The others laughed and Sewell straightened a recently-purchased *Stars & Stripes* newspaper out in his lap. "Hmph." He cleared his throat as tired eyes strained against the dim light. "That goofy Wanda broad almost lost *her* lungs to a B-52 arc-light out Haiphong-way. . . ."

"Front page story?" Chandler asked, his words sounding bitter.

"Yah," Sewell hacked at his smog-coated throat in disgust and spat a load of phlegm down into a tobacco spigot beside the table. "You know them damn journalists aren't any better than the commies," he declared.

"I take it she survived the air attack." Ross tried to sound noncommittal, but Chandler caught the gleam of . . . apprehension? in his eyes.

"Why you almost look like you feel cheated," said Chandler, but he suddenly didn't have the energy to pursue Ross's thoughts or moods. "Anyway, no—she beat feet into a bunker or something and survived to bitch another day."

Sewell groaned, and Ross thought it uncharacteristic of the often-liberal chopper pilot.

"They got a shot of her here on page one posing on top of a surface-to-air missile," he added, turning the paper so all at the table could see. Then, like a professor, "Notice how sensuously she wraps her legs around the rocket's bodytube. . . ."

"Hump away, Wanda-honey," muttered Sewell.

"Pointed right at our boys in the B-52s, no doubt," observed Cory.

"Hands reaching down to jerk-off the rocket launcher controls," added Ross.

"Fucking commie," concluded Chandler after it became apparent Amy was not in the mood to join in.

He ripped the front page off and tossed it over his shoulder. Moments later, "Shee-it! She's on page two too!" He slam-dunked the wadded newspaper into a nearby trashcan and started toward the nearest bamboo cage with a go go girl inside.

"Sit down, Chad." An amused Ross grinned at the former mercenary's antics.

"I need to sink my fist into some pussy," he growled, ignoring Ross.

Their table was at the back of the nightclub, in a corner, and the building had yet to fill up with patrons. There was nobody outside their little group within earshot.

"Chandler!" Ross raised his voice slightly.

"Later." The Korean war vet waved him off without looking back.

"Go drag his ass back here," Ross directed Sewell and MacArthur.

Brent Collins was slowly nursing his beer, immersed in thought. Wondering why he shared none of the hatred for June Wanda his cohorts seemed to have. He considered himself patriotic. Loved his country with every fiber of his being. And wasn't he up on all the current events? But what was it about this woman that spurred a murderous lust in the dangerous men he worked with? Wasn't June Wanda just another rich brat who tired of Beverly Hills and took up with the political activist bandwagon? Wasn't she just another outspoken critic of war who was expressing her right to travel the globe and investigate America's activities overseas firsthand, refusing to rely on the possibly biased reporting of the news media's glamorous foreign correspondents? Was there something about June Wanda that he didn't know . . . and should?

The picture of the sex goddess with her legs wrapped sensuously around the SAM rocket started Collins to thinking. In the photo's background, North Vietnamese soldiers wearing pith helmets were posing with the woman, unsmiling—one even frowning with a . . . a smirk of contemptuous scorn? Did troubleshooting, looking out for her country's interests in Southeast Asia, include posing for pictures with the enemy? And atop something as lethal as a weapon that had already downed several dozen U.S. jets from the skies over Hanoi? Collins shifted his mental gears into neutral and drank the rest of his beer in one long, disenchanted swallow.

"We're moving out tonight," Ross revealed, after Chandler had been led back to the table. He had an ear-to-ear, shit-eating smile on his face, and seemed totally pacifist now—one of the go go dancers had whispered a promise of things-to-come down to him before his teammates had been able to catch up and spirit him away.

"One thing I wanted to mention," Cory looked embarrassed. Ross signalled for him to go ahead with the interruption. "Somebody snatched my watch last night." His eyes fell from Justin's, and he stared into the beer mug on the table in front of him. "But more important: I lost my wallet too. It had my cover ID in it."

"Oh, right." Ross shot a hand down into his thigh pocket. He quickly produced the kid's black, plastic wallet. "The watch is with the rest of my gear back up in the room," Ross smiled.

"But how . . ." Cory opened the wallet to the metallic-green and brown map of Vietnam molded into the inside flap.

"We were all getting a little snockered last night," Ross admitted. "And I have to acknowledge I set you up with a pretty wild lady-of-questionable-virtue . . ."

Cory shot Matt and Chad a half-angry, half-betrayed, and totally disappointed glance. "I'm afraid I wouldn't know," he muttered.

". . . So I kept hold of your stuff there. Just in case she decided to liberate you of your valuables overnight."

"Your guardian angel," Amy smiled approvingly, sounding more like a big sister than a street-tested killer.

"At least young Cory didn't end up with a katoy!" Chandler slapped Sewell on the back and both men erupted into a bellow of laughter.

"Young *Cory* didn't end up with jack-shit," Cory himself explained, and Amy leaned over and got him in a sudden playful headlock, forcing his face against the healthy swell of flesh along the loose edge of her sarong.

"As I was saying . . ." Ross pulled a folded 5x7 manila envelope from his breast pocket. "We've been given another assignment."

"Time to pick up the ol' duffelbag and move out toward new horizons," Sewell mused, somewhat sarcastically, as he stared into the clouds of cigarette smoke with that far-off look in his eyes.

"Not so 'new,' " Ross corrected him. "It's back to Saigon." There was more a hint of suppressed excitement in his expression than foreboding. Like he had been anxiously waiting months to return to Vietnam.

"Aw shit, Justin," Chandler complained. "Don't we get no R&R? For Christsakes . . . we just saved the American embassy a couple days ago."

"And rid Bangkok of one less katoy," Cory chuckled as all eyes switched to Ross.

"You just *had* your R&R," he replied. "And from the smell of some of you, you've yet to wash it off." That was Ross's way of turning a friendly insult around. Everyone, including Amy, tried to act totally innocent as they attempted to casually sniff at the air around them without being obvious.

Ross pulled out two small identical color photos and passed them around the table in different directions. An American full-bird colonel in Army greens was pictured in front of the American flag. A routine military file photo. He was stocky, in his late forties, with head shaved bald and eyebrows a bushy black. And he had what Amy called "a predator's chin."

"Meet Colonel Banks," said Ross. "Commander of the 95-Charlies in Long Binh."

"We're gonna knock off an MP officer?" Collins asked incredulously.

"He's not a street cop, Brent." Ross knew there would be some form of conflict of interest if the ex-policeman knew he was going after an MP. "But officer-in-charge of LBJ—the stockade."

"Long Binh Jail," Sewell whispered the euphemism.

"A cop is a cop is a cop," argued Collins.

Ross didn't bother to bring up the hit a year earlier involving Ngo Dinh Nhu, brother to then president of South Vietnam and head of the secret police branch,

74

and he did not try to make comparisons.

"Banks started out as a stockade guard at Ft. Leavenworth," Ross began the background synopsis. "Worked his way up through the ranks, without incident, till Uncle Sammy put him through OCS and made him an 'occifer.' Didn't make it to Korea, but volunteered for the 'Nam when he got his shoulder eagle, and they sent him to LBJ to revamp the stockade system in this new war zone after it looked like America just might hang around Indochina for a while. Never spent a day in a patrol car.

"Now he's made it known to the brass at Puzzle Palace his wishes to switch MOSs, though," Ross said.

"To what?" Collins cocked his head suspiciously.

"He wants to be the new PM of Saigon."

"Provost Marshal?"

"Right. The big cheese. Might just see some street action after all, if he doesn't spend all day in his office, doing stuff chiefs do. His men call him Bald Eagle."

"So why the hit?" Chandler could care less, but asked anyway.

"CID sent an undercover agent into his outfit as a driver, last year," Ross explained. "It seems his main purpose in coming to the Saigon area was to get involved in the clubs. His secondary MOS just happens to be entertainment services."

"Don't tell me," Sewell ventured a hypothesis. "Slave trader."

"You guessed it," Ross smiled sadly.

"Slave trader?" Cory pressed them for details. The words struck up visions in his mind of a rough-looking merchant seaman holding an auction deep in some mist-enshrouded forest where naked black women, their skin glistening like ebony beneath the full moon, were paraded down through an arena in neck chains, a hundred years ago.

Ross noticed how Amy's eyes dropped to the table as the subject came up. He wondered what she was seeing in the pool of gold that was her beer mug. "It seems some women back in the states have been—*are being* lured to the Orient under false pretenses. Young, white women.

"Some crackpot 'agent' back in The World signs 'em to a contract overseas . . . as a go go dancer—"

"Sure . . ." frowned Sewell.

". . . And they end up strippin' in the bars instead," Ross went on, ". . . getting hooked on dope, and eventually turning into prostitutes."

"White slaves," added Matt.

"Bad news," said Collins, "But I still can't see why _we've_ been called into the affair."

"Banks passed his twenty-year mark back in '58. Apparently he's going for a 30-year pension, with a little Asian spice along the way to fatten up his bank account in Geneva.

"The government hinted to him they were wise he was into something under the table—that he was violating international law. They tried to force his hand and make him retire early, but they didn't have the evidence, and Banks called their bluff."

"But now they've got the goods on him," Sewell decided.

"So why don't they just jerk his ass stateside to do some hard time on the rocks?" Chad asked.

"Once warned, Banks was ready for them," Ross said. "He sent a couple of his own men out to get the goods on those who would have his commission."

"And he dug up quite a few closet skeletons," grinned Cory.

"You know how the military hierarchy can some-times be," said Sewell. "If the general's clean, he'll go after you like a righteous sidewalk preacher. If he's dirty, he'll look the other way for the most part, pray-ing you'll quickly pass on to someone else's duty sta-tion and become some other CG's headache."

"But now," said Sewell.

"But now the Bald Eagle is playing dirty. His driver has 'disappeared.' CID can find no proof he was done away with by Banks, or on the colonel's or-ders. But the clincher: a second CID plant, a woman, is also missing and feared murdered."

"Sent in as a go go dancer?" asked Cory.

"Right," answered Ross. "And she just happens to be the granddaughter of one of Mr. Y's associates, back at the Pentagon.

"The Green Machine is beginning to fear too many unnecessary lives will be lost on this case before they get the necessary proof on Banks to go to court mar-tial. The word is out: hit him with all we've got."

"Can we play with this one?" asked Collins. "Maybe do a little of our own undercover work and see what we can get on the dude before we ice him. It'd sure be nice to get back on the street in a . . . well, investigative capacity, if ya know what I mean . . ."

"I can understand your missing policework, Brent. But no jollies on this one. In quick, hit the target, then beat feet out of the kill zone."

"No ears for souvenirs?" joked Chandler.

"Quick in and quick out," Ross answered him.

"And if that leaves time for a war trophy, have at it," Sewell interpreted.

"Our reservations are waiting," Ross nodded at Sewell, indicating the Huey would be used for the entire cross-jungle trek. Chandler and Cory groaned. They had been hoping for a commercial airliner, so they could harass stewardesses again.

"I suppose we leave tonight." Cory sounded slightly depressed.

"First thing in the morning," Ross said.

"That should leave us just enough time to get you laid by one of the most beautiful women in the world," Chandler told Cory. He stood and motioned for the young man to lead the way to the door.

"Where have I heard *that one* before?" the kid remarked, as Ross watched them leave: like spiders closing in on a fly. Then the night and the noise beyond the swinging doors engulfed them, and all he could hear were the girls of Patpong Road laughing outside as they peddled their love and companionship to the highest bidder.

Collins began feeling uneasy the moment Matt Sewell lifted the chopper off the pad outside their safe house in northern Bangkok. The Huey had been hidden inside an abandoned warehouse that was nestled deep in a maze of burned-out tenements. The housing project had been deserted since a fire swept through the neighborhood in 1946.

His reservations were not connected with the eerie setting that enveloped this edge of the teeming metropolis, nor were they based on any fear police agents might have been watching to see who returned to the black helicopter with no ID markings on its sides. They were, instead, centered around the upcoming mission.

As the team headed for a small mission outpost along the Thai-Lao border, where they would refuel, he felt caught up in a trap of intense emotions and mystery that would quite possibly mean the end of all of them. It was as if the Huey itself had been grabbed by some unseen force and was being dragged, down through space, to its doom. He watched, silently, as hamlet huts, murky canals, and multi-hued stepping stones of rice paddies passed by below. When the flooded fields gave way to the tangled, menacing jungle, that foreboding grew to an ominous level, actually frightening Collins somewhat, though he would never have admitted it. It was almost as if he feared claws would suddenly, at any moment, reach up from the canopy below and snag the helicopter—and him with it—dragging the entire team down into the green evil, the beast awaiting them, and death.

There was another stop at a Special Forces camp in Laos, then a maintenance check and more fuel at Ban Me Thuot. The demon could be waiting for them anywhere along that line of silent Asian wilderness.

But the entire hop across inland Indochina proceeded without incident, and Brent was suddenly watching Sewell bring the gunship in through a maze of fighter-bombers, cargo planes and Phantom jets that were both ascending and descending on all sides.

Tan Son Nhut airport.

They landed on a solitary pad outside the main confines of the base, midway between the southeast perimeter fenceline and the northern suburbs of Saigon. Vietnamese Special Forces troopers in black uniforms and unauthorized camouflage berets were in evidence on the outskirts of the tarmac-lined pad, but they paid the Huey little attention: their eyes and carbine muzzles were all directed out along the fields of man-high elephant grass that extended for miles toward the horizon.

While the chopper was still fifty feet off the ground, Collins had noticed a bunker-lined compound in the distance, at the edge of the airport's east runway, surrounded by leaning palms and probing fingers of jungle. American MPs in sleeveless flak jackets and black helmets were in evidence everywhere: in the towers, leading attack dogs along the inner wire, reclining in parked gunjeeps. He wondered, briefly, why they were there . . . what their mission was, but then the Huey was bouncing across the tarmac, and the Army cops were hidden by the sea of sharp reeds. Some of the Arvins were rushing up to greet Ross, and after the blades slowed down, one of the Vietnamese reached up to grab a rotor to strap it down.

The long blade was still moving too fast, however, and the momentum pulled the soldier off his feet, flung him wildly through the air, and deposited him a good thirty feet away. On his buttocks, in the dust. His fellow soldiers laughed heartily—bombarding him with friendly insults rather than assistance—and, limping, he smiled and returned to the Huey to try again.

Several Arvins joined him, now that the rotors had swished to a stop, and the group pushed the craft back in under a protective shell of concrete that looked like an upside-down "U" with no front or rear walls.

As the Vietnamese set about dragging camouflage nets over the hangar, Chandler said, "I'm impressed, Ross. Quite an entourage to meet you at the airport. It's nice to see all that hardware on *our side* for a change. Old Man Y back at the Big P must have some real good connections."

"They think we're American Special Forces." Ross did not smile back. "They'll keep an eye on the Fly while we're in town, and make sure it's ready if we need it." When the team had originally been issued the helicopter, the thinktank back in Washington had instructed Ross that all radio communications to or from it would use the call sign "Dragonfly," but they had all taken to calling their Huey the 'Fly, because of its black paint scheme and bug-eyed appearance.

"What about that installation on the edge of the jungle over there?" Collins asked. "With all the MPs. Is it one of Banks's monkey houses?"

Ross smiled. Monkey House was a favorite Asian expression for stockade or slammer. And now more and more GIs were beginning to use it too. "No," he said. "That's Fort Hustler. The 18th MPs use it for interrogations and to provide a neutral location for secret negotiations between Premier Ky's people and Uncle Ho's. It shouldn't figure into our mission at all."

Ross spoke a few words to one of the Arvin sergeants in Vietnamese, and the soldier pointed over to a dark blue Peugeot sedan parked behind a laager of APCs.

"What about these ape suits?" Amy asked. Ross told the team they could get out of their black coveralls, and after Sewell slipped off his flightsuit, they squeezed into the complimentary car.

Collins noticed how many of the Vietnamese had been staring at Amy and chuckling to themselves. "They're probably wondering what a beautiful piece of leg like you is doing with a Green Beret A Team," Collins told her, loud enough so the others could hear.

"Naw," replied Chandler. "They're just wondering what it would be like to eat some white meat for a change."

"They probably haven't had any pussy for months," said Cory.

Sewell's grinning expression was saying, "At least they've *had* some pussy," but he argued out loud, "Naw . . . they're just a couple klicks from Saigon. They probably get more cunt than they can handle—"

Just then, as Ross started up the tiny Peugeot and began pulling away from the pad, two motorscooters loaded down with girls in tight hotpants and halter tops sputtered up to the LZ.

Sewell and Chandler began laughing at the almost comical sight of the "handlebar whores" when the windshield of the jeep a few feet away exploded in a shower of glass shards.

"*Nguoi ban trom!*" one of the Asians was yelling at his buddies, ignoring the Americans and the women on the Honda. *Sniper!*

The squad of Vietnamese was suddenly evaporating as men spread out, sprinting away from the hangar

82

and bushes along the kill zone. Uniforms were flattening out within the waves of elephant grass at the edge of the tarmac. Rifles clattered against the ground as some of the Arvins panicked, while the more experienced vets in the group already had their barrels pointed away from the LZ, seeking out muzzle flashes.

Even as he was airborne, diving toward the safety of the concrete structure looming over the gunship, Collins watched as the startled prostitutes drove straight into the free fire zone. Terror registered in the eyes of the girl steering the Honda as she realized what was happening, but her passenger was still smiling and reaching up to catch a butterfly when her doom struck.

The bullet punched her in the back, like an invisible bully suddenly darting from the swaying elephant grass out of nowhere, right between the shoulder blades. It exploded inside a lung, sending shards of lead down into her heart and liver. The single chunk of mushroomed metal that burst forth from her chest tore the front hinge of her halter-top in half, suddenly freeing firm, bouncing breasts. Glistening in the sunlight, they were quickly coated with crimson as a gush of blood followed the rifle slug out the bullet hole. All this happened faster than the blink of an eye—it signalled the direction from which the sniper was shooting, and some of the Arvins took defensive actions rather than retaliatory: they scooped mud out from under their bellies frantically, creating shallow holes in which to hide.

Collins slid in under the Huey, instantly aware now that it was probably the worst place to be, and watched as the Honda slid onto its side, dumping both driver and passenger into the sharp elephant grass. They disappeared from view, hidden by the shimmering sea of endless green.

The women on the second Honda drove right through the crossfire, accelerating, ducking as they raced for what they hoped was safety on the other side of the LZ. A weak ricochet bounced off the metal tarmac and struck one of the women on back in her elbow, showering the area with bone, gristle and red spray. She screamed and almost fell off, but the scooter sputtered off into a ravine and disappeared over a ridge.

Chandler watched, dumbfounded, as one of the South Vietnamese Rangers popped up from behind a bush, sprayed a half-clip of rounds after the women—probably out of frustration more than anything—then fell back behind cover.

Bullets were now zinging into the hangar at the rate of one every few seconds, and Collins knew it would only be a matter of time before the sniper scored a lucky hit and blew the chopper, hangar, and himself sky high.

"Anyone got a mark on that sniper?" Sewell was calling out from somewhere in the elephant grass. Collins glanced around, and felt the wave of sweat break out on his body when he realized he was the only one who had been fool enough to seek cover inside the concrete structure: its shape was ideal for ricochets, increasing the odds of being hit. One tracer in the Huey fuel tanks and the exploding cell would be worse than dropping an M-80 onto a gas-soaked ant hill. The cement hangar would only serve to compress and increase the resulting blast. They'd never even find enough left of him to mail back home in a film cannister.

Another shot bounced into the hangar. The sniper, for the most part, was ignoring the men on the edge of the tarmac.

"He's directly in front of the hangar's north side!" yelled Cory, referring to the guerrilla and answering Sewell's earlier question.

"About seventy-five meters in a straight line out from the Huey's nose!" added Ross. The team was in a bad predicament: their armament was in a sealed case in the trunk of the Peugeot. They wore no side-arms. They had been expecting a cold LZ—granted, an error in tactics—and now, the Arvin Rangers were slow in reacting under fire. "He's behind that knoll in the reeds!"

"Perfect!" responded Sewell.

Ross wanted to warn him not to make any rash moves—it would only be a matter of time before help arrived and the sniper retreated into the reeds—but the Korean war vet and self-acknowledged ace chopper pilot was already on his feet, running a dangerous zigzag sprint toward the helicopter inside the hangar.

Collins watched him approach—it was not in Sewell's character to play hero. He hoped the chopper pilot was not about to make them both minor footnotes in some history book's two page chapter on Indochina, if they warranted even *that*.

"Greetings!" Sewell flashed a toothy grin as he hurdled over Collins and dove into the Huey's open hatch. The ex-policeman, not one to volunteer much himself, was shocked his own legs were lifting him up, driving him toward the open hatch after Matt.

"What's the plan?" Collins felt naked without a sidearm. A bullet smashed into the port window in front of his knee, and as he watched the glass instantly spiderweb into multiple cracks, he also caught the distant muzzle flash in his peripheral vision. "There!" he pointed frantically toward the dull green knoll as another discharge erupted and the shell sparked off the tarmac and bounced around inside the hangar with a Hollywood whistle.

"I see it." Sewell's reply made Collins's observation seem unnecessary as he maneuvered panel knobs and buttons with lightning speed. Between the chopper and the sniper, a few Arvins were slowly moving, on their bellies, toward the muzzle flash. *Finally!*

Collins expected a turbine somewhere to belch smoke, rumbling to life, and the rotors overhead to slowly begin flapping as they cut through the thick, humid air, but all that happened was the console in front of them lit up and some dials began glowing green and red.

"What the fuck?" Collins muttered. He felt so vulnerable to the random sniper rounds. Either the sniper was a terrible shot, or he was just toying with them. Perhaps he was high on dope, or rice wine. Whatever the reason, the longer he remained there to harass them, the better his chances of sacrificing his life for the Cause—*beneath the rolling napalm cannisters of a camo-colored jetfighter!* Why weren't the Arvins rushing him?

Sewell didn't pause to answer—he was busy switching safety clamps out of the way. Putting the grip into RED FIRE status.

86

And then the big Huey burped fire.

The M-79 round shot out from the nose cannon, and it travelled in a slow arc Collins could follow with the naked eye: like a black baseball being batted directly at the sniper!

But the powerful thud both men grinned at during discharge sent the high explosive projectile far over the target, and the grenade disappeared beyond the sea of elephant grass, finally exploding somewhere in the distance several seconds later.

"Too high!" Collins called out.

"No shit, Sherlock," Sewell muttered calmly as he let loose with another HE round. The nose cannon shuddered, and the blur of death popped forth again. Collins found himself laughing this time: there was no ear-ringing discharge like with a carbine or bazooka when an M-79 was used. Just a dull pop that, to Collins, sounded like what an elephant fart must sound like. *Appropriate*, he giggled to himself. *They* do *call M-79s elephant guns, don't they?*

The HE round lost most of its high arc on this trip, keeping close to the ground as it slammed into the knoll. The explosion sent reeds and dirt clods into the air, but no flesh. After the smoke cleared, a crater could be seen where the knolltop had once been.

"Outstanding shooting!" Collins slapped Sewell on the back as both men watched the earth grumble in protest and fling the echo of sound back at them. "Now let's go see if you hit what you were gunning at!"

"Not even a light blood trail," Ross observed as he and Amy stood beside the smoldering knoll.

"Could the explosion have . . . disintegrated him?"

Amy asked cautiously, hoping she didn't sound foolish.

"An M-79 sends little bits of metal out in a wide arc," Cory told her. "Sometimes the victims are barely marked: just countless little puncture wounds they bleed to death from. To get blown to bits you practically have to be sleeping on a satchel of 'em."

"Our field demo specialist." Chad appeared for a look, grinning as he pushed Cory down off the knoll. He glanced about carefully.

"What *you* looking for?" Cory frowned at the putdown.

"Well, I figure that HE round would have literally scared the shit out of our sniper." The remark was followed by scattered laughter as Sewell, Collins and a few Arvins joined them. "But I can't find a turd anywhere around here." Collins noticed that several of the Vietnamese were still cautiously hugging the ground.

"Strange how there's no sign which way he escaped," noted Sewell as he slowly checked the elephant grass in a semicircle behind the knoll.

"Perhaps a tunnel system?" Collins offered, rubbing his chin.

"Doubt it," Ross replied, glancing off in the distance toward a faint rumbling sound. "But the dude probably . . ." his words tapered off to silent thought: several hundred yards distant, in the sea of elephant grass, a small American and Vietnamese flag seemed to be waving back and forth a few feet above the reedtops.

"What the heck?" Chandler locked onto the sight simultaneously.

"A white flag it *ain't*," decided Cory.

As it grew closer, it became apparent the flags were attached to a tall radio antenna, the brilliant red, white, and blue of Old Glory flapping above the gold and red stripes of a bullet-riddled South Vietnamese flag. They were each about a foot in size. The whip radio antenna was attached to a U.S. Army military police gunjeep, and it was heading straight for the team's location.

After several wide furrows magically appeared in the sea of elephant grass and the dust settled, five MP jeeps had pulled up to the landing pad, menacing-looking M60 machine guns bristling atop posts in the back seats.

Ross's eyes locked onto those of a tall, stocky buck sergeant standing up in the front seat of the lead jeep, thick forearms braced against the windshield. Clad in skin-tight jungle fatigues with a faded, 18th Brigade combat patch on his right sleeve, the man did not look amused. He was in his early thirties, with close-cropped hair, a sun-bleached mustache, and jungle green eyes.

Collins watched Ross step forward to meet him, and the ex-cop got the feeling . . . the *weird* feeling, his squad leader was head of a wagon train and was now reluctantly walking out to greet a huge Indian chief after the cavalry had surrendered. Ross, tanned and looking confident, was smiling, but the big MP was bristling like a soaked panther that had been chasing its prey, only to stumble into a river during the pursuit. "Who's in charge of this clusterfuck!" he demanded, jumping out of the patrol jeep.

"Well, unfortunately, it appears as if I'll have to take the bla—" Ross started to say, still smiling and unsure why he was feeling guilty, but the sergeant cut him off.

"Where's the cocksucker with the blooper?" he demanded to know. Blooper, as with elephant gun, was a slang term GIs gave to the handheld M-79 grenade launcher, a weapon that looked like a swollen, sawed-off shotgun. "The motherfucker knocked out one of my guard towers over there!" and he pointed off in the direction of Fort Hustler.

"Now hold on just a minute . . ." big Chad Chandler stepped forward, but the sound of several highly greased Hog-60 swivels swinging around to bear down on him shut the man up and froze him to the spot. Both Ross and the MP sergeant raised their right hands into the air slightly, as if to restrain their men.

"Any of your people hurt?" Ross stood his ground but lost the smile. The rush of adrenaline was subsiding, and his enthusiasm faded.

"Well, no . . ." the MP admitted. He glanced back at the gunjeeps as if counting heads for the first time. "We're operating under strength . . . manpower's down to fifty per cent, and—"

"The Arvins had the M-79," Collins stepped forward when he noticed Sewell was about to explain. None of the MPs seemed interested in the Huey parked inside the concrete hangar—yet. Best to keep it that way. "And they boogied after the sniper, sarge . . ."

Sewell swallowed hard as he sat down on the knoll, perhaps remembering some past encounter with MPs in Korea, and the slammer time that had followed. A visit to the monkey house was never an enjoyable experience.

"Sniper?" One of the MPs in the closest jeep stood up. Chandler started to explain how they had been pinned down by a guerrilla rifleman behind the knoll upon landing when the MP sergeant whistled for one of the gunjeeps in the back of the reaction force to pull forward.

Its driver swerved out of the convoy and rolled up in front of Ross's team. Tied with rope across the vehicle's hood, a skinny Vietnamese youth in baggy GI shorts and a camouflage shirt lay on his back, strapped in snugly like a gutted deer carcass. His entire chest had been ripped apart by a burst of automatic weapons fire, and his head was bent back in an unnatural position, held to the torso by only a few flaps of bloody skin—eyes wide with terror yet lifeless, staring up at the harsh Asian sun.

"We ran across this scumbag on our way over here." The sergeant spat at the ground and began rubbing his temples. The MP in the jeep reached down and grabbed the VC's AK-47 off the floorboards, then held it high over his head for all of Ross's people to see, ". . . sprinting across the elephant grass like a gazelle on the wind, that rifle there his pass to the hereafter."

"Almost crashed into us head on," the private behind the Hog-60 grinned. "But Melodie here cancelled his ticket before he even knew what the fuck hit him!" His words were laced with pride, only slightly cocky, and soaked with job satisfaction.

"Must be your sniper," the sergeant concluded, wiping the crust of grime and sweat from his forehead. Collins noticed that his right hand rested across the .45 on his hip. The holster flap had been cut away so that only a thin strap of black leather held the automatic in place. With bicep muscles bulging below the edge of his rolled up sleeves, and his legs not straight but bent slightly (to better distribute the stocky weight across his frame and keep the blood flowing beneath the sizzling sun?) the man was an impressive figure. "Just who the hell are you guys, anyway?" His narrowed eyes inspected their civilian clothes and lack of weapons, then glanced over at the black helicopter inside the hangar.

"Well . . ." Ross began, but the sergeant held up a hand to silence him.

"Oh . . . Agency spooks," he said quietly, darting his eyes about dramatically as if they now shared a private little joke. He moved to step back into his jeep and gazed over at the swirl of smoke rising from Fort Hustler, where the guard tower had been toppled. "No real damage done. Nice to have a little harmless excitement now and then anyway . . . just to keep my Mike-Papas on their toes."

Ross glanced down at the dead sniper.

"Want him?" the MP sergeant followed his gaze.

Collins and Sewell frowned at the cloud of flies and gnats that had already descended on the deep wounds. "I think we'll pass." Ross scratched at an eyebrow as if the action ended the subject.

"Great." The MP displayed an ear-to-ear smile. "We can use the body count—you know how it is. Stats been kinda lagging behind this month. A hardcore VC sniper'll sure shake up the chairborne warriors back at Disneyland East!"

And the jeeps were gone in a swirl of dust and shredded swamp reeds.

A storm front was rapidly approaching from the west. "Bet that's the same string of monsoon clouds that slammed into us back in Bangkok," wagered Cory.

"Then we better get a move on," replied Ross. "It's about a five mile walk to Saigon from here." He pointed to the three flat tires on the Peugeot. "I doubt these Arvins'll loan us one of their tracks."

"What about these two?" Amy was chest-high in elephant grass, a few yards away, and as the others walked over to her, they could hear the sickening drone of more gathering flies and insects.

The two prostitutes lay at her feet. One dead from the rifle round through her back, the other from the fall. Slivers of translucent cartilage from a broken neck protruded from the swollen skin above her throat.

"Depends on how horny Cory is," Chandler grinned, gently kicking the dead woman with the bullet hole over onto her back with his boot. Her breasts flopped from side to side with the movement, then flattened out across the discolored ribcage, quivering slightly as fresh blood gushed for a few seconds from the exit wound.

"You dudes are *gross!*" Amy sounded disgusted with their antics for a change as she moved away from the bodies. She kept the back of a hand pressed against her lips as she stepped carefully through the tangle of reeds and vines. Collins wondered if she might throw up—it would be the first time, and after all the carnage they had witnessed—but she just made her way over to one of the APCs and sat down on the edge of its aft tread. Collins knew the feeling: no matter how many corpses one viewed, now and then particular circumstances, such as a dead baby dismembered, or pretty women transfigured into grotesque masks of horror, sent the bile rising in your throat. There was nothing you could do about it, except keep your jaws clamped shut, waiting for it to subside. And eventually it would, unless you dwelled on the vomit more than what you had just seen. Funny how the mind worked. Especially when others were watching to see how you would react.

Amy, eyes shut tightly now, tried to think of sights less ghastly than what she had seen. The murders of her parents flashed past her, and the bile subsided.

Ross was lifting the Honda back onto its wheels. "You think it'll run?" he asked Sewell. A few scattered drops from above splashed down around them. Thunder boomed like artillery in the distance, and purple clouds, laced with splinters of lightning, were rolling in off the horizon rapidly.

Collins kicked the tires the same way Chandler had kicked the dead prostitute. Neither had deflated when the scooter flipped end-over-end across the ground. "A product worthy of a damned TV commercial," he muttered sarcastically.

"But can we fit six people on a lousy Honda?" Cory sounded skeptical.

"You, apparently, have already forgotten the scenes we saw last time we roamed the streets of Saigon!"

4

Collins hated bars back in The World. His old girlfriend had always nagged him about never taking her out enough, despite the movie every weekend and a half-dozen fancy Chinese restaurants a month. She was a boozer, though, he had finally figured out, and when one of his fellow cops pulled her over for DUI, he dumped her. Thanked his buddy for the courtesy, (after he directed Collins over the radio to meet him across town, out of his patrol district, at the location of the traffic stop), but told the man to do his duty: lock her young ass up. By the time her parents finally bailed her out, he had changed the locks and piled her belongings out on the porch. *And after all the trouble he had gone through trying to explain to her that he went to a dozen bars every night when he was working the street—to disperse the brawls.* He was sick of nightclubs and the stench of alcohol. He didn't need it during his free time.

But Asia was different. In the Orient, there was something unique about spending time in a drinking establishment. He couldn't explain it to you if he wanted to, but there *was* a difference. Brent Collins could spend all night in a Vietnamese or Korean or Japanese bar, watching the women dancing high in their suspended bamboo cages, bored, but managing a forced smile down at the customers now and then whose peculiar actions—the wink of an eye, a lewd grin—indicated an interest in them. Maybe it was the women.

But tonight Collins was not enjoying himself.

He sat across from Sewell and Chandler, at a table in the back of the bar on Tran Hung Dao, nursing a glass of *Ba Muoi Ba*, and watching Amy at the counter, forty feet away. Wearing the most sensuous outfit in her small, globedrifting wardrobe. "You shouldn't drink so much of that crap," Chandler muttered, "I hear they use formaldehyde in it so it won't spoil in the heat of the tropics," but Collins didn't hear him.

Cory was clashing to the beat of an Elvis medley with a bargirl on the dance floor, and Ross was at a table on the other side of the joint, talking to a woman in hot pants who swore she was just a factory worker, splurging a paycheck. *"But you buy me Saigon tea, okay Joe?"*

Collins's eyes scanned the length of the counter. It was about twenty feet long, with one female bartender behind it. In the center, a closed door led to a back room. Collins saw the small green light blink on next to the cash register the same time that the bartender did. She finished drying a glass, stacked it with others, then moved down to Amy.

"What did you say your name was, Miss?" the Vietnamese asked. Her tone was polite, but laced with disapproval.

"Candy," Amy Atencio replied, brushing her long, ashen hair back over a shoulder. She wore a Chinese *cheong-sam*—a gown that looked ridiculous on most Occidentals, but rode well on her. It was sealed to the throat by a stiff collar, but there was no way the gold silk could conceal the ample swell of her chest. "Candy Marsh."

The bartender ran her eyes up and down Amy's figure one time—the same way women the world over size up the competition, always eliciting a silent chuckle from any men who might be watching. This time there was no envy or jealousy in her narrow, critical eyes. Only stark suspicion. Like she was puzzled by Amy's own subtle hint of Asian features—couldn't decide what nationality she was. She most likely would have been surprised at the answer, if indeed she even knew where Guatemala was. "Colonel Banks will see you now," she said. It sounded like the use of the military rank was common, even in this nightclub, the *Villa*.

Every man on the team tensed as Amy rose and moved around the counter to follow the other woman toward the doorway. Even Cory, whose usually clumsy feet were now magically gliding across the dance floor despite his face being buried in the cleavage of the bargirl holding him up. Amy herself did not appear nervous at all, however. The look in her eyes was one of feigned hope—like she was arriving at a job interview for a position she desperately wanted. Damned good actress, Ross decided.

Amy's eyes checked the door thickness and panel frame as she passed from the noisy bar into the dim, controlled silence of the back room: it appeared heavily reinforced, and might pose a problem if Brent and the others had to charge in—rescue her.

But she didn't expect that sort of problem. Not at this late stage of the game. Not after all the team had gone through to bring her to the attention of Banks.

"Good evening, my dear." A burly man with a glistening tanned crown was rising from behind a large teakwood desk. He was wearing a beige safari shirt that was buttoned only at the bottom. His chest, matted with hair and burnt bronze by years poolside beneath the Asian sun, was decorated with layers of thin Vietnamese gold ceremonial chains that hung from a thick neck. The Bald Eagle in all his glory and splendor. "Candy . . . is it?"

"Yes." Amy displayed her most seductive smile, trying to leave a twinkle of innocence in her wink. It took every ounce of concentration she had not to end the sentence with "sir." The man's expression oozed confidence, power, and just enough skepticism to keep him alive. "Candy Marsh."

Behind and to the left of Banks stood a stocky Chinaman with a wrestler's physique. Dressed in an old fashioned Hong Kong tunic, *his* facial expression was alert but without a visible opinion of her. Amy also knew a second man had followed her into the room from the bar. Bodyguards.

"My people tell me you're interested in an . . . entertainment position with our company here."

"Yes, I am. I dance . . . sing . . ."

"Quite a multitude of talents, from what I hear," he agreed, lifting a sheaf of papers on his desk so she could see them for the first time. The informal application she had filled out earlier. "But sometimes the position requires a sense of loyalty to the association not found in other lines of work . . . or other companies."

"Sort of like the Japanese." The reply came out like she had spent considerable time keeping businessmen in Tokyo happy.

Banks nodded. "A loyalty some might consider above and beyond the call of duty," he grinned mischievously. The phrase made her think of policemen, Brent in particular. "We . . . entertain some very wealthy clients . . . if you know what I mean. . . ." Every sentence was filled with innuendoes.

Amy smiled back. "Yes, I think I know what you mean."

"But quite frankly, Miss . . . Marsh," he spoke the name as if he doubted its authenticity. "I'm a little troubled by your interest in this position."

"Troubled, sir?" There she went: using the word. Ross had told her not to. It made her sound too much like she hung around cops or the military. Amy herself had been a bit troubled, though relieved, when no metal detectors had been activated by her armed entry into the office—perhaps Banks's little group wasn't as sophisticated as they all thought.

"This is the first time an . . . application ever came across my desk, to tell you the truth." His smile faded and condor-like brows focused in on her . . . or was it her imagination? "We usually . . . recruit in other manners. To be honest with you, no one has ever really come right up and . . . volunteered their services."

"Sir?" She crossed her legs sensuously: time for a little flesh.

"I would not be a good . . . manager, if I did not get suspicious about you."

Amy gave her best attempt at showing relief. It was an expression that said, "well, if *that's* all that's bothering you . . ." "Sir, my situation is really no different from the countless other homeless, destitute girls that filter through Cholon, looking for work. It just happens that I'm not Oriental."

"And you have no other skills by which to support yourself?" Banks made his thick eyebrows do a little mating dance as he tried to probe her true intentions. Amy produced a hurt look in reply.

"Sir, I have always been an entertainer. A singer. But I have just not been able to achieve stardom. And a lack of notoriety, in this business, means no work."

"I see."

"Except for the bars . . . the . . . one night gigs . . . (she almost said one night stands), and I heard your people pay handsomely."

"You heard?" Banks rested his chin atop interlaced fingers that accented bruised knuckles. It was an impressive display of intimidation, but Amy did not let it affect her. The same way she did not look over her shoulder when she felt the second bodyguard following her into the room. Taking notice of such things could reveal her street caution. And *that* could end this job interview with a trip down the Saigon River. Face down.

"Word travels fast down the . . . grapevine," she

finally answered. "All I've heard from the other girls for weeks is how good the money is at the Villa in Cholon—"

"Caucasian girls?" Banks cut in.

"Sir?" Amy feigned ignorance of words with more than two syllables.

"White women?"

"No . . . no," she laughed. "I only have Veeyet-Nameese girlfriends."

"As I said earlier," Banks shifted about in his seat. "We require a great deal of loyalty from our employees. We compensate such dedication with ample sums of money." His eyes fell to the jutting swell below her throat. "Greenbacks, piaster, MPC. But I think an . . . audition of sorts would be necessary before I could make the final decision on you, Candy."

"You mean you want me to sing for you?"

Banks hesitated only the briefest of moments. "I want you to take off your clothes," he finally said, matter-of-factly.

"So you can inspect the goods." Amy's reply was made with a straight face.

"It is only fair to ask . . . and purely business of course."

Amy could see the sweat beads of anticipation and arousal forming at the base of the man's adams apple. For the first time, she glanced back at the bodyguard behind her. "With these two men present?"

"They are members of the association, Candy. Highly trusted. And like I said, the job requires a high degree of devotion from all its employees." The man in the Hong Kong tunic smiled slightly.

"That comes with the territory," Amy agreed, smiling herself now, but then she made the smile disappear, "and the paycheck. I don't put on floorshows for free."

Banks moved his shoulders about, as if the action allowed him to see something from a different point of view. "I guess it all depends on how bad you want the job. . . ."

Amy's eyes dropped to the floor for a few seconds as she appeared to consider everything. "I'll drop my shorts if your gorillas take a hike," she said bluntly.

Banks almost laughed, and he glanced at the two other men in the room as if in agreement that precautions were in excess that day. He waved the bodyguards out of the room. One man left immediately, but the other gave Amy a suspicious frown before making his exit. *He* will pose the biggest problem later, she decided. Then the panels behind the huge desk slid shut, and they were alone.

Banks rose from his chair and sat along the edge of the desk. "Well now, Miss Marsh," he began unbuttoning the rest of his shirt. "Let's not waste any more time with bothersome formalities . . ."

"I'm ready any time you are, honey." She slipped her high heels off and removed the silk scarf around her throat.

Banks ran his eyes along her chest, mentally calculating the size of her breasts from the swell under the blouse. Amy ignored the zipper, however, and lifted one foot up onto the white plaster elephant statue in front of Banks's desk. She pulled her skirt up to her crotch, revealing firm golden thighs, and began rolling down the nylons.

Banks's eyes jumped slightly when they caught sight of the black bikini briefs in the shadows under the skirt. In the dim room they made her look like she was wearing nothing, and the colonel hastily threw his shirt off. With his arm out straight, he swept his wrist across the desktop, knocking all the papers and curios onto the hard teakwood floor. Amy shook her head slightly: here was another john who liked doing it on desktops.

When Banks looked down to struggle with an uncooperative buckle, Amy brought the other leg up onto the elephant, pulled the skirt back again, and drew the commando knife strapped to the inside of her thigh.

As his pants fell down around his knees, she flew over the desk, plunging the blade deep into his chest even before he could look up.

They both toppled backward onto the floor and against the wall, but Amy landed catlike, one foot on either side of the man's spasm-filled body.

The last thing Banks saw before he died was the inviting dark shadow inside the skirt over his face—where the long, tensed thighs above him came together. He wanted to smile—to laugh at the irony of it, but suddenly the shaft of cold steel was being jerked out of his sternum and forced back down into his heart like a hot poker, fresh out of the fireplace at his lodge back in Rhode Island. Banks could not even cry out: now she was ripping his throat open with the gleaming, crimson-lined blade, from ear to ear. *A true professional* Banks decided, moments

103

before Amy roughly rolled him onto his stomach, punched the dagger up into the base of his skull from behind, and scrambled his brains around with it.

It was the last thought the Bald Eagle would ever have.

Amy, always anticipating the worst, recovered from the stress of the kill as if she was expecting no assistance from outside the room: she slid a sturdy bookcase against the panel through which the bodyguards had exited. Moments later, they were pounding on the sliding doors from the other side, creating a racket that was not quite hidden by the floorshow speakers blaring outside in the bar.

Collins was first through the front entrance into the room, and the sight of Amy's face—streaked with blood and whirling around to face them, dagger in hand—was a mental picture of her he would carry the rest of his life. Ross was already brushing past them, going down on one knee beside Banks for the fraction of a second it took to determine the man was dead. Then a CS grenade was out and rolling across the floor toward the rear door, thirty feet away.

"All right, let's move out!" he directed.

Chandler's eyes were locked on the far panels, shaking about with each pounding fist from the bodyguards. "How 'bout I lace 'em with a burst of tracers, Justin?" His cut-down AK was out of its side sheath. There came a dull pop, and gas spewed forth gray and wet along the far side of the room.

"No need for it." Ross was digging through piles of paperwork on the colonel's desk, then quickly but cautiously sifting through the two drawers whose locks he had to tear out.

A minute later, as the teargas began to fill the entire room and the team strapped handkerchiefs across their faces, braced for any surprise intrusions through the front door, Ross was scooping a handful of papers in under his shirt and motioning the others out.

Momentarily troubled by the lack of additional guards confronting them via the front door, Sewell decided the two Amy had barricaded in the back room were the only ones aware of the disturbance. The room was probably sealed for safety, except for the panels, which were now also blocked. Any bodyguards out in the main section of the bar should have seen the Americans rushing into the office however. Would they be met with a hail of bullets upon exiting? All these thoughts went through Sewell's mind as one, but he gritted his teeth, took in a deep breath, and started out the door.

At the same time, Ross broke the fire alarm switch on the wall above Banks's body. The Villa was soon a chorus of ringing bells.

Sewell saw the four bodyguards waiting outside the second he opened the door. Pistols drawn, they restrained firing blindly as the nightclub patrons passed between them in a mad, noisy rush for the exits.

The last one out into the lobby, Ross dropped two more CS grenades, and rolled a mortar simulator under Banks's desk in all the confusion.

When the simulator began its harsh whistle, most of the customers still in the bar dove under tables, uncomfortably familiar with the sounds of war and the signs of a sapper attack. The explosion that culminated the shrill warning was multiplied several times over by the small size of Banks's office, and it sent several bargirls screaming. Chandler sent a burst of red glowing tracers up into the giant revolving chandelier above the dance floor, and amid a shower of multi-colored glass shards, the nightclub fell dark except for some of the tabletop candles flickering in the corners. Ross's team slipped out of the building without further incident.

Later, as they sat at umbrellaed tables along the edge of the Bat Dat Hotel's rooftop terrace, watching the street below fill with Vietnamese firetrucks, Ross said, "I'll have to be getting these documents over to the Provost Marshal's office. I'll slip 'em to a gate guard or something. Banks was smart: didn't keep much incriminating evidence around. But maybe the white-hats can find a clue here somewhere as to their female agent's current status."

"I doubt even somebody as smug as Banks would put in writing where he holds hostages or how he snuffs female CID agents," Amy was still wiping a handkerchief across parts of her face—where Banks's blood had long ago been cleaned off by Collins.

"I realize that," Ross sounded irritated. They all seemed in bad spirits. Though the hit had gone down without casualties, they had all been against sending Amy into such a dangerous situation alone. "But the guy had a big ego."

"Probably kept notes somewhere." Cory felt the responsibility to come to Ross's defense. "For a future bio."

"He'd have to PCS to Brazil to get a bio like that printed," Chandler muttered.

"Don't you think you'll be jeopardizing the mission by making contact with the MPs?" Collins asked. Ross had glanced through some of the documents he had taken out of Banks's desk, but now was sealing them in a large manila envelope he had scrounged from the hotel receptionist.

Ross made a show of writing "PM" in large letters across the face of the envelope. "Just going to hand this to a buck private at the gate," he said. "Or maybe give some cabbie a couple dong to carry it to the gate guard."

"Just so you keep an eye on the cabbie from Point A to Point B." Collins was still frowning.

Ross's smile faded and his expression turned serious, but his voice retained a mildly humorous tone. "You're all sounding like a truckload of mother hens. Perhaps you'd like to accompany me over to the MP compound, wherever it is, and make sure I do things by the numbers."

The others remained silent.

"Brent, why don't you remain here and monitor things going on down there in the street for awhile," Ross said. "The rest of us will head back over into Saigon proper and take care of this," he patted the thick envelope, "before curfew."

"Too many round-eyes up here," Chandler agreed. "Best we filter out around town before the canh-sats start canvassing the neighborhood for witnesses. Shit's gonna hit the fan when they find that dead colonel down there. . . ."

Almost mechanically, Amy and Sewell rose from their seats with Ross and Chandler. Down in the street, more sirens were arriving, until Dong Khanh Boulevard was clogged with idling motors and red lights flashing bright beams through the mist.

"I'll stay behind with Brent," Cory MacArthur said. "In case he needs any cover," and he patted the sawed-off Ithaca under his jean jacket.

"Won't be necessary," Collins said softly. His eyes were glued to the activity below. A truckload of Vietnamese QCs had pulled up, and a squad sergeant was directing the military policemen to secure the block and prevent any spectators from entering or potential witnesses from leaving.

"We better get a move on," Sewell motioned to a set of gunjeeps turning onto Dong Khanh from Cong Rung, up the street a half dozen blocks. Their lights and sirens were not on, but there was no mistaking the white "MP" letters glowing on the black helmets.

Ross hesitated. "Come on Cory," he motioned to the youngest member of the team. "You'll come with us." Then he turned to face Amy. "Atencio will remain behind with Collins. A caucasian female face will only attract attention at this time. If things don't cool down by curfew—and they probably won't—see if you can get a room in this dump for the night."

"And if they're full up?" Amy asked.

Ross didn't supply an immediate answer, and Collins said, "Perhaps Matt could pick us up with his whirlybird."

Ross frowned and turned to start for the stairs.

An hour later, as curfew approached, and the street below remained clogged with law enforcement personnel, Collins glanced over at Amy for the first time. "I better go down and pay for a room," he said.

She nodded her head, but said nothing.

Not wanting to be seen in a dim stairwell by any of the security forces, Brent took the elevator at the edge of the terrace. On the second floor, two British foreign correspondents with shoulder-length hair and wire rim glasses stumbled into the elevator, laughing hysterically. One was trying to keep his balance as he stared at the ceiling, eyes tightly shut, singing a Beatles' tune loudly. The other leaned on Collins for support with one hand. He was carrying an opium ball in the other. "Lobby, mate," he laughed. "Hope you're goin' down, that is." Neither journalist looked the American in the eyes.

"The lobby it is, gents." He forced a smile. He gently shifted the man on his elbow over until he was leaning on his friend instead. He didn't wish to be associated with the dopers in the event there were policemen waiting in the lobby for the elevator doors to slide open. "You'd best pocket your chow there, though," he talked with a mild British accent. "Lot of activity down there right now. I imagine the lobby's full of canh-sats right about now."

"Who do ya think we scored *this* from?" The man with the opium laughed louder, still not facing Collins eye to eye.

"Some Yankee general or something bit the dust

109

across the street," the other reporter revealed, singing the words instead of talking them as he continued his medley of current hits.

"We tried to get some shorts for the wire," the first man said, "But the white mice aren't letting *any*body in there, mate!"

When the elevator slid open, Collins was pleasantly surprised to find the hotel lobby practically vacant. A few old Asian hands sat in sunken rattan chairs with felt cushions, reading their copies of the *Vietnam Guardian* and ignoring the goings-on outside. There were no police uniforms immediately visible, though beams of flashing red light filled the frosted windows of the hotel restaurant on the far side of the lobby, down the inner steps from the check-in desk.

Standing in front of the mail bin, a pretty receptionist was leaning across the check-in counter, watching the activity out in the street. Hair piled up neatly on top of her head, she wore thin, nearly invisible eyeglasses. Sensing his approach from the side, she automatically slid the glasses off and prepared a facial expression of greeting. When their eyes locked for the first time, she was momentarily unable to speak, so taken aback was she by Brent's ruggedly handsome features. Collins kept his eyes on her as he glided up to the counter, and was soon towering over the slim, petite woman.

Embarrassed, the woman's eyes fell to the counter, and Collins could sense her swallowing hard. "Good evening, my dear." He said the words in his most romantic tone. The woman was blushing now. Collins was confident that, even if there were no rooms available, by the time he was done with her, she'd abandon her post and take him home to her hooch. Although that wasn't in the plan.

"Hello, sir . . . How can I help you?" Her voice was high-pitched. Each syllable coming across sing-song, like a bird high in tree branches somewhere.

Collins ran his eyes from her chin to her dress's edge and back up. Her figure was cleverly concealed by an unflattering hotel uniform, composed of dull browns and reds. "I'm hoping you might still have a room available at this late hour." His expression was not desperate like his tone, but humorous.

The receptionist produced a frown perfected by years of turning away potential customers as she glanced back at the empty keyboard. "Sir, I'm afraid it appears as if—"

"Surely you can find me . . . *some*thing." His eyes now told her he wouldn't mind spending the night cuddled in her arms at some cockroach-infested flat overlooking the Ben Nghe canal.

The woman checked her watch. Was she feeling guilty at turning away a foreigner so close to curfew—and how did he get in that elevator in the first place? "We had a room only five minutes ago." Her lip trembled as if she were about to cry, "but some reporters rushed in and took it—"

"What *is* all the activity about out there?" His eyes darted to the collage of flashing lights against the restaurant windows.

"I don't know." She did not now seem interested in all the canh-sat jeeps skidding up in front of the Villa. "Probably another raid on prostitutes, or perhaps—"

"What about that key?" he interrupted, leaning over the counter slightly as he pointed up to the bamboo framed keyboard. "Is anybody using that one?" He was almost brushing against her ear, inhaling the fragrance of her in a way that told her exactly what he was up to. She smiled at the closeness of him, but backed away a few paces. She glanced up at the lone key at the top of the board, and started to nod her head from side to side.

"I am afraid that key is to the penthouse," she started to explain, turning back to face him, "and it is being used by—"

But the woman's lips froze in mid-sentence, and her eyes went wide with fear as they focused on something behind Collins. Before he could move, a powerful arm shot around him, over his right shoulder. A thick forearm wrapped itself around his throat, cutting off his windpipe in a classic chokehold as his assailant's left wrist clamped in firmly behind Collins's head and he was slowly lifted off his feet.

5

Brent Collins felt the desperation that comes with being caught in a headlock by a bigger man. He could still concentrate—the pretty receptionist in front of him was backing away, unable to scream though her mouth was open slightly—but he knew it would only be a matter of moments before he blacked out and became helpless.

He took the first defensive action that was called for in this sort of situation, realizing his energy would quickly be depleted if he didn't act fast: he moved his hip to the left and brought his right fist down and back, aiming blindly for his attacker's groin.

But the fist sliced into only air and nothing more.

"Gotta be quicker than that, Brent!" The voice behind him was chasing his consciousness down into the swirl of black, and then Collins could feel the hold on his throat being slowly released.

Where had he heard that voice before? The man had obviously pivoted out of the way when Collins brought his fist back—had he gone through police training with him somewhere?

No, he knew no cops who could make such a fool-ish, risky move in an Asian city, and after dark at that. The man was now draping an arm around his waist, to keep the smaller American on his feet. Collins half expected him to say *Guess Who?* next.

No, it could only be a GI . . . a *marine* who would engage in horseplay like this, despite the passage of years, the maturing, the lessons learned.

"Guess who?"

Collins concentrated on the two words, but he could not attach a face to them.

He was becoming angry. And he just might spend the next few seconds silently catching his breath in preparation for whirling around and decking the damned sonofa—

"It's me, Brent-baby!" Collins was practically pushed over the counter into the arms of the recep-tionist. And just like that, the memories rushed back at him. . . .

Inchon. The gray, overcast sky . . . the drizzle, the railyards extending to the sea. Ocean-front bars filled to the brim with combative sailors, drunk GIs . . . the two of them pulling Shore Patrol to-gether . . . raising more hell than the servicemen they were supposed to be policing. . . .

"Why Hank, you sonofabuck!" Collins was whirl-ing around now. "Is it really you?"

He suddenly found himself facing a bear of a man with his hair combed back into a short flat-top, his barrel-framed torso straining at the seams of his short-sleeved nylon shirt, and his face an ear-to-ear flash of teeth. His arms were outstretched, frozen in mid-air like the startled expression on the receptionist behind him.

The men embraced, and the friendly hug was punctuated by a lot of loud backslapping. Hank was then dragging Collins away from the lobby and down the carpeted stairs into the hotel restaurant.

Brent glanced back at the receptionist helplessly and smiled, winking an eye. But she was still too shocked by the whole incident to react.

Entering the restaurant was like leaving the old, boring world behind. Except for the flashing lights and bustle of activity outside, the only illumination came from orange glass candle holders on the tables and glowing Chinese lanterns suspended from the ceiling. The counter along the bar was full, but Collins observed that only a quarter, at most, of the tables were occupied. There was a stage in the distance, but, except for a set of drums with *The Dreamers* stenciled across the bass, it was dark and abandoned. A jukebox in a far corner glowed purple and blue as it churned out several soft tunes in slow succession. There were no bargirls in sight, and the number of men without partners would have made a pimp's mouth water.

Collins smiled: Hank was leading him directly to a table occupied by a young woman with jet-black hair that fell to her waist and shimmered like silk beneath the lanterns. The scent of her perfume was mingling with alcohol and noodle soup fragrances as both men drew closer. "I spotted you in the lobby from my table here," Hank said.

"Good ol' Hank O'Leary," said Brent. "As eagle-eyed as ever. And you just couldn't pass up the ol' bearhug approach after all these years, right?"

115

O'Leary shot him a what-do-you-think? look.

They had spent three years in the Marines together. In Korea. When cannons kept the night lit up and American boys wagered whether they'd wake up the next morning dodging a mortar barrage or bayonets from a human wave of mainland Chinese shock troops. The early fifties, when life was much more simple, and death was a far cry from the black-and-white movies of World War II Hollywood. Collins and O'Leary had shipped over to Inchon late in their tour of duty, and with their non-com rank intact, the majority of their time overseas was spent with the SPs, where they worked nights and slept days, usually during lulls in the constant fighting. When their units stood down, everyone exchanged addresses and phone numbers, but the men drifted apart and never wrote or called. O'Leary had remained in Korea, until ETS, where he lived with a young masseuse and spent his time filling out job applications with American firms in the Land of the Morning Calm. After the money ran out, he returned to the Land of the Big PX, minus his lady friend, and, like Brent, became involved with civilian law enforcement. Though both men eventually became dues-paying members of the Fraternal Order of Police, neither learned the fate of the other, though Collins had once sent him a postcard from Guadalajara, and O'Leary had once tried to phone Brent in the states from Seoul.

"My dear." Hank gently brought the Vietnamese woman's hand to his lips and kissed it. "May I present an old friend . . . Brent Collins."

Collins was already sitting down. Obvious callgirls

116

did not impress him, regardless of their manner or wardrobe. He nodded and smiled as he picked up a menu, but the woman ignored him, busy with her makeup case.

"So what brings you to South Vietnam?" Collins was genuinely surprised at meeting his old friend in Cholon.

"Oh, I'm back on active duty, hombre." He reached across the table and slapped Brent on the side of the arm. The woman between them slipped her mirror and lipstick back into her purse and frowned at the scene.

"Active duty?" Collins asked incredulously. "In the Marine Corps?"

"Yah." O'Leary dropped his chin and nodded, almost embarrassed. But then his expression perked up as he announced his advance through the ranks. "But I'm a major now, buddy. Got me a little gold oak leaf and everything."

"A fucking officer? Naw . . . you're shitting me, Hank. I don't believe you'd forsake all your old jarhead pals by becomin' a damned occifer!"

"Wait till you hear this, amigo," and he slipped his wallet out of a back pocket and flipped it open dramatically until Brent was staring at an impressive ID card. "Military Intelligence."

"Naw."

He tossed the wallet across the table and Brent caught it in the air, despite the poor lighting.

"I don't believe it," Collins maintained.

"Believe it, bucko. Got tired of all the boredom stateside. When this Vietnam thing heated up, I re-en-fucking-listed for MI training and an Indochina

117

post, turned in my shield, and—"

"Turned in my shield?" Collins straightened up in his seat. Only cops used the term shield, instead of badge. "You were on the cops?"

"Dade County, Florida."

"Naw. . ."

"Was a damned good deputy, too. But I got burned out on all them crazy Cubans down there, you know what I mean? Miami ain't even a part of the United States any more, Brent."

"So you came to Saigontown to mellow out," he replied sarcastically.

"Hey, you know how it is overseas. I missed that certain something connected with a duty station in the . . . mysterious Orient."

Collins flinched at the overused stereotype. Amy's face flashed through his mind, but he didn't mention her, waiting up on the rooftop terrace. She could take care of herself. "Yah, I know how it is."

There came a scattering of yells outside the restaurant, some isolated shots, laughter, and then several police jeeps were pulling away. A waitress appeared beside Brent. "Can I take your order, honey?" She was running the edge of her tongue along the eraser on her pencil.

"See what I mean?" O'Leary laughed at the girl's remark. "Only in Saigon."

"I suppose you're on some kind of secret war-related assignment," Collins handed the big man his wallet back.

"Nope . . . not really. In between missions right now—you know how it is."

"Can't really talk about it."

O'Leary picked up a slab of barbecued ribs with his chopsticks and tore a slice free. Juice trickled down into the stubble on his chin. "Right."

Collins wondered if he already knew what was going on across the street—if he knew anything at all about Bald Eagle Banks's white slave market—or if he just happened to be staying at the out of the way, back-alley Bat Dat Hotel.

"Come to think of it," the MI agent paused, looking up from his meal. "What the hell brings *you* to the 'Nam?"

Collins's brain felt like it was suddenly beginning to overheat, as he struggled to come up with a convincing reason. He never in his wildest dreams had foreseen the possibility of encountering an old friend in a country like South Vietnam. "How 'bout the sweet-and-sour shrimp?" he finally placed his order with the patient waitress. It would give him more time to think. The woman sitting between him and Hank frowned at his selection, and the waitress made her little pug nose do a funny jig, like she had just strolled past an open sewer unexpectedly.

"Sweet-and-sour shrimp?" O'Leary feigned intense disappointment in his choice. "There you go ordering like a goddamned white boy." He reached over and grabbed Brent's menu, eyes scanning the inside pages more like an after-action report than a food list. "Try some *Goi cuon* for an appetizer— that's rubber shrimp rolls, for you civilians," he smiled, looking up temporarily. "and some *com-tay-cam* for the main dish—sliced pork in ginger sauce with mushrooms and chicken on rice . . . say, how hungry are you, anyway?" But without allowing a re-

119

sponse, he glanced up at the waitress, who was busy writing on her pad. "And he'll take some *Dua xanh banh lot* to drink—"

"*Dua xanh banh lot?*" Brent wasn't in the mood for liquor.

"Coconut bean drink, Marco Polo," he laughed. "Don't you know anything?"

"I just don't want any booze tonight, Hank."

"Oh, that's for later." The big Irishman's eyes lit up. "When we get down to some serious war stories. By the way . . . you never answered my original question: what brings you to the Pearl of the Orient?"

Collins feigned a semi-embarrassed expression and let his shoulders droop slightly. "War is romance." The words came out almost in a whisper. "And romance is literature. . . ." O'Leary replied with a bewildered frown. "I've come here in search of the great American novel, Hank."

"Huh?"

What else could he say? A man from MI just might check up on him, out of boredom, if he came up with a more exciting story. "I made a few grand back in The World on some magazine articles—"

"Congrats," O'Leary's frown broke into a tense smile, but his eyes said he was not impressed.

"And I'm using those funds to tide me over until I can freelance some pictures for the wire services or—"

"A lousy photojournalist, eh?" O'Leary now seemed pleased with Brent's explanation. Reporters were something he could comprehend, deal with. They were everywhere—up to everything, just to get a story. He'd seen them accompany advisors out to the field for a week, only to come back with a short story, two rolls of film, then have to wait six weeks for possible acceptance by a publication stateside, and even longer for that elusive paycheck. "I just never figured you much for being one of them news media types," O'Leary shook his head. "Bunch o' lousy bloodsuckers, Brent. Tell me you aren't like them."

Collins watched him glance about the room absentmindedly, bored, seeking out more flesh: he was tiring of the woman's attitude beside him. His expression told Collins he didn't really care what kind of story Brent concocted. Saigon was a neon fantasyland, powered by lies. "Who knows, Hank. Might just score that book contract without even having to resort to venturing out into the field—won't have to disappoint you."

"But you should be over at the Continental, covering the war from the rooftop terrace with those other clowns. Why the Bat Dat, Brent, of all places?" He glanced out at the few police jeeps still in the street, and revolving red lights danced in his eyes. His expression changed back to one of challenge: *answer me that one, buddy.*

"Cholon seems to have a little more flavor to it than Tu Do, don't you think?" he replied. "More culture . . . and less flesh." O'Leary just snorted back lightly in response as his eyes now followed one of the waitress's bouncing bottom as she glided by, a tray of empty glasses balanced across a tiny palm. "*I* should be the one asking that question, pal: what's a bigshot clandestine type like yourself doing on Dong Khanh street?"

121

"Gorgeous here," he motioned to the woman sitting beside him, "dragged me down here. Claimed they had a good band, but all I see is an abandoned drumset over there . . . " A black sedan was pulling up across the street, and what appeared to be two CID agents got out. O'Leary showed no new interest in the goings-on outside the restaurant window, and he made no move to join them. He glanced at his Rolex wristwatch. "As fate would have it, I'm working graveyards this month . . . almost time to move out, actually. Just coming off my three day break." He looked sadly over at the prostitute beside him again, then at Brent. "Forty-eight hours in the sack with this cunt, and I never succeeded in wiping that defiant smirk off her face . . . " He smiled broadly then, thinking back to their days in Korea. "And you know how I like challenges, son."

"Yah, but nightshift can sure put a drain on you," Collins smiled back.

"Well," he made a move to rise from his chair, "it's easy duty the next few weeks. Just a bunch of paperwork I got piled up on my desk . . . field agent notes I gotta sift through—we're following this June Wanda bullshit pretty closely. She's due in to Saigon again in a few days, you know . . . "

"No, I didn't know that."

"By the way," Collins had risen also, and O'Leary draped a big arm around his shoulder, "I heard the receptionist telling you they were out of rooms—just before I ambushed your young ass. Well, I'm paid up through tomorrow, amigo. You can have my suite."

The woman still seated at their table showed some interest in the conversation for the first time. She flashed irritated eyes up at O'Leary. "What about me?" she demanded in halting English, her accent heavy, yet sensuous. Her chest jiggled about slightly with the movement.

O'Leary's devilish grin returned. He had been planning to tell her she was on her own, despite the curfew, but instead, he said, "Well, if Brent here has no objection, maybe you could give him one of your notorious massages . . . then the two of you could see what develops from there." He winked at both of them.

Collins thought of Amy, waiting overhead, on the roof all this time. The prostitute at the table was running her eyes over him, appraising his build. Her scowl turned suddenly friendly, but he said, "Well, actually Hank . . . I've got a lady friend waiting for me upstairs. On the terrace."

"What?" he feigned insult and injury. "And you didn't bring her down here to meet me?"

"But how could I know—" he started to explain.

"Viet or Chinese?" he interrupted.

"Round-eye," he answered, biting his tongue too late. The woman at the table picked up her glass of rice wine, downed it with one final, angry swallow, and got up and left the table without saying a word. She made her way over to the few remaining patrons at the counter, careful to make her hips shift about erotically with each footfall before she reached the bar and leaned across the nearest stranger's shoulder. He responded with a startled but pleased expression and invitation to be seated on his lap. The woman never once looked back at Collins or his friend.

123

"So screw her, anyway," O'Leary said loud enough for everyone in the restaurant to hear. "Lead me up to meet your—"

But a jeep had rolled up outside and a marine non-com was laying on the horn. "Ooops. . . have to make a raincheck," the man from MI said. "There's my driver, bud. Tell you what," he reached down in his pocket and produced a room key. "I should be back around eight a.m. or nine o'clock the latest. Stick around so we can talk some more, and I'll buy you both breakfast."

Collins took the key and smiled. "Sure, Hank . . . sure." O'Leary was already halfway to the door. "Thanks."

"Oh, and Brent," he paused before walking out into the night.

"Yah, trooper?"

O'Leary produced his brightest smile. "Go easy on the sheets, okay?"

Collins nodded his head sheepishly and made a mental note to have them both out of the hotel by six in the morning.

Justin Ross counted fifty thousand piasters from the pile of currency notes on his hotel room desk and slid them in front of Collins. "Don't spend it all in one whorehouse," he smiled.

Chad Chandler was next in line, and as he moved up anxiously, Collins slowly walked back to sit down on a bed, his eyes glued to the bills as he recounted them slowly. "A hundred lousy bucks?" he said, even before Ross had started divvying out Chandler's paycheck.

"What do you expect?" Sewell waited patiently in line, looking more tired and depressed than usual. "This *is* the Green Machine, you know."

"But a hundred lousy bucks?" his eyes shifted to Ross, who did not look up, but just kept smiling and counting. "All the heads I've sent rolling in the last month for Uncle Sammy, and all I rate is a fucking C-note?"

"You forget." Amy was beside him now, dropping out of line in hopes of comforting her undercover lover. "We're lucky to get jack-shit, remember? Very little separates you and me from the boys doing hard time back in Folsom or San Quentin. . . ."

Ross's smile faded, but nobody seemed to notice. He kept counting out the wrinkled brown notes.

Collins sat down on one of the two beds in the room and stared at the money in his hand. He went stubbornly silent, realizing Amy was right but not wanting to admit it. What could one do with a hundred dollars?

Actually, quite a bit, in Saigon. But that was not how Collins looked at it. He was recalling his days with the police department back in the states—how he struggled from paycheck to paycheck financially, but enjoyed the freedom to live his bachelor life the way he saw fit. Now he was back in the military, and his activities were strictly monitored and regulated. It didn't matter that the team was probably one of the most elite counter-insurgency units in American history, empowered to take life without fear of public repercussions or earthly consequences. Only God.

And how many of them even believed in an Almighty? Sure, Sewell had his weird beliefs in the power of soaring, flight, and a supreme being of sorts waiting above the clouds. And Chandler was into reincarnation. All those years in the Orient had made him a convert, and now and then—as a joke, he maintained—his hotel room filled with incense and the sounds of chanting. The thought of coming back in an afterlife—potluck decided your race, nationality and even whether you returned as a frog or a prince—made Collins cringe, even though he knew he'd choose Buddhism over Western religions if he were forced to. And who would force him, anyway? Nobody knew what went on in Ross's mind, and Cory professed mankind sprang forth from games played by the gods in ancient Greece. And the gods themselves could just conceivably be alien astronauts or time travellers from another world, thank you. Then there was Amy. She never talked much about God, either, but Brent felt she had probably been raised a Christian in her youth.

And Brent Collins? He was beginning to wonder about a Jesus who wore long hair and preached pacifism. All these years, he had done his job as a cop should—confident that if there indeed was a God, he would judge Brent one of the good guys at his death. But was he, Brent, now becoming an enemy of Christ? Would following his beliefs eventually lead to damnation at his death? Or was he right in leading a warrior's life—and to hell with the consequences! Perhaps the life awaiting him after death was what he made of it: a mental existence soothing to the soul, yet devoid of both heaven and hell. What thoughts went through the minds of young, impressionable, religious soldiers the government was sending off to Vietnam—while the same priests who had taught them catechisms throughout their childhoods now protested the war though violent demonstrations in the streets across America? Did these mortals really represent the Lord . . . the Almighty Creator? Was Jesus Christ a long-hair who sat at the foot of the Divine Being's throne, frowning down at his children in soldier uniforms? If this was the case, Collins was repulsed by the thought of worshipping such a creature. Satan, if he existed, was not the answer, for Brent had spent his entire life fighting evil in all its forms and manifestations.

The collage of thoughts, theories and contradictions always left him with a headache and days of depression. All he could do was live life boldly, doing what was *right*—not what other mortals told him was the correct or humble way of surviving day to day. What happened at the point of death—be it the beginning of another life on the other side of earth, heavenly bliss, flames, or a mental awareness confined only to the outer limits of the cosmos—was inconsequential. Collins knew he possessed a shade of conscience that was separate from his upbringing or the teachings of any god. It was an instinct of survival that other men had shared long before there were any temples or crucifixes to regulate their lives.

"Ninety-nine . . . one hundred." Chad Chandler smacked his lips and folded his paycheck, then walked over and joined Collins on the edge of the bed. "What say we go down to the bar and toast our sudden accumulation of wealth," he said sarcastically. They had relocated to another hotel after the hit at the

Villa, and none of them had yet to visit the building's restaurant or bar.

"Stick around," Ross mumbled as he proceeded to count out Cory's money. "We got things to discuss . . ."

"Not another hit," Chandler looked up from recounting his piasters. He was separating the notes into little piles: so much for booze, this much for women, that much for a silk shirt he'd never get to wear.

"Something like that." Again Ross did not look up.

"Christ, Justin—how long we gonna stay in Saigon-town. I was hoping we could get back to Tokyo before the games—"

"Dream on," said Amy, recalling the geishas the men had sauntered in with their last night in Japan.

Collins watched them all preparing their little retorts and bounce-back insults, and he found himself thinking back to what Amy had said about San Quentin. She was right, he hated to admit. And not only were they seeing the world instead of a jail cell—Brent had to chuckle to himself when he came up with that thought—but the government was supporting them. Justin always came up with money from somewhere to pay the hotel bills, food and entertainment costs, and miscellaneous underworld fees that came with passing from country to country undetected.

Cory was still giving him that goofy-kid look. It was an expression the youth produced when he was troubled by something someone had said. Today, Brent noticed, it came about when Amy mentioned the prisons back in The World.

Was young Cory curious about his background?

Even after all these missions, the team members remained secretive about their pasts. Sure, there were a few remarks about Chandler's days as a mercenary in Africa, and everyone knew Sewell had piloted choppers during the Korean War. But nobody really knew what mistakes had caused the others to be sentenced to life under the watchful eye of Justin Ross.

Brent thought back briefly to the arrest back in that small steelmill town in the Rockies a lifetime ago. Where the prisoner had shot it out with them and could have died anyway—only a fluke in the manner he was captured spared his life. It had been a bad week all around for the policeman, and after his prisoner spat on him, ran the gambit of burn-down-your-house-and-rape-your-wife threats, and kicked him in the head from the back seat of the patrol car, ignoring the handcuffs, Collins had pulled the patrol car over and gone to work on the punk. As luck would have it, the prisoner died. The supervisor in charge of the watch that day had known Ross from his old war days. He knew Collins was an otherwise good cop who had made a regrettable mistake and overreacted to a bad situation. But he had a dead prisoner on his hands. As it turned out, Collins was spirited away to the team's training camps at LZ London and the Panamanian jungle, and the incident was covered up. Though the prisoner was a transient with no family, Collins was never told this, and the body—the evidence—was kept on ice in the event the ex-cop ever tried to leave the team or betray their missions to the press. Five months after leaving the department he loved with all his heart, Collins's watch commander—the man who had originally contacted Ross—died in a traffic accident during a high speed chase, but Brent was not told about this turn of events either.

Perhaps someday the others would also relive the tragedies that had brought this most recent death squad together. Perhaps some rainy night down along the road, when they were all gathered in an Asian bar, therapy group fashion, feeling sorry for themselves, one, then another and another would open up, revealing it all. . . .

Ross himself had been in and out of the death squads for the past ten years, beginning in Korea, when he was searching tunnels and his squad sergeant sealed the entrance with a grenade. Scrambling away from the blast, through the dark, he had smashed into another person beneath the surface of the battle-scarred earth. With visions of a Chinese soldier, bayoneted carbine in hand, flashing through his mind, Ross fired his pistol into the dark. Exploding light from the deafening discharges revealed an unarmed Korean woman, child in hand, taking the brunt of the fire in the face and chest.

Cory MacArthur, born wealthy and destined to follow his parents on their travels across the globe, ran away from home at seventeen and joined the U.S. Army after years in Greece. After his friend in boot camp was harassed to the point of suicide by a relentless drill sergeant, Cory confronted the man right in his own office, and killed the DI after a round of hand-to-hand combat. Confined to a psycho ward for observation, a therapist noticed the boy possessed a cold, calculating mind that would better serve his country on the battlefield than behind bars. Shortly thereafter, the youth was liberated from his holding cell and padded room by one Justin Ross.

Matthew Sewell saw himself as an aspiring entertainer after his hitch with the Army during the Korean war was over. But failure after failure on both the stage and screen tests sent the chopper pilot on his first attempt at smuggling drugs into the country through the Florida Everglades. Not only was his craft shot out of the sky by crack drug enforcement agents, but the young woman accompanying him—a mob kingpin's daughter—fell out of the helicopter. Right into the jaws of a hungry crocodile. Impressed with his evasive flying talents, members of the Coast Guard chopper that had chased Sewell brought him to the attention of Justin Ross. Matt chose life with the team over a dim future trying to elude Mafia hit men.

Chad Chandler, another vet of the police action in Korea, quickly tired of life in America upon returning to the states. The Dark Continent was where all adventure lies in wait these days, his friends in the know told him. So it was off to Africa. But Chad was unable to hitch up with big-time mercenaries currently making their fortunes in the Congo or Ethiopia. And after several years working ranch security for a wealthy Dutchman in Rhodesia, he led several of his fellow guardsmen on a cross-border raid into Mozambique where they planned on robbing a communist-owned bank in the small community of Botzwan. The B.S.A.P. got wind of the caper, however, and sent one of their own crack commando units in to arrest the group. Impressed with Chandler's ability to withstand the British Police Constabulary's interrogation techniques, a senior B.S.A.P. official saw to it the soldier-of-*mis*fortune was heavily fined, then deported with a five year suspended prison sentence—after three of the members of his team were gunned down resisting arrest, one received a 20 year sentence of hard labor, and another was given the firing squad. Justin Ross met Chandler at the Customs station in New York's Kennedy airport. At first the ex-merc told the Army lieutenant to jump in a lake. Then Ross produced the photos of Chandler in the buff with a naked negress on the floor of the barracks in Rhodesia. Which was nothing to have a heart attack over. Except that Chandler's wife thought he had perished in a fiery car crash ten years earlier and 125,000 dollars worth of insurance money ago. And of course there was that money-hungry mistress back in Seoul. Chandler reluctantly accepted Ross's offer to re-up, and *be the best he could be.*

Amy Atencio felt no guilt at working the streets of New York City as a prostitute. There was no pride in her life either, but only that gut instinct for survival. A refugee from the jungle skirmishes around Guatemala City, she was in the United States illegally when a pimp tried to beat her up because she wouldn't join his corral. She shot him four times in the chest with a Saturday Night Special and blew up the gas tank of his pimpmobile—with him still in the front seat. The following night she was back on the same street corner when a maniac terrorizing the ladies of the evening that winter pulled up in front of her. Known in the news media as the Bronx Basher because of his method of mutilating his victims then slamming their limp bodies into the sharp edges of granite buildings, the john produced a phony police badge and ordered Amy into his car. Not one to be fooled quite so easily, she laughed and told him to get lost, only to be pulled by the hair in through the man's car window. He then raced off down the street, ignoring the screams of her startled girlfriends, and pulled into a dark, deserted back-alley. Two undercover policemen, positioned atop a rooftop across the street from the kidnapping (on a stake-out totally unrelated to the activities of the curbside hookers) gave chase on foot, but Amy needed no assistance. After the madman nearly ripped off her breast with an icepick, she shot him in the face with her pistol. And as the vice cops were rushing up to the scene, she fired the rest of the cylinder into the already defenseless suspect—an act that nullified any future claims of self defense against a murder charge. Amy was sewn up at a Veterans' Administration hospital after word reached Ross's people about the incident and the woman's cold, calculating skill with firearms. At first defiant, she submitted to the team contract after Ross explained the alternative meant dual homicide charges—the police had matched her pistol to bullets from the earlier shooting—probable deportation to a prison in Guatemala, and certain death in a homeland where she no longer had any family. She certainly would never work the streets of any big city again—who would bed down a whore with a jagged scar running diagonally across her chest? Ross promised plastic surgery. Eventually.

Amy glanced at the wide scar on Chandler's chin—souvenir from the interrogator in Rhodesia—and felt a chill run through her as she remembered how long it took her own grisly wound to heal. As if to combat the depressing thoughts, she blew a large purple bubble with her gum. Amy had a way of chewing bubblegum and smacking her lips that made the usually fluid motion look more like an act of violence. A loud *pop* cracked across the room.

The sudden noise made Matt Sewell whirl around in his seat. It made him think of the incident back in the Everglades, when the state trooper's shotgun cracked in front of his face, sending a blast of double-00 buck into his chest and leg. He felt himself turning red as Amy smiled and winked at him—always the cocktease. The purple sphere expanding again in front of her face made him think about the time he was bounced out of the Army's helicopter program for dropping paint-filled water balloons from his Huey down onto a two-star general's cocktail party at Diamond Head in Hawaii.

Cory MacArthur rubbed the lucky medicine man's pouch hanging from his neck as he breezed through a recent copy of the English-language *Saipan Post*. "Says here ol' June Wanda had another brush with death," he announced.

Ross handed out the last bundle of piasters and folded his fingers together, looking up. "Oh, really?"

"Yah. Says here a, quote, mentally disturbed veteran of the Korean conflict, end-quote, was attending voluntary therapy sessions after several unsuccessful attempts at suicide. See, they got a whole sidebar here on the guy next to the Wanda story . . ." He turned the newspaper about for all to see. Ross caught sight of another photo of the starlet with her fist raised in the air—next to a file photo of her posing with North Vietnamese anti-aircraft gunners in Hanoi.

"Says here the vet finally realized—after all the rap sessions with the counselors and fellow soldiers—that suicide was just a waste of his life. After all he had gone through . . . all he had experienced—the war and all that—how could he just end his miserable existence without making some kind of public statement?" Cory read on.

" 'Like all the war protesters lining up outside the White House these days to parade against American involvement in Indochina'—seems the dude had an apartment across the street from the capitol."

"*Had?*" said Ross, looking more interested every second.

"There's a long background story here on the vet." Cory continued scanning the front page, as if he was now sorry he had mentioned the article before he had time to consume and digest it. " 'Apparently the man slowly came to realize suicide was not the answer—wasteful suicide, that is. He still had no desire to live—flashbacks of the war and nightmares of his friends dying . . . survivor's guilt kept him up all the time. The only answer, to his way of thinking, was an act of weapons-related violence that would shock the world and at the same time reveal a certain public figure he had come to despise for what she really was—a traitor who should have been publicly executed by a society-trained marksman long ago . . . ' "

"I'm beginning to get your drift," grinned Ross.

"Poor guy," said Amy, her lips still cracking the bubblegum.

"Anyway, the dude did some research on every GI's dartposter pin-up and found out where she was holding her news-release interviews and public fan receptions."

"And our vet took some pot shots at her from a rooftop?" Chad sounded hopeful as he scratched at the scar on his chin.

"Not quite," Cory frowned. "Seems he was packing only a revolver—"

"Shoulda had a fucking carbine with a telescopic sight," interrupted Chandler again.

"And when he tried to get close to the cunt, a plainclothes bodyguard in the crowd next to Hanoi-June was warned in the nick of time by a metal-detector."

"Bummer . . ." muttered Sewell. Ross's surprised eyes shifted to the chopper pilot at the comment.

" 'His efforts weren't wasted, though,' " Cory continued. " 'A shoot-out ensued, and though Wanda escaped into an armor-plated sedan parked nearby, two bodyguards sustained serious gunshot wounds.' "

"Another commie bites the dust," snarled Amy.

"The story goes on to describe Wanda's outspoken views on American involvement in Southeast Asia, and says—this is old news now, of course—that she plans another trip to North Vietnam in the near future. She's quoted as saying, '. . . After this incident in front of the White House, *Vietnam* will probably be the only place I will feel safe . . . ' The reporter noted that she was laughing sarcastically when she made the statement."

"What happened to the vet?" Chandler shifted about in his seat.

"Being held for observation, under heavy guard. It says here several right-wing rich guy types are pooling funds to get him the best available lawyer— they're gonna claim 'postponed mental combat trauma' or something as his defensive. They've already hired several private investigators to look into Wanda's activities so her crimes can be documented and then publicized. They want to make finding an impartial jury impossible."

"They're saying all that in a newspaper that's not published by the military?" Sewell was both astonished and skeptical.

"After they caught her channeling funds from one of her supposedly all-charity fund raisers to her boyfriend's revolutionary underground organization, Wanda lost a lot of credibility with the press," Chandler explained.

"I just say it's too bad the guy with the gun didn't get the bitch," grumbled Cory, tossing the paper in a trashcan.

Yes, Ross thought, smiling to himself as he closely watched his team members falling silent to contemplate the story. *Too bad*. . . .

PART II

6

East Saigon . . .

Brent Collins gripped the thin cable tightly with both hands and pulled, but the brace, wrapped around several stout TV antennas, held.

He stepped over to the edge of the hotel roof and peered down the five flights to the street. Blue and yellow Renault taxis, headlights lancing through the dense smog hugging the curbs, passed back and forth below. He could hear their horns now and then, but the engine noise was lost in the din of activity overflowing onto the streets and sidewalks from the storefronts along ground level.

He sniffed at the air—moist with humidity and thick enough to cut with a machete—and glanced over at Chandler. Also clad in black coveralls, with ammo pouches bristling along his web belt, the former mercenary raised his rifle in casual salute and grinned. The teeth flashed with white brilliance against the charcoal-greased face and pitch-black background. His AK-47 sling was over his right shoulder, and the weapon fell back down to rest against his waist.

141

Collins checked his watch and glanced up at the stormfront moving in across the northern half of the city. Clouds were quickly covering up the crescent moon.

When a vast shadow finally fell across the block, Chandler pointed over at the edge of the roofline. "Let's do it," Collins read his lips.

As they slowly, silently rappelled down the side of the brick hotel, Brent was not concentrating so much on his freelance mission as he was on the conversation the two of them had had earlier that day. . . .

"A hundred lousy bucks." Chandler was still upset over the small paycheck. "All that goofy blood-and-guts, and what does it get us? A hundred lousy bucks."

The newspapers had been full of articles about the up coming trial of a Saigon narcotics czar. So confident was the man that his notorious bribes would get him off without any hard time at Chi Hoa prison, he went so far as to notify reporters he would sell a kilo of heroin right in front of his hotel lobby on Le Loi street.

Notepads at the ready, newsmen watched in disbelief as the transaction took place precisely on time—and right across the street from two uniformed canh-sats walking their beats. The policemen appeared to ignore the entire incident, turning away to walk off in the opposite direction, though an official would later proclaim the officers were imposters—some of the kingpin's own men, in fact.

Chandler had come up with the brainstorm of raiding the man's room after dark, looting the premises of its drug money, and killing the elderly Vietnamese if he resisted. Ross would never have to know a thing—it was all extracurricular, an after-hours activity.

They had hoped to make their move after curfew, but the man had returned from his underworld exploits ahead of schedule and retired early. Any delay in pulling off the heist could see the day's booty spirited out of town by his hired guns, unannounced.

A recon down the crowded corridors of the fourth floor had revealed an army of henchmen with an arsenal of concealed firepower. Entry would have to be from outside, through the window if they were only going to operate with two midnight commandos. Risky, with a potential for unexpected obstacles once inside, but the element of surprise was definitely there. And hopefully a small fortune in daily profits awaited them also. Spending-cash to keep them occupied between the real missions. Booze money to slow the adrenaline after a crossborder chopper flight, a hot LZ, or a bloody hit.

A police siren wailed in the distance, artillery rumbled along the horizon, and flashes of heat lightning lanced down into the clusters of tenements on the opposite edge of Saigon. A few drops of rain sprayed across their headbands, and clouds of mosquitoes drifted in, only to buzz away in an angry flurry upon hitting the men's potent, invisible bug screen.

Collins waited until Chandler was suspended beside him, level with the fourth floor, each man's boots braced against bricks on either side of the balcony railing.

Chandler nodded his relief: no activity on the balcony. Not even a sleeping sentry.

Soft music drifted out from the suite, however—an old Chinese love ballad—and inside, off to the right, a ceiling lantern shaped like a dragon floated about on the evening breeze, casting an orange shade of light against the silk shades.

Silk shades! Collins thought, as he gave the thumbs-up and both men sprang back several feet and crashed through the open bamboo shutters.

Both men released their grips on the roof cables at the zenith of each swing, were propelled a considerable distance through the air by sheer momentum, and landed on their feet, rifles fanning in wide arcs away from each other as eyes darted about, seeking sources of potential danger.

A Eurasian woman was sitting up in the bed on the far side of the room, staring past them with a dazed expression on her face, eyes blank, forearms a railroad track of syringe punctures and collapsed veins. She wavered slightly from side to side, trying calmly to focus on the intruders. Satin sheets covered her legs, but she was nude from the waist up and her breasts, moist with sweat, bobbled about with the movement. Overhead, a ceiling fan swished about slowly. Featherlight shards of bamboo from the damaged shutters were still fluttering into the center of the bedroom. The fan tried unsuccessfully to blow them back toward the window.

Chandler and Collins hestitated only for a moment—outside, flares drifted along the shifting wind currents, sizzling against the drizzle now blanketing the city. Jets could be heard in the distance, racing their reverse thrusters upon landing at Tan Son Nhut airport—and both men's eyes came to rest on the bathroom door to their right, a crack of light visible along its bottom edge.

A split second later, the door burst open.

A plump Vietnamese man, wearing only a bath-robe, leaped out through the doorway into the bed-room, an ear-to-ear grin on his sunken features and a long cigar dangling between his teeth. "Here I cooooome, baby-san!" he announced in English, pull-ing the flaps of his robe apart to reveal his aroused genitals.

Chandler almost cracked a smile of his own at the sight of the old pervert, flashing his erection at the un-announced guests.

The elderly drug-runner's smile slowly faded, and his glowing cigar rolled off the edge of his lips and bounced off the teakwood floor. Embers scattered and went bright for a second then died out.

"Spread-eagle on the floor!" Collins ordered in En-glish, moving the barrel of his rifle up and down to emphasize his point.

"Who are you?" the man demanded.

Chandler was upon him immediately, slamming him to the floor.

Collins rushed across the room and grabbed the woman in the bed by a wrist. He flipped her onto her stomach, tied her arms behind her with twine from his belt, and wrapped a strip of electrical tape across her mouth and around her head.

"Your money," Chandler hissed. "Where is it?"

"Whatever are you talking about—"

Chandler stomped a boot down into the small of the man's back. "Your dope money, fool!" he threatened the drug czar further by jamming the AK muzzle up in under the back of the man's head.

Collins frowned at two things: this was taking too long, and Chandler was enjoying it too much. He now

145

had the old man's arm twisted back behind him, and was forcing it up farther than nature had ever planned for. Joints popped and cracked about.

Collins's eyes darted about the room again. There were a hundred places the old man's cash could be hidden.

"Should I break it?" Chandler was grinning evilly as he pretended the drug czar's wrist was one of those new, twist-off beercaps he had come across in Capetown.

Before Collins could answer, something happened that neither American expected nor had planned for. The sixty-year-old buzzard on the floor spun around a couple feet until he was on his back, then kicked a leg out rigidly and pulled Chandler off balance.

The big 200-pounder would have fallen upon and crushed the Vietnamese, except that Chandler felt a rough foot heel digging into his stomach, knocking the air from his chest as the old man yanked hard.

Collins watched Chandler sail through the air in a slow-motion somersault, landing on his back across a floormat several feet away. And that quick, the old man sprang into a standing position, using his backbone like an accordion. His hands flew out into a martial arts defensive stance, and he started moving about from side to side in front of Collins, grinning himself now.

"Christ," the American muttered, as his partner groaned in the corner and struggled to roll over. *I've no time for this crap.*

Someone was knocking at the door, obviously curious—finally—about the sound of Chandler's bulk sliding across the teakwood.

146

The old man advanced a couple feet closer to Collins. "Hyai!" he yelled dramatically, moving his feet apart farther as he presented his adversary with his left side, protecting his frontal area.

"Where's . . . your . . . money . . ." Collins spoke the words slowly. His tone was menacing, unruffled by the unexpected turn of events.

The doorknob was moving about now, and someone was calling out in the hallway, using Vietnamese.

"Hyai!" the old man shifted his feet about, as if choosing to respond only to the American and not his associates. And only in a physical way. He showed no sign of cooperating.

"Have it your way," Collins muttered. The barrel of his rifle fell a few inches, and when the weapon suddenly barked lead, the muzzle flash lanced out so far that powderburns sank into the old man's plush bathrobe. The bullet took his right kneecap completely off.

His startled screams sent several men outside pounding on the heavily bolted door, and Collins fired a twenty round burst horizontally along the wall beside it. Bodies tumbled about outside as men raced to safety or died on the spot.

Collins expected a splash of tracers back through the bamboo to follow in answer—erupting into the room from outside, seeking him out blindly—but the pandemonium in the hallway would now afford him a few extra precious seconds to locate what he had come here for.

He slowly walked up to the pitiful form thrashing about on the floor—the AK round had splintered through the center of the kneecap, sending bone shards out in all directions and inflicting a wound probably more painful than any others except for being gut-shot. Collins pinned the old man to the floor by placing a boot down onto his chest. Then he rammed his rifle muzzle down into the fleshy sack of the man's scrotum, between his testicles.

"Is it worth it?" Collins knew he was rapidly running out of time, but he took slow pleasure in the dramatics of the situation. He nudged the man's mutilated leg with the other boot. "Is it worth it?" he repeated, depressing the mechanism that releases the rifle's clip. The metal magazine, still heavy with bullets inside, clattered across the floor as Collins pulled a fresh, fully loaded one from the canvas pouch on his web belt. He briefly displayed the top orange-tipped rounds to the man before slamming the clip into the rifle—careful the whole time to keep the barrel tight against the man's groin so his senses could feel all the smoothly oiled yet cold and harsh movements of the weapon against his trembling frame.

"Tracers," Collins grumbled. "*Hot, sizzling* tracers, papa-san. They'll light up your life and make pizza outta your meatballs . . . Is it worth it?" Both hands back on the stock now, he pushed in slightly, as if tensing to fire off a short burst.

The old man was staring up at him with eyes wide in terror now—his earlier cockiness completely gone. He motioned over to one of the brass bed posts.

"Don't move." Collins hissed his warning like a snake. This was the most dangerous time—when he was so close. He knocked the ornamental phoenix off the top of the post with a leaning heel kick, and started to reach down, then hesitated.

He glanced back over at the dope kingpin, who now

had both hands tightly around his shattered knee, trying to stem the flow of blood. "A trap, perhaps, honorable papa-san?" The old man shook his head violently in the negative. "An oversized mousetrap, maybe . . . with razorblade teeth to relieve me of my selfish little fingers? Or a grenade, all hooked up with fishing wire?"

Across the room, Chandler was getting back to his feet, shaking his own head now, and groaning.

"Look alive, Chad," Collins called out.

Outside, men were starting to pound on the door again. *Fools*, he thought, preparing to spray the wall a second time, but he hestitated—there could be innocent people . . . police, out there by now. He held off, telling Chandler instead, "Cover me, bud. If the bastard there's got this bed rigged up to deliver the ultimate orgasm, I want you to shatter his face with a banana-burst on rock-n-roll . . . got that?"

Chandler was on his feet now.

Collins produced a small military flashlight from an empty canteen pouch. It was operated by a hand-generated power pack, and after squeezing the handle a few times, he pointed the concentrated laser-like shaft down into the bed post. Suddenly smiling, he reached down and pulled out a small rice bag, wrapped with twine. He shook it up and down a couple times for Chandler. The sound of large-denomination gold coins shuffling about filled the room.

Chandler grinned too, and let loose with a burst from his rifle that splattered into the Vietnamese's chest and catapulted him on his seat across the floor and back into the far wall with a dull thud.

"Christ!" muttered Collins as he stuffed the bag

down into his pack and started for the window. "Whatja do that for?"

Chandler laughed out loud. "Oh sorry," he said. "I thought you said to smoke the dude if that bed post delivered the ultimate orgasm." Collins frowned but did not look back. ". . . And it sure looked like you got the climax of your career when those coins jingled about."

"You're a regular one-man comedy act." Collins did not sound enthused. He glanced back at the old man leaning against the wall—several weak fountains of blood were springing forth from the bulletholes beneath his chin, reminding Collins of a statue he had seen in Europe somewhere . . . a statue of a young boy urinating onto stone penguins clustered in a wishing well.

"You done sold your last sack of shit, dopescum!" Chandler laughed loudly at the dead drug kingpin. His heart had finally stopped, and the gushing of blood quickly died with it.

Collins glanced over at the woman on the bed—the sheets were now wet and discolored where she had released some of her sobering tension—shook his head in mild disgust, then both men climbed through the window, latched onto their roof cables and disappeared into the night.

"Wonder what's goin' down over there across the street?" Chad Chandler produced his most convincing expression as the waitress arrived at their table with the drinks. She placed the glasses in front of the two Americans, leaned over to both look out the win-

150

dow and give the burly foreigner a free shot down her blouse. Chad's feigned innocence never failed to both amaze and astonish Brent Collins.

"Mus' be cop trouble, mista," she said in a deep, throaty voice that did not really go with the dainty body. It would have fit a mini-skirted hooker perfectly, but not this waitress with baggy, unflattering pantaloons.

Chandler suddenly seemed no longer interested in all the police jeeps rolling up outside. "How's about you and me givin' each other a massage tonight, honey?" He laid a heavy paw across her wrist.

"I married." The woman's businesslike smile faded as she recoiled, trying to draw her hand free, but Chad wouldn't let go.

"I don't see no ring, honey." He ran his tongue along his bottom lip, aware most Vietnamese men he had talked to were repulsed by the idea of cunnilingus while the women secretly yearned for it.

She promptly slapped him full across the face, though Chad only let his chops jiggle about slightly like some clownface attached to a tall spring little boys beat with their baseball bats. His grin remained intact, as if the waitress had only slapped some aftershave lotion on. "You don't see no ring, *honey*, because I don't wear it on a job like this!" She held her fist in front of his eyes so he could see the white tan mark left on her ring finger by the harsh Asian sun. "Okay, GI?"

Chandler was about to launch into his I-ain't-no-fucking-GI testimonial, but the girl was gone.

"I thought we weren't supposed to bring no undue attention to ourselves," Collins reminded him.

151

"*You're* the one with the goofy idea to come here so we could watch the fiasco across the street," Chandler retorted loudly. Then he softened his voice and leaned closer to Brent. "I say we should be up in our room dividing the loot, *partner*."

Collins had yet to surrender or even count the stash they had liberated from the old man a few minutes earlier. They had hidden their coveralls and gear on a rooftop several buildings down from the target location, then slid down the fire escape and sauntered back up to this hotel to watch the proceedings across the street as if out of boredom.

A bargirl in tight hot pants and a loose halter top was suddenly hovering next to their table. Chad leaned back in his seat cautiously. His eyes took in the full breasts straining against the fabric to stretch out and meet him. Her nipples were already taut at the ends, and Chad felt himself growing instantly hard. "You buy me Saigon tea tonight?" she cooed, jerking her head around slightly without taking her eyes off his—her long, radiant hair, black as midnight, was tossed over a shoulder by the movement.

Chandler was already getting to his feet. "I think we can come to some sort of agreement," he giggled, draping an arm around her and winking back at Collins. They started in the direction of the lobby, where Chad could get a room key and an elevator ride to Oriental heaven.

Collins smiled slightly and shook his head from side to side. Already two other hookers had observed the *catch* and were maneuvering through the dance floor to be the first over to his table.

The women tried to lock eyes with him, but he made

152

a convincing show of ignoring them, and stared out the window instead.

Brent Collins sat bolt upright in his chair at what he saw through the frosted glass: his broad flattop bristling with perspiration, Hank O'Leary, the marine from Military Intelligence, was waving as he crossed the street, approaching the hotel nightclub Collins was sitting in. There was no time to turn away, no chance to duck out—the barrel-chested American had already spotted him.

A few seconds later, O'Leary was slapping him on the back and breathing hard like he had just run a marathon or chased some back-alley criminal through the Saigon underworld. "Funny meeting you here, Brent." His eyes were flooded with sarcasm and suspicion.

"Whatever do you mean, Hank?" Collins felt himself going red, but he was confident O'Leary couldn't see the blush in the dark room. "I'm just fuckin' off, suckin' up some suds . . ."

O'Leary's skeptical grin remained intact, but Collins could practically read his mind: *First the Villa and the dead stockade colonel . . . now I find you sitting right across the street from a big time narcotics hit. . . .*

"All by yourself?" O'Leary surveyed the bar. Collins glanced over at the two prostitutes, who had skidded to a stop in mid-stride upon seeing the white gorilla burst in through the swinging front doors. He briefly considered claiming he was with one of the girls, but he had watched them both lead a steady procession of customers through the back doors, and the thought of *sloppy seconds* or even sitting with a woman who hadn't bathed yet repulsed him.

He opened his mouth and almost said, *I came in here with a partner but he slipped away with some boom boom girl*, but thought better of it at the last moment—just wouldn't do to have a man from marine intelligence learn who his associates were. Not yet, anyway. "Yes, I'm alone," he finally said, after his mouth had hung open for half an eternity. He instantly knew his words did not sound very convincing.

"Not even a cunt ya been workin' on, ol' buddy?" O'Leary was hard to convince.

"Nope."

"Then drink up!" He reached over and grabbed Collins's glass, downing it with one gulp. Brent could not tell if Hank even noticed the two sets of napkins on the table. *Thank God Big Chad took his fucking drink with him*!

O'Leary was on his feet, leading Collins toward the door. "Paid your tab yet?" he growled, but they were out in the street even before Collins could answer. "Can't bear to see you wastin' your time in a dive like that," he added, heading straight for a military jeep parked in between two canh-sat landrovers.

"Don't suppose you'd know anything about the bloody mess in there?" O'Leary motioned toward the hotel lobby, filled to overflowing with police uniforms, as he twisted the starter toggle. The jeep's engine rolled over and came to life, and O'Leary gunned the accelerator a couple times. A few canh-sats glanced his way, then resumed what they were doing upon recognizing the American.

"Why would I?" Collins answered the question with a question, sounding defensive. "I just happened to—"

"No problem . . . no problem!" O'Leary broke into his usual raunchy grin. "Just a horserunner and half his corral bought the farm is all, anyway."

"Oh really?" Collins decided he had better act curious.

"Yah, looks like a simple cache rip-off between competitors," he continued. "I don't even know why the mice called me in, unless they found a contact sheet or customer log they're not tellin' me about." O'Leary backed the jeep out of the collage of multi-jurisdictional police vehicles and started off down a side street that would take them to busy Pham Dinh Phung.

"So what's on the itinerary?" Collins felt strange relief at the warm breeze slapping at his face, compared to the muggy atmosphere in the bar.

"Just happened to be on my way to the embassy for a coffee break when this call went down, matter o' fact," he said, "Care to join me for a mug of real brew?"

"Still working nights, eh?" Collins was wondering when his marine friend would bring up their first reunion, asking why the aspiring novelist didn't hang around after being loaned room and board.

"Yah . . ." O'Leary let his eyes inspect two women strolling down the busy sidewalk in their form-hugging *ao dais*. "Same old crap."

A few minutes and three miles later, they were coasting up to the embassy on Thong Nhut. Two Army MPs sitting inside a mean-looking gunjeep outside the main gate gave them the silent once-over, then waved them through to the next checkpoint. Collins turned to stare at them as O'Leary shifted into second gear and rumbled away—the white letters glowing on the black helmets beneath the dim street lights were almost mesmerizing.

A marine with a Thompson machinegun stepped in front of the jeep as it rolled to a stop mere inches in front of the sagging strands of concertina. He had recognized O'Leary from far off down the street, but sentries got nervous when unfamiliar faces in civilian clothes invaded their posts. "Evening, sir," the big marine stood almost as tall as O'Leary. His bushy mustache, Fred MacMurray expression and thick black glasses gave him a grim look. *A drooping pipe would make him look scholarly*, Collins decided.

"How ya doing, Big-Jim?" O'Leary responded with a Bugs Bunny impression that made both leathernecks laugh while keeping Brent totally in the dark.

"Oh, okay, I guess . . ." The embassy guard kept eyeing the rooftops all around them apprehensively.

"Looks like something's troublin' ya, Big-Jim . . ." He turned off the jeep engine with his knee, jumped out of the unit, and draped a thick arm around the non-com. "Talk to papa . . ." But before the sentry could reply, Hank was sniffing at the air—like he had just detected a hint of mother's home cooking on the hot Saigon breeze. "That cordite I'm breathin' in right now, Big-Jim?"

"Shrapnel smoke," the corporal answered. "That's what I was just about to tell you: damned if Charlie didn't walk some mortars right up the block at us again tonight." Big-Jim's eyes remained on the dark shadowy skyline as he spoke.

O'Leary frowned, and his eyes also began darting

about along the tops of the tenements. "Funny . . ." he muttered. "But I didn't hear nothin' about it, and I'm on fucking call tonight." He rested his hands on his hips and closed one eye as he followed a distant flare floating along the edge of the city. Glowing green and gold as it sizzled down through the mist, it eventually burned free of its parachute, and as it plummeted to earth, like some eerie falling star, O'Leary asked, "Anybody hurt?"

"Naw . . . not really, sir." Big-Jim scratched at the slight stubble on his chin. "Fabian-The-Worm and Bullwinkle caught some shrapnel in the ass, but Twiggy shot 'em over to 3rd Field Army Hospital ala-*code*, and I think they're gonna be all right."

"The installation's under Red Alert, however, sir. I'm gonna have to see your passenger's pass before I can let him on the embassy grounds."

"We were just going to share some of your fine nightwatch coffee, friend." O'Leary frowned at the formalities. Collins was still bewildered by the nicknames all the embassy guards seemed to have.

"Rules is rules, sir." Big-Jim seemed just as bothered by all the precautions.

"Sure . . . sure, I understand," O'Leary said. "Brent here's a buddy from way back . . . my old Korean days. He's here to write the great American novel, son. Maybe make your young ass famous or something."

"A civilian?" Big-Jim cocked his head suspiciously. "Then no way can I allow him on post, sir. You know that. Not with a Red Alert on, no sir. . . ." The sentry shifted about with his boots to show he meant business.

"Sure . . . sure, partner. Just tell me where the gang's at tonight. Someplace where's I can mooch a free cup of brew."

Big-Jim looked suddenly relieved. "Just got a land-line from San Diego Sy," he said. "From the Fire House at the MACV annex. He took one of the para-medics back there who originally responded to our call for help here," Big-Jim pointed to a shop across the street that had been hit by one of the mortars, burned to the ground, and was still smoldering. "Said he was gonna take a coffee break there, then return to 3rd Field after they patched up Twiggy and the others, and bring the whole load of them home."

"Then the Fire House it is." O'Leary glanced at his watch. "Couple more hours till curfew anyway. Maybe we can score a piece of ass on Tu Do, Brent-baby . . ." Collins wondered how Chandler was doing right then: if he was in the sack, and if he had any piasters to pay for it later.

Big-Jim whipped a salute on them as O'Leary forced the protesting gears into reverse and backed out onto the busy boulevard despite a barrage of horns and tire skids. Collins covered his head with his arm, but there was no collision.

"Yah, ol' Big-Jim takes the cake," O'Leary smiled as he turned southwest and headed for Cong Ly. He would take the scenic route back to Phan Dinh Phung, then jet up Le Van Duyet. "Found himself an honest-to-God, genuine VC flag hanging on the bar-racks perimeter fenceline couple weeks back. Snatched it up for a Numba One Saigon souvenir, GI! Damned near coulda got his family jewels snatched right back," he chuckled.

"Boobytrapped?" Collins did not realize he was rubbing affectionately at his groin.

"Yah. A good quarter pound of C-4 at the end of a tripwire. I'll never figure out why the damned thing didn't detonate."

"Maybe he's just religious or something," Collins started counting all the beautiful women with firm thighs hiked up on the curbsides.

"Yah, maybe he is," O'Leary didn't seem pressed to dwell on the matter for long. When they came to a crowded stoplight, a young boy darted through the bumper-to-bumper traffic, dragging an only slightly taller girl in and out of the cars behind him. Collins tensed, remembering all the stories he had heard about little VC kids rushing up between parked cars just to lob a live grenade in your lap.

The boy stopped on Brent's side of the jeep and pressed his older sister close to the American. "You want cherry girl, Joe?" the kid appeared desperate—after all, time was tight. Curfew was only an hour away. "Clean cunt, mista! Make you feel goooood all over, ching!" As if on cue, the girl—maybe twelve at most, with filthy brown hair and a dirty face streaked by old tears—reached into the jeep and gently grabbed Collins's crotch.

"Beat it, ya little bastards!" O'Leary leaned across as if to swat at them. The children recoiled a safe distance back only momentarily, then, as the lights turned green and horns began honking, they both reached back in and tried to grab O'Leary's briefcase. The marine slapped them back, away from the vehicle and let the clutch out.

"Cheap Charlie!" the little boy yelled after them,

waving his fist, but they didn't try to chase the Americans. Collins noticed that an older youth, standing at a busy intersection close by selling flowers and newspapers to passing cars, had ceased peddling his wares to direct an icy glare of hate at the two foreigners.

"No sweat," O'Leary reached down and tugged at the briefcase as he swerved into the fast lane. The briefcase barely budged—it was apparently chained to a latch along the floorboard. "Nothin' in it but fool efficiency reports, anyhow. . . ."

"Crazy kids got eagle eyes," observed Collins. His own eyes shot up as a fleet of gunships flapped past low overhead.

"Yah, damned runts don't miss much." O'Leary also gazed up at the six choppers, only fifty yards or so above the earth—they appeared to be following the boulevard in the same direction the jeep was headed. Collins could see men sitting along the edge of the open hatches, jungle boots and baggy fatigues hanging out over the edge, M16 rifles and older carbines balanced across knees. Above the gleam of deadly metal could also be seen, now and then, the flash of smiling teeth. Then the ghostships were just shadows against the moon. The whop-whopping roar of their rotors beating at the warm, sticky air blanketing the city could still be heard long after the Hueys faded into the night.

"Welcome to Magic Mountain." Four firefighters were sitting on folding chairs outside the engine house, watching swing-shift nationals filing off post, when Collins and O'Leary coasted down through the MACV annex a short while later. O'Leary had hoped to sneak up on the firemen with his lights doused, so he could hit them with the tiny siren bolted to his front bumper, but a guy in the end seat had spotted them several blocks away and splashed a beam of light from a powerful fluorescent searchlamp across his windshield, long before he could startle anybody.

"Heard through the wait-a-minute vine that you clowns went and brewed up a fresh pot of Army-green for us," O'Leary told the civilians with his best shit-eating expression.

The firemen all wore dark blue pants—*just like policemen*, Collins mused—and white T-shirts, and the one with the lamp, in his early thirties with wire-rim glasses and an arm wrestler's physique, said, "Don't go parkin' that heap of shitmetal in front of our firehouse now, you hear me O'Leary-san?" His hair bleached a sandy color by the tropical sun after four years in Asia, he folded sinewy forearms across his chest and flared massive nostrils out at the marine like an irritated water buffalo, smiling the entire time.

"Aw, come on, Kamberman," O'Leary drooped his shoulders an imitated a defenseless puppy seeking shelter from hungry mongrels in a rainstorm. "Gimme a break. I heard tell one of my jarheads is in there, anyway." He turned the jeep off, positioning it diagonally in front of both the shed doors.

One of the other firemen, his brown hair over his ears and uncombable, jumped onto his feet and directed and insane, wide-eyed glare at O'Leary, feigning both shock and insult. "I don't believe you done went and blocked my exit ramp!" he bellowed, stomping around in circles, only to lock eyes with the marine officer again. "I don't believe—"

"Aw, put a cork in it, Mister Merradyth! Can't ya

161

guys just direct me to San Diego Sy and that excuse for poison ya call a coffee pot?'' As if by magic, the automatic dual doors to the engine shed began cranking upward as chains and pulleys lifted them toward the ceiling. A red turret light on the wall above the firemen's chairs began revolving lazily, and a loudspeaker emitted whining static, then a fire alarm.

"Move that crate!" a slender lieutenant with businesslike eyes and a half-smile shot up from his folding chair. "Move it! Move it! Move it!"

"Pumper two, pumper six, truck one, rescue two, Chief-7 . . ." the intercom blasted into Collins's ears after a set of complex tones screeched out of the wallspeaker, " . . . Regular alarm, at the Outdoor Theater . . . your run is Code 3 . . ."

"Let's gooooo!" the Fire Lieutenant was bringing both hands palm up repeatedly—Collins wasn't sure if he looked more like a traffic cop shooing away a rabid dog or some native worshipping flames at a sacrificial altar. *Can't fucking believe this is actually happening to me!* O'Leary's mind was overheating as he twisted at the starter switch and the engine refused to turn over. A fireman was climbing up into a monstrous pumper unit, and soon its diesel engine was rumbling to life. The intercom was repeating the truck numbers and the location of the alarm, and the lieutenant was shrieking for O'Leary to move his fat ass out of the way.

"Okay, Freestone! Okay, okay!" Already, a half dozen men had appeared from the shadows of the firehouse—where they had been waiting to turn a hose on O'Leary after Big-Jim back at the embassy had warned them by landline that the MI marine was enroute—and they began pushing the protesting jeep back out of the driveway.

"Regular alarm, pumper two, pumper six, truck one, rescue two, Chief-7 . . . at the Outdoor Theater . . ." the central dispatcher at Tan Son Nhut was airing the call for the third and final time, "Report of smoke in the projectionist's booth . . . got a near riot at that Ten-twenty . . . some GIs tossed a molotov at the silver screen and projector room . . . MPs seventy-six to cover you . . . Time out: 2320 hours."

"Them fools are showing that June Wanda flick!" an anonymous firefighter from the back of the pumper called out, as if the eight-word sentence would describe an act of arson that would eventually cost several tens of thousands of dollars.

As the first fire truck roared down the drive and into the street, O'Leary hiked up his pants leg and dangled his hairy knee in front of the second pumper starting out the shed. "Going my way?" His thumb was out.

Collins decided he had better climb out of the jeep. The firemen had rolled it back out of the way; now life was passing him by. He watched the driver of the second truck, sporting an engineer's badge, glance up to see if the lieutenant in the lead pumper was watching—he obviously wasn't—then motion the two GIs aboard. "Thanks, Gunne!"

O'Leary was waving him aboard now, onto the tail runningboard. Collins glanced up at the broad, stocky, baby-faced engineer with the thin mustache and perpetual grin—*shoulda been a cop*, he decided, *with a name like that*—then caught hold of a canvas strap and swung around beside O'Leary. The lone fireman on the other side of the big intelligence agent held on with one hand as he fastened his glowing asbestos jacket with the other.

163

"Bet you wanted to ride a cherry-red fire truck all your life, right?" he yelled at them proudly above the roar of the motor and exhausts.

Shee-it! Collins thought back. He respected the courageous men who fought fires, but it was a job they could have! He'd never forget the time when—long, long ago . . . it seemed now—he was back on the police force, and they had responded to a fire alarm at a mobile home park. The unit was totally engulfed in flames when he and Sutton arrived on scene—the nearest fire truck five miles away, snowed-in by a howling blizzard's drifts. They had heard screaming somewhere beyond the wall of billowing silver smoke, and donning their riot helmets—who knew why?—they charged in over the hip-deep blanket of white, visions of heroism medals in their heads. Both had been quickly overcome by the poisonous fumes and smoke inhalation, and damn if that crazy watch commander hadn't dragged both their asses out of the kill zone seconds before the propane tanks went up, leveling half the trailer park. When he came to, firemen looking more like martians in their buggy-eyed O_2 masks were huddled over them both. It was a nightmare scene from hell.

Eleven people had died, after the final tally was taken, including two infant twins, and the mother who had screamed her lungs black, before the blast claimed her too.

No, they could have the glamor. And the pain. Scars. Memories that would last through the hereafter. Hell's gates were barred to them. They had already seen what it had to offer. Satan wasn't shit.

"Make way!" O'Leary was leaning out to the side, terrorizing Vietnamese workers from the eleven a.m. to

164

eleven p.m. shift who had just gotten off work and were scampering to the checkpoints, rolls of toilet paper and GI soap hidden deep beneath their foodpacks and rice baskets. "Make way for Big Red!" he snatched the straw conical hat right off a young woman who worked in the post laundry and was notorious for returning one less article of clothing to her regular customers every other week. Several teenage girls in tissue-thin *ao dais* scattered out of the huge truck's path at the last moment. Too shy to look back at all the commotion, they acted more from some mysterious feminine sonar, O'Leary believed. He plopped the straw hat down onto his head and slipped its strap in under his chin.

"This rates me a damn overtime card!" he told Collins. "Damned June Wanda movie! Can you believe that? Who the hell'd be fool enough to show a Wanda flick on a fucking GI post during crazy times like these?"

Collins didn't immediately answer, though he was inclined to challenge O'Leary about the overtime remark. Instead, his eyes were locked on the shapely hips of a woman moving through the angry crowd as they rolled up to the theater walls.

Amy was wearing one of her form-hugging sarongs again, and she was following Justin Ross through clouds of smoke, away from the brawl.

7

Big Hank O'Leary leaped off the fire truck as it was still rolling. He bounded over firemen struggling to pull endless lengths of waterhose off the heavy rigs toward non-existent plugs. Notebook in hand, the agent from Marine Intelligence abandoned Collins in the midst of the smoke-clogged ruckus, and set about detaining potential witnesses.

Collins brushed through the mob, elbowing several angry GIs out of the way, trampling an equal number of bewildered civilians—mostly hookers signed onto the installation by boom-boom happy soldiers. One intoxicated master sergeant tried to swing out at him, but Brent was already fifty feet way, rapidly gaining on Ross and Amy from behind.

They were merely sauntering out along the fringe of the disturbance, making a good show of appearing non-involved, innocent. Police whistles sliced through the dense air from all sides as additional units from the Fire Department continued to scream up on the scene.

"I gotta admit I ain't seen a pitch like that since I last watched the Mets lose in New York!" He overheard Amy laughing when he was still a few feet in back of them.

"You're a baseball fan?" Ross was smiling back. *Acting like they had just left a movie without incident*, Collins felt like smiling himself at their cool confidence at slipping from the scene of so much havoc.

"Naw . . . I was trickin' a busload o' tourists outside the stadium."

Collins's thoughts were still wondering if, perhaps, these two crazy clowns from his team had actually tossed the molotovs as a silent unofficial protest aimed at June Wanda, when Amy's words flashed back at him in instant neon replay. *Naw . . . I was trickin' a busload o' tourists outside the stadium . . .*

He skidded to a stop just as Ross whirled around, feeling his approach from behind. Amy's eyes went wide briefly, then narrowed as she tried to conceal her concern: *had he heard?*

"Brent!" Justin Ross wrapped a steel-strong arm around the ex-cop. His face was all smiles. "Funny finding you here," he said wryly. "Wasn't *you* who torched that Wanda festival back there, was it?"

Amy's eyes avoided both men as they continued up the grassy slope toward the annex cafeteria. Collins remained silent, forcing a smile though his guts felt like they were being torn out through his rectum.

"Ran across an old friend," he finally said, choosing not to elaborate. The words came out more like he was talking about an old, exotic girlfriend from his past than some burly marine buddy.

Trickin,' eh? So that's what she's got hidden in her past . . . The cunt's nothing but a burned-out old whore. Collins hoped his remark about meeting an old friend hurt Amy. Burned into her heart like only a fireflash of jealousy could. But he was beginning to doubt anything could penetrate her rough exterior. *A hole is a hole is a hole.*

"So what are your plans tonight?" Ross's smile was slowly fading, and his eyes displayed that uneasy look which always came about with surges of anxiety.

"Oh, won a large bundle of *p* back in a Cholon card game," he said. His tone was cocky. "Thought I'd see if I could blow it all tonight."

"Just don't get too zonkered, all right?" Ross broke away from them and walked up to an old papa-san manning an ice box. "We got important things to discuss tonight." He handed the Vietnamese a few piasters and carefully watched as the vendor wiped off a glistening bottle of Coca Cola and produced a bottle opener and multi-colored straw.

"Chop-chop," the old man pointed further up the hill, where a group of women were closing up a rice and beef food stall. "Numba One!"

"But they're closed," Collins heard him argue mildly.

"No sweat!" the Vietnamese insisted. "Numba one chop-chop!" and he pushed the big American away gently, in the direction of gossiping girls.

"Want some . . . chop-chop?" he smiled over at Brent and Amy as he started up the hill. They both remained silent, choosing to stare down at the cluster-fuck within the Outdoor Theater complex: bright crimson beams of light from a dozen firetrucks slashed in and out of the thick smoke as line officers ran around trying to maintain order. "Okay . . . then hang tight. I'll be right back."

Out of the corner of his eye, Ross saw a large shadow rushing up the slope toward his two team members, but before he could react, the man was upon them: an American.

"Thought I lost you in the crowd!" Hank O'Leary wrapped the ever-present bicep around Collins. "And who, may I ask, is this lovely princess?"

Justin Ross decided to ignore the group of women on the hilltop, and chose to sit down midway up the grassy slope instead, watching the trio from shadows.

"Oh, this is the young lady I was telling you about last night," he responded after a few seconds of indecision.

"Ah . . ." O'Leary took Amy's slender hand and slowly, dramatically kissed it. "I am honored to meet such a lovely flower in a land of so many vicious thorns. Hank O'Leary."

Amy glanced over at Collins for guidance, and when he looked the other way, she said, "Candy Marsh."

"Will your services be required here much longer?" Collins's tone was hopeful, but O'Leary's answer was disappointing.

"No, no, no," he didn't catch the hint. Motioning down at the smoke still belching from the projector building, he said, "Just some disgruntled patriot unhappy with Miss Wanda's politics. Appears to be no connection with hardcore elements rumored to be—" but his statement trailed off and the man from Marine Intelligence bit his lip.

"Candy here was dumped by her date," Collins muttered sarcastically, fully aware how embarrassing the statement came across for her. "So it looks like we're *all* without transportation. I doubt the firefighters would be so kind as to run us back to your jeep."

"Piece o' shit's dead anyway," he blurted out. Then, "Oh, but please excuse my language, Miss Marsh." He sounded sincere.

"Hell, you don't have to worry about little ole Candy," Collins said. "I'm sure she's heard every word in the book." His words came out mean. Amy glanced at him with a look of intense hurt in her eyes but looked away. "In fact, I'm sure that, at one time or another, she's probably talked pretty . . . *dirty* to some of her . . . clients herself. . . ."

"Oh?" Hank was feeling suddenly mischievous. "And what type of business are you in, Miss Marsh?"

Collins answered for her. "She's into . . . escorts," he said. "*Body*guard work and all that." Amy refused to look at him, though Brent could see her facial muscles tensing. He wondered if she was angry or just trying to hold back the tears. He couldn't understand why he was being so hateful—he was falling in love with this woman . . . had probably fallen in love with her months ago, but now he was tearing her down in front of a virtual stranger with cryptic references and innuendoes. Yet wasn't that the way it always happened . . . when you found the woman of your dreams wasn't so virginal after all. What the hell had he expected to find in a damned war zone?

"Ah . . . of course," O'Leary winked at her knowingly. "Executive . . ." and he massaged his crotch so only Brent could see, " . . . protection."

"So are we walking back downtown, or what?" Amy sounded irritated as she ignored their he-man games and pushed her chest up from within so that the breasts pointed straight out. *Was O'Leary's mouth actually watering—in this heat?*

"Never fear . . . O'Leary's here!" he stepped out in front of a passing MP jeep and displayed his credentials.

The vehicle skidded to a halt and the soldier in the back swung the menacing M-60 around to bear down on them. The two men in front cast immediate scowls of grim concentration at O'Leary and made it known with their narrow eyes they were rarely impressed by fancy little ID cards.

"Marine Intelligence, boys," O'Leary produced his brightest smile. "Don't suppose you'd be en route to midnight chow via downtown Saigon, would ya? We seemed to have lost our jeep in the confusion down there," and he motioned toward the storm of swirling smoke clinging to the structures at the bottom of the hill.

Collins focused his eyes on the driver's nametag and felt his heart skip a beat: Cain. One of the MPs who had met their chopper out at Fort Hustler after Sewell dumped a perimeter tower with the nose cannon accidentally. Would he recognize them? How could he not, what with Amy's bristling chest, straining to break free of her blouse, something few war zone cops would soon forget.

Already, the MP riding shotgun was moving flak jackets aside to make room for at least one of them: *her!*

"I imagine we can swing down into Sector Eight," the driver muttered softly, still unsmiling, eyes as narrow as before. He glanced at Collins, and his expression said *Why don't you spooks keep your fool games*

171

outta our territory.

"Yah, we'll run ya downtown," his partner said importantly. "The guys working Tu Do will raise hell if they catch us on their beat, but fuck 'em if they can't take a joke, right? You *are* staying down on Tu Do, aren't you?"

"Dong Khanh," replied O'Leary. "The Bat Dat . . . know the joint?"

"Cholon?" the Hog gunner in the back seat asked. "Sure pops, we all know Chinatown like the back of our hands!"

Collins almost laughed at the pops reference, and started to climb into the back of the gunjeep. He could understand it too: the oldest vet among them was the driver, and he couldn't have been nineteen at the most.

Later, after Saigon's Finest had dropped them off in front of O'Leary's hotel and their jeep rumbled off into the mist of night, all three checked their wristwatches.

"Half past curfew," Collins grumbled. They glanced down the street both ways. Motorscooters and a rare taxi were sputtering about, searching out hookers who had not found a home and GIs who had outdrunk themselves and couldn't find their way back to camp.

"Did you two ever find a hotel room?" O'Leary sounded hopeful. It was evidently his night off, but he wouldn't mind loaning them his hooch again—*if* they'd let him watch. O'Leary chuckled to himself, prepared suddenly to make the offer, but Collins answered.

"Why don't you buy Candy here a drink?" He

172

pushed Amy toward him roughly, and O'Leary's smile vanished. "She's real good at giving massages, Hank-honey . . . and I'm sure . . . if you talk real sweet in her ear, she might even show you one hell of an all-nighter!"

"But Brent—" both Amy and Hank whispered in mild protest and shock.

"Oh, Brent-baby'll be okay," he grinned, flagging down a slender Vietnamese Honda Honey on a 50cc scooter. She was in her early twenties, with hair down to her kickstand.

"Where you go, GI?" She spoke the words like a dream come true.

"But it's past curfew," Amy argued. "Some canh-sat catches you on her back seat and it's gonna mean—"

"Oh, I'm gonna ride her back seat all the way to Thai Heaven." His eyes burned into her as he hopped onto the cycle and wrapped his arms around the driver's waist.

"But where are you going?" The concerned look on Amy's face actually made him feel terrible inside—his gut did a bellyflop—but Brent kept the grin on his face.

He moved his wrists up slightly so that they pushed his companion's breasts toward the edge of her loose tanktop. "*Di di*," he motioned with his chin for her to pull away from the curb and proceed in the direction she had originally been heading. The Honda Honey produced a somewhat nervous, naive smile that told the two men present she was not a Honda Honey at all, but just some schoolgirl trying to make an extra buck as a two-wheeled taxi. Or perhaps a seamstress from an 18 hour-a-day factory, moonlighting for extra scrip. It was doubtful Amy even noticed her facial expression—Brent was confident her eyes were glued to the younger woman's healthy figure. Collins buried his face against her shoulder as the scooter sputtered off down the street, inhaling her scent as the warm night breeze flailed her hair against his eyes like strands of fine shimmering silk beneath the floating moon. He made a production of holding her tightly as the bike dipped to the side to take a corner, gaining speed as it swerved around a bum sleeping in the gutter.

And Brent Collins never looked back or he would have seen the tearful expression of anguish and concern on Amy's face as the jovial Big Hank O'Leary draped his massive arm around her and led the lady into the cavernous dragon's den of a hotel on Dong Khanh street in lower Cholon.

Brent Collins felt himself floating on a cloud of silver incense. He took another swig of the *Ba moui ba* beer and left his head back as the liquor raced down a throat drawn tight and seemed to lift him higher off the teakwood floor. He felt increasingly dizzy and light-headed, but he was confident he wouldn't fall backward—someone was holding him up. His entire lap was tingling from her effort to both please and keep him still.

"Elephants!" Collins's speech came out slurred as he struggled to stare at the blur of an orange Chinese lantern suspended from a ceiling corner over the bed. But his eyes kept dropping to the tapestry on the far wall—an elephant trumpeting through a bamboo thicket with hunters in straw conical hats in pursuit. The tapestry was composed of fine, rich grains of multi-hued blues and green that shimmered about like waves in a restless sea, he decided . . . when he could keep his eyes focused long enough. Joss sticks in front of the makeshift altar above the dresser bureau glowed faintly as thin wisps of the incense drifted out to assault what remained of his other senses.

Where am I? He let his head drop back to its natural position. The bedposts looked vaguely familiar, but they were probably identical in hotels throughout the Orient. Some little Chinaman in Hong Kong had cornered the market decades before Dien Bien Phu. The comparison made him laugh out loud for the first time: while the bedposts appeared to remain stationary, the tapestry and the altar honoring dead relatives seemed to be wavering like a reflection of trees surrounding a pond after a stone was cast into the middle of the water.

The woman on the scooter! Had he actually followed her home?

The wet slapping below his field of vision ceased, and an unfamiliar voice taunted him. "Why you laugh? I would not think this is so funny were I man same-same you!"

He forced his head to look down toward his lap—the neck muscles responded shakily, without any semblance of coordination—and the girl's face materialized in front of him so magically he was almost startled. The soothing sensation along his crotch that had propelled him above the clouds of incense was draining away, like energy after a long patrol through the jungles of Asian heat.

"Oh no . . . no, don't stop now . . ." he whispered, cupping his hands gently against her ears as he guided her lips back where he felt they belonged. The woman worked slowly, teasing . . . totally engulfing then abruptly pulling back . . . withdrawing, just as the tingling returned, nearly peaking.

"You are no longer laughing," she whispered back sarcastically after running her tongue along the outside of it.

He let her broad, cocky smile back down, keeping his hands against her ears. "You are certainly not the novice I thought you were," he replied, wondering if she could even hear him. He began rubbing her temples as she responded to his mild groans with a sudden rapid quickening of the pace. As if on their own, his fingers shifted to the back of her head, clasping together under the curve of her skull, until he was forcing her down farther and farther, away from the irregular motions she had been torturing him with and into a smooth, almost choking rhythm more to his liking. "No, definitely not the naive cherry girl you portray while cruising the streets of Saigon atop your trusty motorscooter."

She was pulling away again, and he had to fight the urge to force her mouth back in place. "Yes," she sounded somewhat over-confident, "Uncle Ho teaches his daughters how to master the art of cocksucking from an early age," and she was grinning evilly as she allowed her head to drop back down. "As well as the skill of castrating the enemy with deathly silence."

Collins's ecstatic smile vanished as he felt the edges of her teeth gliding down his shaft. His eyes popped

176

open in terror, but when the woman could not take in any more, soft lips replaced the gentle clasp of sharp incisors, and she giggled with her mouth full.

"Lousy cunt!" He found no humor in the jest and flung her away from him, across the floor. How was he supposed to keep it up after a scare like that?

The girl, rubbing her neck dramatically, was staring back up at him. She frowned for a few seconds, then jumped to her feet, modest breasts bouncing about wildly, and snatched up her blouse. "I go now!" she pouted, switching to pidgin English.

Collins stared back at her, suddenly aroused by her anger and indignation. He rolled off the bed, vision unfocused and head swaying, and pulled her down on top of him. "Now we're gonna do this right!"

"I said I'm going!" she protested. "Fun over! I *am* a cherry girl—forget the tricks I learn with my lips! We stop now."

"Horse shit!" he responded, flinging her blouse away as he rolled on top of her and pushed her panties down tense thighs. When Collins rammed a knee between them, forcing her legs apart, visions of every rape victim he had ever questioned as a cop flooded back to haunt him. Faces, wounds, scars, crime scenes. Smoking weapons and corpses. Blood stains on windowsills. Evidence kits.

When he lowered his body against hers, his eyes were seeing not some beautiful woman stretched out helpless beneath him, but a hospital emergency room back in The World, and some ER doctor running a comb through a victim's pubic hair, collecting evidence left behind by her attacker.

Brent rolled off the woman before achieving pene-

177

tration, and came to rest on his side against the cold, teakwood floor. Moments later, the hotel door creaked open, and Justin Ross stood silhouetted in the frame, silenting scanning the room.

The woman lying beside Collins swallowed her sobs and took the unannounced intrusion as her opportunity to flee unchallenged. She swept up her clothes and dashed out into the hallway past Ross, semi-nude. They had never once discussed money. It had been the typical college girl lark gone awry.

"Everything all right in here?" Ross stepped inside and closed the door without turning on the light.

"What are you doing here?" Brent detected the anger in his own tone after the words left his mouth. Had Justin followed him from the scene of the fire?

"Whatta ya mean what am I doing here?" He walked over to the window and drew the shades. Starlight drifted in, giving the room an elusive radiance. The candles on the nightstand had burned themselves out seconds after Brent and the Honda Honey had moved to the floor. "This is my hotel room, clown. You shoulda warned me you were bringin' a little beaver aboard, and I woulda found another pad to spend the night."

Collins glanced around the room. There were no tapestries on the wall, no worship altar surrounded by pictures of dead ancestors . . .

Had he dreamt her?

But no: Ross's own words proved she had existed. And by his foot, the undergarments he had ripped away in his passion.

Collins shook his head back and forth violently—the maneuver had never worked in the past, but the effort at trying to do *something* often served to clear his head—and tried to focus on Ross's eyes. In the courtyard below, both men could hear the girl kick-start her scooter frantically, and sputter off into the night. "This has not been one of my better . . . dates," he admitted, trying desperately to remember the woman's face.

"Yah," Ross picked Brent's pants up off the chair and tossed them down to him. "If only I had a dollar for every cunt who picked up and rabbited whenever—"

Police whistles sounded several blocks in the distance, and after a barrage of rifle and pistol fire further shattered the night silence, there came the sound of screeching metal against blacktop, and a terrific crash. Neither man, both far from the window now, could tell in which direction the disturbance came from, or what was the cause of it. Visions of the topless girl racing through a curfew roadblock in her panic only to be gunned down by a squad of startled militiamen flashed through Collins's mind, but he did not stir.

After Ross watched the Honda Honey smash into a parked truck (after catching a dozen rifle slugs in the back) in his own mind's eye, he said, "Shield your eyes," and an instant later, the lone lightbulb dangling down over the nightstand came to life.

"Like I was saying earlier tonight," Ross continued, and Collins was glad that, though he glanced about the room suspiciously, he never asked about Amy. "We got things to discuss."

"Oh?" Collins felt sore as he slipped the pants on.

"A new mission."

179

"In Vietnam?" A lone siren was growing in the distance.

"Yes. Saigon."

"Convenient."

"Of course."

A movement along the edge of his peripheral vision caught Brent's attention, but when he glanced toward the window, it was only a greenish-gold flare, floating along on the night breeze fifty yards above the rooftops on the other side of the boulevard.

There came a slight grating noise from behind—a key being inserted into the doorlock, and Ross allowed his hand to rest against the automatic in his shoulder holster.

"Knock knock," came a voice from out in the hallway. Ross and Collins instantly recognized Chandler's sarcastic tone.

"Who's there?" Ross played along, bracing a boot against the door so it would stay shut. His hand fell away from the .45 pistol.

"Mother," came a husky voice. It sounded like Sewell.

"Who's mother?"

"Mo-fucking' baaaaaadest mothers in the valley, son . . . gonna kick this door down in your face if ya don't expedite unlockin'—"

Big Chad and Matt Sewell staggered into the room, carrying young Cory in a sitting position between them. After they shuffled past, Ross leaned out into the hallway, glancing up and down the corridor.

"No Amy?" he asked, closing the door quietly.

"Haven't seen her since she left with you this afternoon," said Matt, his words slightly slurred. "Weren't

180

you two gonna catch a flick at the cinema or something?"

Ross looked across the room at Collins, as if to say "And from there she was with *you*."

Brent answered the questioning expression with, "Last I saw of Miss Atencio, she was leading some john off toward the sack. Deja vu and all that, eh Justin? Just like the good old days, when she was bobbin' for tricks in the Big Apple back in The World."

The others didn't seem to notice what Collins had said. They were busy making themselves at home—all three collapsed across the bed, face down. Ross directed an annoyed glare at Brent but said nothing.

"Hey!" Cory suddenly came alive as he slid his face around on the sheet. "I smell pussy! Right here in front of my face, I swear to God! I smell—"

"You wouldn't know the scent of cunt juice if Big Bertha in the massage parlor down the street sat on your face, cherry-boy," Sewell interrupted, rolling over onto his back. His eyes locked onto two margouillas lizards stuck together in sexual intercourse upside-down along a corner of the ceiling. GIs called them "fuck you" lizards because of their peculiar mating call that sounded somewhat identical to the obscene directive. Sewell began giggling. Chandler, still flat on his face, fell into an authentic sounding snore.

"Roust his ass," Ross said as he pulled a pocket notebook out and positioned himself on the edge of the dresser. He glanced at his watch. "We'll have to begin without Amy."

"She'll make it," Cory was all smiles as he remained face down on the sheet, "or I'll be happy to bring her up to date with my own personal briefing in

181

the morning."

"Shee-it," muttered Sewell as he pulled Chandler toward the edge of the bed. The big soldier-of-fortune rolled off, onto the teakwood floor with a loud, painful-sounding thump, and Ross winced.

Thirty minutes later, after he had phoned downstairs for a coffeepot and tray of mugs, Ross checked his watch again. Amy was still missing, but he was more irritated than worried. He knew she could handle herself out on the street. He stared at the four men precariously balanced on the edge of the bed across from him now. Chandler and Sewell were cautiously holding their steaming cups, eyes half closed—both men looked like they were already suffering numbing hangovers. Collins had a depressing mask on his face, and just sat there nursing his coffee mug, avoiding Ross's eyes. Cory was the only one sitting up straight, and with a far-off look in his eyes, his head jiggled about atop shoulders to some silent tune while his teeth flashed a permanent, ear-to-ear grin. *You'd have though he just bedded down a king's harem*, Ross thought to himself.

"I've recently received orders for a new mission," the team leader finally revealed.

"Outfuckinstanding," muttered Chandler. He almost fell over onto his face, but Sewell reached out, grabbed, and steadied him.

"Back to Bangkok?" Cory sounded hopeful, but his eyes remained locked onto some distant vision in another world . . . some experience on another plane of thought. *Perhaps memories of the maidens of the Kingdom of Siam?* Ross wondered, *Rumored by some to be the most beautiful women in the world.*

182

"No, we stay right here in the Pearl of the Orient," he announced. There were none of the groans of protest Ross had expected. Only silence. "I'm sure you're all aware of our notorious Beverly Hills-born brat who poses on SAM missiles in Hanoi and makes kiddy-bopper records back in The World."

"Jungle June?" Cory's smile faded, and his eyes shifted to Ross.

"Recently Miss Wanda has fallen from grace with her innumerable fans," the team leader continued.

"Why I saw her on the tube just this morning," Cory said, "on that contraption they got in the lobby. Black and white. They showed her arriving at Tan Son Nhut airport," and he released a slight chuckle. "Some clown in the crowd hit her smack in the chops with a water balloon filled with commie-red paint— least the announcer said it was red . . . black and white TV, you know. Fuck if I could tell . . . Got all in her hair and everything."

"Her recent arrest in New York drew large crowds after she loudly claimed police brutality," Ross said. "She turned the whole fiasco against herself when she used the opportunity to publicly call for a Viet Cong victory in Hanoi."

"But the VC are South Vietnamese," Cory commented.

"The broad don't know her politics very good," Chandler agreed, sobering somewhat, but his chin just as quickly fell back down against his chest and Sewell had to keep him from tumbling over.

"What was she arrested for?" Collins was beginning to take a sudden interest in the conversation.

"Well, you heard she married that low-echelon

Black Panther from Cleveland . . ."

"Yah . . . that's carrying being a bleeding-heart liberal a bit far, isn't it?"

"That, and all her protest rallies and subversive get-togethers at the GI bars in small military towns across the country put her smack dab on the government's shitlist."

"And rightfully so," belched Big Chad Chandler.

"Far fucking out," Sewell was searching his pockets for one last match. He already had four of them placed between the comatose mercenary's stubby toes.

"And that meant that when Customs at international airport found all kinds of unidentified pills in her luggage Uncle Sam jumped all over her."

"Far fucking out," Sewell repeated. He had found another book of matches. His grin faded, however, when he opened it to find only three very old matches folded up inside.

"Even those clowns in Hollywood who snatched her from the recording business to transform her into a tinsel town starlet turned against her last week," Ross continued. "Seems she made some kind of pro-Arab statement—they got another skirmish raging between Egypt and Israel or something I guess—and since most of the movie moguls are Jewish, they told her to stick her politics up her ass, and are now slamming doors in her agent's face."

"What's a mogul?" Sewell was feeling feisty. He scratched the first match against the strip of sandpaper on the book, but it only fizzled and shot a spark across the room.

"And just before leaving on her most recent jaunt back here to Asia," he ignored Sewell except to visually gauge how much attention the chopper pilot was allotting the briefing, "several of her closest friends even turned against her after it was revealed publicly that her last rock concert—touted as a fund raiser where all proceeds would go to charity, specifically cancer research—ended being nothing more than a scam: all the money has ended up in her husband's hands and is to be used for his budding political aspirations. . . ."

"A Black Panther in parliament, eh?" Chandler was now making no sense whatsoever as his eyes focused on Sewell trying to light his last match. The big man's expression said Let me show you how to do it, but after leaning forward slightly, then hesitating altogether, the ex-soldier of fortune remained silent.

"No wonder she came back to the 'Nam again," said Collins. "With enemies like that, she's better off with her friends in Hanoi."

No one, including Ross, smiled at the play on words.

"Against her husband's advice," the lieutenant continued, "she has decided to stop off in Saigon on her way to Hanoi to . . . entertain the troops."

"Bob Hope's already here to do that," said Collins.

"Exactly. Wanda feels his sexist USO acts only serve to influence young soldiers to escalate their pillaging, plundering and raping—in her words. So she's brought along her select troupe of socialists to try and compete with the likes of Ann and Lola."

"Fat chance," muttered Brent.

"If the paint attack on this morning's newscast is any indication of her dwindling popularity," Cory said, "she won't even have an audience . . . except for maybe the jive monkeys in the platform shoes, boppin' each other with their made-in-Zululand concealed-sword walking sticks."

"You're right again," Justin Ross broke into the smile he usually saved for special occasions. "June Wanda's popular support back in the states has eroded drastically. She put out three singles last month, but none even made the Top 40. Mr. Y back at the Big P has decided the time is right. The order has finally come down from the mountaintop, gentlemen . . ."

Cory and Collins sat up straight, concern, apprehension, and excitement alive in their eyes.

Ross slowly drew his .45 and handed it, butt-first, to Brent Collins, as if merely shuffling some papers . . . assigning someone a shit detail. "We are to proceed with our primary objective in Vietnam: the termination of a new target. *Hit June Wanda!*"

Brent Collins, carefully taking the automatic pistol, nearly triggered a round into the ceiling when Big Chad Chandler exploded into a sudden roar and began hopping around the room on one foot.

PART III

8

Waves of heat were dancing about between the hotel entrance and the rooftop where Collins was lying prone along its edge, making it difficult for him to keep his eye against the riflescope for more than a few minutes at a time. Every now and then he would pull away, rub at his shooting eye for a second or two, glance up at the sizzling orb of an orange sun overhead at twelve o'clock high, mutter a few muffled obscenities, then sight in on the lobby doors again.

He hated daylight hits. Oh, he didn't mind all the extra bystanders, or the odds-increase in being spotted by a diligent traffic cop on a TCP somewhere. No, Collins just hated the heat. He always worked better after dark, enjoyed the streets more when the sun went down. And he'd even tell you his eyesight was better beneath the stars, though a good optometrist would argue that point. He'd claim it was unlikely and probably just his imagination, since humans weren't designed to prowl through the night. They were made to cower in the back of a cave somewhere, safe behind a raging campfire.

Below, on Nguyen Trung Truc street, shoppers

were crowding along storefronts, spilling out off the sidewalks at the end of each block—though he couldn't tell you where they got the money to spend so much time browsing. O'Leary had told him even some of the high ranking policemen on the Saigon force only took home around twenty bucks a month—after taxes and before graft, of course—and O'Leary seemed to be one who knew about such things. Yet day and night, the tamarind-shaded, flower-lined boulevards of the city were always alive with a bustle of people and activity. Of course it could just be they were all only *looking* at the items which were intended for the GI market all along—dreamers, like refugees fresh off the boat in Brooklyn, awed by an American grocery store.

Tires skidding a couple blocks away took his attention from the sniper scope again, and Collins watched as a blue and yellow Renault taxi smashed broadside into a black, Russian-made Moskwa saloon sedan in front of the open air market. The Moskwa's windows were all tinted black, and its door remained closed while those of the tiny Bluebird sprang open. Three U.S. soldiers, snockered to the gills, spilled out. Sporting platform shoes that almost caused them all to lose their balance in their rush to confront the driver of the other car, the blacks launched into a barrage of unintelligible jive that could be heard all the way to the fifth floor perch. There Brent Collins was seeing not the street scene taking place below him, but the pair of Vietnamese women, holding hands, pausing in front of a melon display at the open-air market.

The markets of the Orient. Now *that* was where a tourist found the true heart of Asia, both he and

Hank agreed. Where even the poorest peasant could afford *something* to eat; where the prices were gauged to the Vietnamese, and not the ignorant GIs. Where a round-eyed tourist (and even the Japanese, who were hated and despised after WWII, still managed to show up in the strangest places, and could be recognized blocks away) were overcharged three or four hundred percent as a matter of policy. If you knew what the prices should be (your best bet was to latch onto a lady-of-questionable-virtue for your Tour 365) you could gorge yourself on a dollar or two, and live like a king on a private's pay.

Two women holding hands—or two men for that matter—was a sign of simple friendship in Indochina, not hormonal imbalance. Collins watched the two girls in the market release each other to squeeze, smell and inspect the lush watermelons laid out before them. He watched the warm afternoon breeze grab at their filmy, almost transparent *ao dais* and tug the garments against breasts that pointed straight out, refusing to sag. He did not notice that the dap-darlings beside the Moskwa had ceased hostilities and were instead throwing smiles of admiration, and black power fists at the sole occupant in the rear seat of the sedan. (Though the thought did cross his mind in the beginning to take a bead on the tallest buck private and see if he could knock both platforms out from under him with just one shot.)

Brent Collins, ex-police SWAT sniper, Korean war vet, notorious international adventurer (now) and dapper, all-around good guy, rubbed his shooting eye again and glanced up at the sun. Not a cloud in sight. The thunder he had been hearing all morning was not thunder at all, but Arvin artillery north of Gia Dinh somewhere. *Crazy Viets probably fighting over drug-running territory again.*

With the naked eye, he carefully examined the waves of heat hugging the pavement in front of the Park Hotel lobby, trying to gauge any discrepancy that might exist—it just would not do to aim high to compensate for distance only to find, after the echos of the discharge sent every bystander within fifty yards of the target zone scurrying for cover, that you had fired at a phantom heat apparition all along.

He brought the scope down onto the face of the female porter standing in the deceptively cool shade of the lobby archway—early twenties, the traditional seven bracelets of intricately carved Vietnamese gold on one wrist, high cheekbones, slightest hint of a smile that curved downward on one side hauntingly, long black hair fanning out across the unflattering brown tunic management made her wear. The essence of all that was beautiful to Collins. Until Amy came along.

Damn, he mentally reprimanded himself as he shifted about on the hot tenement rooftop, rearranging his trousers in an attempt to get comfortable again. *This was not the fucking time to get a hard-on.*

She had sauntered into the restaurant shortly after dawn, smiling at Ross and the others gathered around two coffee pots. She reserved a mean, mysterious twinkle in her eye for Brent, knocking Cory off his chair after he made a snide remark about her grin, meaning she must have discovered the secret about those sinister-eyed Vietnamese Don Juans with their battery-powered, exotic aphrodisiacs.

192

She hadn't offered a word of explanation to Ross, and after a Saigon breakfast of pho soup, croissants, puff, and iced coffee, she attentively listened to his briefing. She dispersed with the others toward the target location afterwards, remaining silent the entire twenty block trip.

The porter's arousing, almond eyes disappeared from his scope suddenly. The black Moskwa was pulling up right in front of the lobby.

Ross had said Wanda would be returning from her meeting with the news media in a camo-flocked land-rover.

This couldn't be her, but he sighted in on the rear door anyway. The lens magnification brought the dragonfly hovering in front of the window into sharp focus but did nothing to penetrate the thick layers of black tint.

He felt the urge to shoot up the entire sedan, making mincemeat of every window and occupant inside, but he restrained himself. The Park Hotel was not grandiose or fancy, but it did cater to several French plantation owners, and destroying the wrong car would only serve to put Wanda and her entourage back on the defensive.

When the door finally opened, and June Wanda—wearing a camouflage-design scarf and peasant's sarong—brought one leg out, Collins hesitated for the slightest instant. As her blonde curls were brought into sharp focus in the center of the scope's crosshairs, he was seeing not the target Ross had ordered him to terminate, but one of his favorite album covers in a priceless collection it had taken him nearly a decade to put together.

Artillery thundering on the horizon woke him from his briefest of daydreams—slammed him back to the matter at hand, the purpose of the mission, the *wrath of Ross* if he failed. But before he could hold the breath necessary for a smooth quick-kill, the sight picture in his eyepiece was suddenly a blank wall of green!

Collins jerked his eye away from the scope—a long, doubledecker Saigon municipal bus had pulled up between him and the target vehicle!

Collins jumped to his feet, panicking for the first time since he could remember, and nervously paced from one end of the rooftop to the other, uncaring if someone spotted him on high, a suspicious prowler toting a menacing superrifle.

The usual intricate network of traffic jams was keeping the bus motionless, which in turn completely obscured the semi circular driveway that led to the hotel lobby. Collins could just see Ross's expression after the team leader realized his so-called sharpshooter had botched the hit. He could already hear Chandler and Sewell chuckling about the foul-up . . . could sense Sewell's silent mocking. His smiling eyes. And what of Amy? What would she think of her hardcore hero now? Would she ignore the whole regrettable episode, or just—

A bullet zinged up at him without warning, impacting against the line of red French style shingles at Brent's feet, sending shards of stone and plaster up at him—an instant later he heard the discharge from the street below . . . saw the tiny traffic cop on his pedestal in the middle of the closest intersection . . . staring back up at him now from behind the swirling cloud of gunsmoke.

The bus was lurching ahead . . . pulling away amid the din of screams all around the excited canh-sat private.

June Wanda had slipped into the lobby, protectively encircled by her ring of bodyguards, and was nowhere in sight.

The small porcelain teacup flew across the room, out the window.

Justin Ross pounded his fist across the top of the coffee table and shook his head from side to side. None of the team members had ever seen him so upset. It was as though he was taking this mission—or their latest foul-up—personally, and the lieutenant had never done that in the past. Failures or setbacks in other missions had just been part of the overall game. *Game.* He had usually responded with a shoulder shrug and we'll-get-em-next-time-around expression. But this time there was no mistaking his vibes: *Roscoe was pissed!* "You only hesitated for a moment?" he roared sarcastically. "I can't believe it, Brent! I just can't believe that was *you* up on that rooftop today. We should be on our way to Cambodia by now!"

Chandler was chuckling in a corner, a newspaper across his lap. "And *I* can't believe how our trigger-happy canh-sat had such a change of heart," he smiled in relief. "Says here, in a little box sidebar on page 49 I might add, that a Saigon policeman took a pot shot at a cat burglar making his rounds in broad daylight. No mention of June Wanda. No mention the cat burglar was occidental."

It appeared June Wanda was not even aware of the incident—when it went down, even her bodyguards had assumed the toylike crack of the .38 caliber discharge had just been one in a series of automobile backfires in front of the hotel. Ross was uncertain whether Wanda would read about the incident, or even connect it to her afternoon travels earlier that day. Hopefully she only read *Pravda* releases and would ignore the complimentary copies of the *Saigon Post* lying around her hotel lobby.

"Few South Vietnamese in this town hold any love for Wanda," Sewell surmised. "To most of them, she's just Hanoi June, the VC Queen. That poor canh-sat still probably doesn't know how close he came to getting greased by me or Chad . . . probably didn't even realize who the cunt was in the Moskwa. Probably fired at Collins out of gut reaction . . . purely a street reflex to correct something not right: in this case, a giant elephant gun atop a downtown rooftop," he commented philosophically. "He probably never even noticed Brent—just the fucking Ruskie router against his shoulder."

"And if he did," added Chandler, "he probably figured he was screwing something up—shooting at a white boy and all," Sewell giggled and Amy grinned, "and fabricated the whole cat burglar yarn to cover his ass."

"I still can't figure out how the bitch got a visa for South Vietnam in the first place," MacArthur said, pouring himself another cup of coffee.

"Money talks in this part of the world," Sewell lamented somberly. "Money talks."

"Ain't that the truth," muttered Collins.

Cory stared at the wisps of steam rising from his coffee cup and had a change of heart. He reached down into the cooler beside the bed and rummaged around in the ice until he came up with a bottle of "33" beer.

"Put it back," Ross said with zero emotion.

"Huh?" Cory reached for a can opener anyway.

"We're going out tonight." The lieutenant remained unsmiling.

"And I get the impression it ain't to no floorshow at the Miramar," Amy said, popping a large purple gum bubble with snarling lips.

"June Wanda is making a guest appearance at a Buddhist student movement meeting," Ross explained.

"And we're going to finish what we screwed up this afternoon," Collins ventured a guess.

Chandler cleared his throat. "What *you* screwed up, Sherlock."

"The place is gonna be crawlin' with cops." Sewell was brooding with one of his most solemn faces.

"No more games,' Ross's lips curled up into a death's-head grin. "It's going to be an open-air affair. Tonight the dragonfly kicks ass from on high . . . we attack from the sky."

The site of the gathering was a soccer field half a block from the massive golden temple towering over the intersection of Le Van Duyet and Chi Lang. Normally reserved after curfew as a med-evac LZ and dustoff point for the GIs, and evacuation pad for

197

American officers' wives in the event of an all-out communist attack, it was now crammed with row after row of folding chairs that had been arranged into a colorful "fist" that stretched out for some three hundred yards. The field was in an area well outside the metropolis of downtown dwellers and within sight of the southern runways of busy Tan Son Nhut airport.

June Wanda was requested to limit her guest lecture on women's rights and oppression of the student movement by the current regime to ten minutes of inspirational religious rhetoric, but everyone knew the woman was an atheist who would waste little time in launching into a verbal attack against American foreign policy in Southeast Asia.

The area was cordoned off by whole platoons of Vietnamese National Police and plain clothes undercover agents—no doubt, if Collins had his way, they'd transform the whole affair into a sticktime jamboree as soon as The Man back at Doc Lap palace gave the go-ahead. Armored personnel carriers loaded down with eager QCs rumbled back and forth along the perimeter of bright field lamps towering two stories above the field and pointed at center stage.

"Think you can pull it off?" Ross glanced over Collins's shoulder at the sight-picture taking shape a thousand feet below and four hundred yards out. The three men all wore headphones. The flapping rotors above their heads were a mere hum. It was doubtful the people on the ground—with all the crowd chatter and clanking APC treads lumbering about—could ever hear the helicopter hovering motionless overhead. Painted black, it was invisible against the moonless night.

"Gimme a break, Roscoe," Collins muttered into his mouthpiece as he sat in the open hatch, legs dangling over the side, rifle against his shoulder. "A hit at ten hundred feet is hard enough when you got a tripod, zero breeze, and mother Earth beneath your balls—but with sucklips Sewell up there flying this tub? Don't hold your breath."

For the first time in over a year, Justin Ross wanted to slap Collins in the head and tell him it was *Lieutenant*, not Roscoe. He wanted to boot the insubordinate sonofabitch out into the pitch-black of never-never land, but he kept his cool and forced an unemotional mask across his features.

"It will only be necessary for you to unload all you got on the speaker's platform if Cory fails in his mission on the ground. Blast the fuck outta every white woman running around on that stage when the shit hits the fan . . . think you can handle that?"

Collins slowly took his brow from the telescopic eyepiece, looked up at Ross, and gave him a cocky, overconfident grin, but didn't say anything—he knew better. Already, June Wanda was clapping along with all the applause, in the common Oriental tradition, as she climbed the steps to the speaker's platform.

The plan was simple enough. MacArthur was to imitate a VC mortar squad by lobbing a single 60mm projectile (the Americans and Arvins used eightyones) along a carefully pre-determined arc into the area directly behind the platform when Wanda rose to give her speech. Injuries to innocent bystanders would be minimized since the area was a dead space empty of audience and cordoned off by the soccer field backstop netframe. It was piled high with audio equipment and stacks of propaganda leaflets, but would remain deserted until after the scheduled ninety minutes of speeches, according to one of Mr. Y's informants Ross had been in contact with.

Only June Wanda's back, and possibly a few choice leaders of the radical Buddhist movement would be in the kill zone.

And after it was over, all the carnage and mayhem could be blamed on the VC queen's own loyal though misguided subjects.

Collins waited beneath the clouds, high in the humming dragonfly, with Ross by his side, and Sewell at the controls, ready to pick off the woman if she survived the lone projectile sailing in from the hills overlooking the tenements along Le Van Duyet.

Chandler and Atencio sat parked in a souped-up Alfa Romeo across the street from Wanda's black Moskwa. If Cory's commie mortar and Collins's Russian sniper rifle (he had temporarily sidelined his M40 favorite) failed to do the job, Chad and Amy would fill the sedan with enough Chinese AK lead to sink the bloody Bismarck!

"There it goes." Chandler smiled when he heard the dull thump signal the mortar had left its tube.

"There it goes," Ross tapped Collins on the shoulder with one hand as the other gripped binoculars which caught Cory's green flashlight signal from the ground.

"Thar she blows," young Cory had giggled to himself as he let the mortar slide down into the launch tube. Already he was sprinting down the opposite side of the hill, and would disappear into the maze of alleys below the tenements that towered all around, abandoning the remaining mortars in place, as planned.

The twirling projectile generated a slight whistle as it plummeted to earth, ignoring the vehement rhetoric being shouted, gospel fashion, by the American communist. Saigon policemen manning the gates to the soccer field immediately recognized the death warning and began blowing out panic through their whistles. Women with children in their arms and golden-robed monks with their heads shaved bald began screaming and running for cover. These people were Vietnamese. They had known what descending mortars sounded like since the days they had sucked on their mothers' breasts. Now they were scattering like dust in the wind.

Except for June Wanda.

Mouth agape, eyes darting from side to side frantically, she stopped in midsentence and watched the audience parting before her like the sea from some Hollywood Bible epic.

The mortar's spiraling whistle increased to a deceptive shrill of a scream as it shot to earth directly behind the startled starlet—right on target.

And landed with an ugly sucking thump in the pool of soft mud and muck between the audio system and tables full of pamphlets.

A dud.

"*Well, fuck me!*" Cory MacArthur bit his lip and poured fuel on the fires in his feet as he increased the speed of his sprint. *A goddamned commie dud. Leave it to Ross's sorry-assed contacts to sell us bad ammo!*

"Aw fuck." Chad Chandler's smile of anticipation faded when he heard the screaming mortar ker-plunk and fall silent without detonating. He started up the engine.

"No explosion." chopper pilot Matt Sewell whispered disheartened confirmation into the others' headphones. "Repeat: no flash."

"A fucking dud!" Ross roared, wishing to God Cory would drop one more mortar into the tube, but well aware the plan had called for him to rabbit the second his fingers dropped the first one down the tube. Escape time was all important—they could not afford to have one of the team killed or captured by a lucky security guard.

No shit, Sherlock, Collins mentally shook his head from side to side as the crowds scattered under the bright field lights below. This time he would not screw up—this time he would not hesitate. But even before his mind could send the command to his finger to pull the trigger, a bodyguard on the ground was sailing through the air like a leaping jungle cat, knocking Wanda from between Brent Collins's crosshairs, out of sight.

9

"She's all yours," Chandler muttered as he received the commo code from the 'Fly (seven scratchy clicks on VNP channel 4) and shifted the Alfa Romeo into neutral. He slowly let the clutch up so the sedan would sit idle, its powerful engine purring patiently. They both donned clear nylon masks that were barely noticeable in the darkness rubbing at the intense glow around the ring of field lights.

Amy kept the AK47 rifle barrel just below the open window of the passenger side door. June Wanda would kiss Saigon goodbye under a barrage of thirty sizzling tracers set to rock-and-roll on full auto.

It would have to take place as the starlet bounded toward the Moskwa thirty feet away. If she made it into the rear door—now being opened by a wide-eyed escort with a submachinegun cradled in one arm— there'd be little chance of taking her out of the picture: the car would surely be armor-plated.

"Jesus H . . ." Big Chad suddenly muttered.

"What the fuck else can go wrong!?" Amy abandoned her manners and made her purple bubblegum explode repeatedly as she threw her lips into a snarl:

the Moskwa was backing up in reverse, shooting gravel and dirt out from under its tires as it disappeared from between the two sights on the end of her gun barrel.

The driver was trying to get the large sedan closer to the throng of bodyguards surrounding the stage, where her escorts were attempting to whisk Wanda to safety.

The rear door, still open, caught onto a huge speaker after bowling over two fleeing spectators, and snapped partially off. It dragged across the ground throwing sparks, as the sedan's motor roared against the din of screams and clamor of scurrying feet.

"No way! No fucking way!" Chandler was trying to see through the mob of terrified Vietnamese . . . was looking for a route through the fleeing masses that could bring him closer to the stage and afford Amy a righteous shot. "This is unfucking real, woman! How could I ever listen to Ross? How does he get us into these nightmares!"

The Moskwa wasted little time in squealing backward into the limelight—a half dozen students were not quick enough in their effort to get out of the way. Legs fractured as tires spun over sudden victims. Amy closed her eyes at the gruesome *thump-thump* sound of warm flesh being rolled across by hot rubber. "Just drive, damnit!" she yelled in an uncharacteristic display of emotion. Just as suddenly, her eyes popped back open—burying whatever the flashback had been deeper in her subconscious—and she leaned out the window, brandishing the automatic rifle.

Chandler laid into the horn and shifted to second gear before letting the clutch fly. The front tires of the

Alfa Romeo took the sports car into a powerful side spin through the crowd and nearly struck a Vietnamese policeman with gun in hand.

When he saw the two masked men and the AK muzzle staring back at him, his eyes flew wide and he turned in the opposite direction, vanishing in the sea of terrified faces.

Amy was practically knocked out the window as the Moskwa smashed into them head-on without warning.

They had successfully hustled Wanda into the car before Atencio could fire on them!

Metal screaming in protest as bumpers grated and collapsed, the more powerful Moskwa pushed the Alfa Romeo backward and out of the way as if a linebacker had knocked a careless cheerleader flat on her pom poms.

Amy let loose with a half-clip burst that stitched the sedan from hood ornament to rear license plate, but the tracers all ricocheted into the ground or skyward in a fantastic show of deflected pyrotechnics. It was just as they had suspected: bulletproof.

"Don't look good," Justin Ross decided as he watched the rounds spark off the Moskwa and arc up into the heavens. The back sedan, horn blaring, raced out of the soccer field with its headlights off, leaving a cloud of dust in its wake. It was impossible to tell just then if Chad's sportscar had been disabled. "Better take us down," Ross said grimly. "If all else fails, I guess we'll have to pop some '79s up their ass."

"There's the Alfa!" Collins was ecstatic, arm extended out the hatch of the descending craft as he pointed. The sportscar was rocketing out of the dust-

205

bowl, swerving in and out of bystanders and skidding onto Le Van Duyet. "Right on the money!" he added when Chandler turned down the same direction as the speeding Moskwa. "Good ol' Chad . . ." They were already gaining on the car carrying June Wanda, and were now about two blocks behind it.

"Take out its tires!" Chandler yelled over at Amy as he swerved from side to side even though they had yet to encounter return fire, but the woman needed no coaching. Already she had expended two banana clips, using five round bursts, and was slamming another magazine into the well of the weapon. Ross had taught them all that in a streetfight, a round blasted into the blacktop rarely bounced more than a foot off the ground but travelled inches above the pavement in a straight line until striking something or losing power. Amy didn't waste time and energy aiming at the rear tires—Ross had also told them shoot-outs between moving cars rarely saw any lucky hits and fewer skilled ones—but fired in a fanning motion at the pavement stretching out between their two vehicles.

Still no results.

Come on, Amy-baby . . . Collins was sucking on a knuckle as the chopper dropped to only a couple hundred feet above the chase and remained above and slightly behind the cars. He and Ross could clearly see her leaning out the window even at this distance, and the tracers spewing forth from her AK against the black of night and pavement were a sight to behold.

"What about Cory?" Collins listened to Matt ask Ross the question over the metallic intercom system. He grimaced at the prospect of abandoning the pursuit just then, but he also worried about the kid waiting longer at the EP than they had planned—he'd get antsy for sure.

"He passed the confidence course at LZ London," Ross said after a lengthy pause. "He can weather an extra hour or two in lower Saigon after curfew."

Sewell checked his console clocks. *Uncanny!* It *was* almost eleven already. Time . . . sunsets, sunrises—they all crept up on you so fast. How could Ross keep track?

"My God!" Collins nearly tumbled out the open hatch as the three of them watched two men suddenly lean out the back windows of the Moskwa and unleash a combined burst of red and green tracers back at the Alfa Romeo. A slug caught Amy in the shoulder and catapulted her out of the sportscar—she was sent rolling across the edge of the roadway by the impact. More sparks flashed off the pavement as her rifle clattered beside her and slid along for a half block at fifty miles per hour. Trying to roll into a protective ball with her head cupped in her arms, she disappeared from view down the hillside beyond the line of dim amber street lights.

"Take her down!" Collins yelled into his mike. "Take her fucking down, Matt!"

"Negative!" Ross in no way hesitated.

"But Justin—"

"She's dead, Brent." Ross did not look back. His next sentence was directed at Sewell, "Stay on 'em. . . ."

"He's right," Sewell said grudgingly. "You don't survive a fall from a speeding auto going *that* fast, Brent . . . I'm sorry—"

The thought of leveling his pistol at them both entered his mind briefly, but he shook it free and just sat there on the edge of the open hatch, wishing the dull rhythmic beating of the rotors would clear his head. The warm downblast slapped at his hair, and he couldn't hear the shooting below. He wanted to throwup.

"Prepare to lob some HE rounds at 'em." He heard Ross's voice come over the earphones again, but he was seeing Amy's face. The way she looked when he was on top of her in bed, both of them slick with sweat, her throat tight and her breasts flattened out beneath him, nipples taut, rubbing his chest. Her lips drawn back like something wild, eyes tightly shut as he swirled around inside her the way she taught him to . . . the way she said felt best. He tried to hear her voice, but visions of an Amy with her face torn away by unyielding blacktop kept creeping in, and the only sound was the turbines overhead and the roar of racing engines below. Chad would not pull over. It would hurt even a man as bad and tough as he claimed to be, but he would proceed with the mission. Duty and country came first. Honor was something they often joked about. He wondered if he would do the same thing—he didn't think he would . . . he'd swerve to the side of the road and run back to her. Of course he would. But Brent Collins knew that, if Amy was driving and *he* was the one shot out of the window, she would never have eased up on the gas pedal a hair.

The chase proceeded southeast along Le Van Duyet until it approached the hilltop at Hien Than. Once across, they'd be dazzled with the skyline view of the countless city lights. And a hundred police checkpoints.

Ross couldn't allow that.

Sewell read his thoughts and brought the craft down further until it was a mere fifty feet above Chandler's sportscar. "Here goes nothing." He activated the weapons system and directed a cannon shot at the back window of the Moskwa.

"Wrong choice of words," Ross muttered when nothing happened.

"Aw, fuck," Sewell ran a cross-check of his panel and frowned.

The controls appeared to be functioning, for they were treated to the noise of clicks when the nose cannon armed and activated itself, but the snout remained silent. Misfire.

"Chuck it and try another round," Ross said, some urgency creeping into his voice.

"You don't understand how these babies work, Roscoe." Sewell was not smiling.

The situation below was deteriorating rapidly: Chandler's Alfa Romeo had taken a radiator hit and was spewing steam. A few seconds later, sparks flew off his hood when a burst of tracers again connected, and silver smoke began belching from the undercarriage and top vents.

"I say cut 'em off at the pass," Collins spoke loudly, but still as if from a world of hurt.

"Perhaps overly dramatic, but to the point," Sewell responded to the suggestion without coaching from Ross and slammed fuel into the chopper's motor, taking them swiftly ahead of the ground chase. He banked to the left, pushed the collective stick down, pulled back on the cyclic, until the Huey was hovering in the roadway a half block in front of the Moskwa and three feet off the ground. Sewell brought the craft slowly around until the open left hatch was facing the rapidly approaching sedan.

Collins fired off a burst from an AK he had ripped from a wall case, but the rounds ricocheted off in a shower of sparks, and climbed toward the stars in a glowing, dreamlike arc of hot green. *Don't miss, or you'll paste Chad to his car seat*, Sewell was thinking as he concentrated on keeping the helicopter steady, but Ross's words quickly shattered his thoughts.

"Motherfuck! He wants to play chicken . . . *take 'er up!*"

The driver of the Moskwa had switched on his bright lights and floored the gas pedal—was barreling straight for the center of the chopper.

Sewell's pride made him hesitate for a few seconds, but when it became quickly evident to even the Korean war vet that the bodyguard in the hurtling auto was not balking, he finally tilted the rotors and brought his craft barely above the roof at the last moment.

Collins leaned down under the Huey, supporting himself with one hand gripping the skid as he fired after the Moskwa with the other. Tracers sailed away, some bouncing off the back of the car, and then Chandler was racing past beneath him, smoke still pouring from the Alfa Romeo as pistons knocked and rattled loudly in protest, and Collins let up on the trigger with only a couple of rounds remaining in the magazine.

He ejected the clip, listening to it clatter against the pavement below, and as he fought to keep his balance while pulling another magazine from the ammo pouch on his web belt, Sewell whirled the craft around. Collins thought he would fall out into space but then they were levelling out and pulling up in front of the Moskwa again, and he found he was still gripping the skid with white knuckles, and was still alive.

"Give 'em everything we got!" Ross told Collins as Sewell hovered directly in the path of the black sedan again.

"What about Chad?" Sewell was asking above the roar of the downblast, but the two men behind him were already firing, and he concentrated on keeping the craft steady.

"He's going for broke again," Collins muttered, a sudden tension in his voice now as it became obvious the driver was aware a first win at this game of chicken insured perpetual glory.

"Keep her steady!" Ross yelled back to Sewell, more in response to Collins's statement. Matt found himself wondering if the sedan driver felt confident his vehicle's armor-plating could survive a crash with a floating tank.

The men behind him switched magazines again—the car was a half block away now, gaining speed the whole time, it seemed—and unleashed another thirty round burst at the front of the Moskwa.

"He ain't gonna pull off, Justin!" There was a tone of urgency in Brent's voice now, but he kept himself busy with slamming fresh clips home instead of worrying or preparing to bolt.

"*Steady!*" Ross sounded confident as he smoothly replaced his fourth empty clip. Smoke drifted in front of the barrel until he pointed the weapon out the hatch again and sent flame out the muzzle in scattered, five round bursts at the blacktop in front of the car. "Steady . . ."

"Well, fuck it!" Collins muttered as the car roared right up to them unabated. The windshield was tinted black as all the other windows or Collins and Ross would have been able to see the look of terror in the driver's astonished eyes when the huge helicopter failed to pull up again.

The top edge of the bulletproof windshield shattered as it slammed into the chopper's metal landing skids. "Damnit, Roscoe!" Sewell called out as the impact forced the craft out of his control. It dipped down to the left after the sedan passed underneath, and the rotors dug and gouged into the pavement, snapping off in a scream of flying blades as the Huey jerked about uncertainly then dropped heavily onto its side, powerless, its frame collapsing under the weight of the heavy turboshaft.

"Sayonara, you sonofabitches!" Ross almost sounded like he was smiling as the chunks of flying steel and fiberglass sliced in all around them, and the chopper collapsed in the middle and folded across the roadway. A muffled explosion lifted the cockpit up off the ground a few feet, forcing it back onto its bottom, and a secondary blast threw Collins and Ross clear of the wreckage, but the disabled craft failed to catch fire. *Going out, burning bright!*

Brent Collins folded his forearms across his face as gravel was thrown into it by Chandler's tires skidding to a stop inches from his head. He wanted to just close his eyes tightly and kiss it all goodbye—*Fuck the Nam and thank you veddy much!*—but steam hissing from the damaged radiator was engulfing him in a silver cloud and stinging his left ear. Collins forced the side of his face off the warm blacktop and turned to survey the carnage behind him: Ross was twenty yards away, also on the street, teetering back and forth on his buttocks as he held a bloodied knee with both hands and grimaced in pain. To his left, Matt Sewell, his coverall torn to shreds and body coated with soot and ash, crawled from the pulverized cockpit, his white toothy grin quite a contrast against the charcoal-black face. "Anybody get the wing numbers off that Learjet that cut me off?" he laughed, ignoring the pursuit. Collins was amazed he could joke at a time like this.

"This ain't no damn airport!" someone was yelling off in the distance, and they turned to discover what had just been a dim line of gray in the darkness below was now a heavily populated neighborhood, with locked and shuttered storefronts stretching out along the edges of the wide boulevard as far as the eye could see. Vietnamese awakened by the crash were crowded on countless balconies watching the drama unfold in their front yards.

Ross was fairly certain none of the people had heard Sewell's comment. Quickly wrapping his wound with an empty ammo bandolier, he took the .45 from his shoulder holster and fired four rounds up at the closest rooftop. "Back into your homes!" he barked in Russian. It was doubtful few if any of the Vietnamese spoke the language of the Soviet Union, but everyone understood *Colt automatic pistol*, and bystanders quickly dissolved into the shadows of cracks and crevices at the back of the balconies or between the leaning tenements.

Collins glanced over his other shoulder, expecting to

213

see the fading tail lights of the triumphant Moskwa—
and was treated to the sight of the sedan sitting on the
side of the road a block away, one tire shredded and
the rim melted, finally disabled.

Sewell had already abandoned the temporary
adrenaline high that came with discovering he had not
gone to that great pilot limbo beyond the clouds, and
was now back at the Huey, setting the three C-4
charges that would further destroy the gunship. It
would be difficult to conceal the fact the craft was
American-made, impossible in fact. But at least he
could remove any trace of their commo capabilities
and command affiliation. He briefly thought of
Cory—sneaking about in some dark back alley miles
away—and wished the kid's magic medicine man's
pouch had been on the Huey tonight. It hadn't pre-
vented the mortar from malfunctioning, and probably
wouldn't have kept his Huey in the air, but maybe it
would convince the spectators out there in the night
that the three men crawling about in black coveralls
were Ruskies and not a trio of Agency spooks or SOG
seals down on their luck. Yes, a charm would come in
handy just then—it surely couldn't hurt.

Brent Collins was already on his feet, rushing past
Sewell and his dead child, firing from the hip at the
two men emerging from the car.

The bodyguards, both tall and burly, were heavily
armed and returned the fire as two more brutes rolled
from the back door and joined the spectacular exchange of tracers and smoking lead. Collins rolled behind the nearest concrete lamp post, and Ross was
soon beside him, sucking in lungfuls of the hot, sticky
air, his leg soaked in crimson from the knee down.

214

"Wouldn't you know it?" He glanced up at the dim yellow bulb glowing thirty feet overhead. "Only fucking streetlight working in this whole neighborhood and we both gotta roll under it."

"Don't mean nuthin'." Collins frowned as he set the butt of his rifle stock on the ground between his legs and fired off two rounds into the sky. The two foot diameter plexiglass shade above snapped like corn popping and with the sudden darkness, glass sprinkled down on them.

"What's your plan?" Collins muttered after he leaned out around the post and fired a three round burst at the Moskwa, keeping them pinned down.

"I don't *have* a fuckin' plan!" Ross responded with a similar discharge of bullets from the opposite side of the concrete pillar. "Just kill that bitch any way we can."

"You got any frags?"

"Shit, Cory's got all the grenades." Ross buried his face in the gutter as a concentrated barrage from three rifles zeroed in on their position, kicking pieces of cement and shards of lead at them.

"Bad mistake." Collins's words did not come across as insulting as he leaned toward the edge of the post again but was forced back by the heavy fire before he could shoot.

"Bad sequence of events," Ross conceded. "We should still be hovering above that damn soccer field, watching the white mice shovel pieces of June Wanda into a body bag."

"Yah, for sure." Collins's reply was soaked in sarcasm.

A squealing of rubber on blacktop behind the two

215

men forced them to shift their attention from the black sedan down the road to big Chad's sportscar. "What's Chandler up to now?" Ross muttered aloud as the Alfa Romeo, still smoking as heavily as ever, roared past at high speed, headed directly for the other vehicle.

Timing himself almost perfectly, the ex-mercenary dove from the passenger side door as the sportscar shot past the lightpole protecting Ross and Collins. Cradling his pistol against his chest, he rolled as hard and fast as he could until he had slammed into Brent's left side.

Moments later, the Alfa Romeo—its accelerator jammed to the floorboard with a heavyduty flashlight—piled into the back of the Moskwa and burst into flames with a dull blast. A secondary explosion was much louder, and as a fireball of orange and black colors climbed the skyline, lighting up half the block for several seconds, Collins, Ross and Chandler unleashed a heavy barrage of lead on the four men dragging a hysterically screaming American woman from the back seat.

They were expert shots. There was no reason for missing their targets, despite the return fire. Despite the crowds growing all around again and the deafening noise. But the clouds of smoke billowing forth from the wreck and the manner in which the evening breeze was whipping it in and out of the kill zone provided just the small amount of visual cover needed to save June Wanda from death's grasp again.

Her bodyguards began hustling her away from the vehicle, down toward the rolling hills that led to abandoned railyards, and, on the run, Ross and his men kept up the steady rate of fire as they quickly traversed the stretch of ground between the two groups.

"Score one!" Collins cried out as a lance of tracers from Ross's rifle reached out and slammed into the head of one of the bodyguards. The five rounds tore off his lower jaw and severed his neck an inch above the breastbone, and as his skull flew from his shoulders and slammed into Wanda's back, splashing her with a spray of crimson, Chad cheered, ejected an old and inserted a new banana clip, gave a war cry and fired another burst—all before the dead man's body had a chance to topple over onto its front.

"Take out the fucker on my romeo!" Ross ordered Chandler, all business now, unsmiling, switching to military jargon. "Brent, you dust the one on the lima . . , I'll take the fuck in the middle! Leave Wanda alive!" he decided. "I want her taken in custody, got that?"

The bodyguard whirled around and sent a wild burst of soft-nosed slugs Ross's way, but they flew high and the man turned back in the opposite direction to flee. Ross placed a single bullet between his shoulder blades as he was midway through the clumsy maneuver, and the thug flipped to the ground.

"Alive!" Collins sounded incredulous. But this was no time for conversation. He brought his rifle up to his shoulder and took aim—enough of this shooting off the hip dramatics (*that* was nothing but a waste of ammo, he decided).

Collins's eyes flew wide with surprise when a round punched him in the belly and flopped him down onto his bottom heavily. His trigger finger jerked off a burst of tracers that flashed up into the night sky in a wild arc.

"Brent!" Sewell called out from the other side of the road as he fired three shots and killed his friend's assailant with the first shot. "Ya-dumb-fuck! You trying to get yourself killed or something?"

But Collins did not immediately respond. While Chad Chandler was busy exchanging a frantic sustained burst of ammunition with his opponent, Collins was engrossed with his own sudden predicament. He slowly opened the fingers that had been clutching his gut, stared down at the torn shreds of cloth, over at his sweat soaked but bloodless fingers, then back at the faint curl of smoke drifting up from the bellytear in his coveralls.

He was severely bruised underneath and it hurt like hell, but Collins had yet to entirely comprehend the situation: his life had been spared not by any lucky charms, but by the thin layer of molded body armour Ross made each of them insert into their work clothes since the incident in Tokyo.

"And motherfuck you too!" Big Chad Chandler had bounded up to the man he had just shot in the nose and left eye, and was commencing to kick him around on the ground.

Ross and Sewell ignored him for the time being— better to let the monster vent his penned up frustrations on the genuine bad guys rather than some loudmouth whore back on Tu Do Street.

June Wanda was sitting in the midst of all the blood and carnage, coated with crimsoned bits of bone and gristle, soaked below the belt in urine. Her long blonde hair was tangled with portions of eye muscle from the dead man Chandler had shot up and was now mopping the gutter with, and, with her face buried between her knees, she held her trembling hands up over her head as she screamed incoherently about life, death, and *God save this lowly, ignorant, foolish atheist!*

"Some revolutionary," Sewell spat at the ground next to June Wanda, nothing but utter contempt and disgust in his voice. Collins had finally staggered up to the rest of them, and as he too stared down at the woman he couldn't help but compare her to the teammate they had abandoned several miles back: Amy, so confident, fearless, downright ruthless at times, yet beautiful. And Wanda, unmasked—a sniveling coward who was all talk, no guts, and even less self pride . . . your typical political radical. He hated himself for comparing the two of them in the same thought.

"Aw, shit," muttered Chandler as a police landrover, siren wailing, rolled up to the smoldering helicopter blocking the road. "This side show has just come to a screechin' halt."

Only one canh-sat jumped out of the mint green emergency vehicle.

"Not yet," replied a grinning Justin Ross confidently. He strode up to the Vietnamese policeman, draped a husky arm around the shorter man's shoulder without saying a word, and led the canh-sat over toward the front of the Huey.

"Your weapon!" he barked in Russian without warning.

The canh-sat's eyes did a double-take on the nasty looking sawed-off carbine in the occidental's hands and cautiously surrendered his service revolver even though he didn't speak Russian. "Aw . . . good!"

Ross said in heavily accented English as he slipped the Smith & Wesson under his belt—it was a Soviet accent he was sure the policeman would not soon forget.

Ross handcuffed the canh-sat to a lightpole, took the revolver back out, unloaded it, and slipped it back into the tiny guy's holster. Then he trotted back over to the rest of his group. War was hell, but a .38 Special was government issue, and worth three months' salary. The canh-sat was not so depressed after all.

"Whatta we do with the VC bitch?" Chandler was sincere with his label. He didn't like the idea of dragging her all over Saigon with the authorities lurking around every corner. Already a chorus of sirens was growing in the distance.

Ross slipped a set of wire-like plastic flexi-cuffs out from underneath his web belt with one hand and grabbed Wanda's shoulder with the other. She jerked away and kicked out at him. "Some spice in the cunt after all," he muttered as he kicked her over onto her stomach and forced her arms behind her back. He quickly wrapped the flexi-cuffs around her wrists and yanked the ends tight. Several buttons along the front of her blouse snapped off, and as Ross pulled her up onto her knees and steadied her, Juna Wanda's breasts, sweat-slick and propped up from below by a Hollywood Boulevard bra, swayed slightly from side to side, catching the eye of every man standing above her. Big Chad decided maybe it wasn't such a bad idea to drag her along with them after all.

Ross jerked her to her feet. Wanda's knees swayed slightly as she struggled to keep her balance, and Ross allowed her a moment to compose herself, then he was dragging her across the street, through the wreckage in the middle of the road, to the police landrover.

"Where do we go now?" Sewell was biting his lower lip when he asked the question; two canh-sat jeeps had skidded around a distant corner and their revolving red lights could be seen about fifteen or twenty blocks away, rapidly approaching.

He used his hands to double the prisoner over, then held her face-down in his arms and threw her into the back seat of the landrover. His eyes told the others to keep their voices down: more bystanders were congregating curbside again.

An empty beer bottle flew several feet over Chandler's head and smashed against the cement lightpole against which the frightened policeman was handcuffed: these people would tear up an unarmed canh-sat with their bare hands if they thought they could get away with it.

"We head for the safe house on Thanh Mau street," Ross answered finally, jumping in the front seat behind the steering wheel. Collins flew in beside him, and Sewell and Chandler tumbled into the back seat, crashing into either side of June Wanda and designating themselves her new escorts.

"What about Amy?" Collins asked, fighting off the vision of the woman he loved being catapulted out of a speeding automobile by a rifle slug to the shoulder.

"We search for her on the way there," Ross conceded.

He surveyed the angry mob of misfits and back alley scum gathering around the policeman handcuffed to the lightpole, and waited a few more seconds before throwing the landrover into gear. When it appeared

221

help would arrive at the scene before the young street hoodlums could do the cop any serious harm, Ross popped the clutch and raced off in the opposite direction with his headlights off, the hot humid breeze in his face, and the electricity in the air that is Saigon excitement forcing his lips to curl up in an almost demonic grin.

"Damn!" Justin Ross slapped the dashboard of the powerful finely tuned landrover carrying his team off into the night. The job satisfaction he experienced at times like this was better than a rush of firefight-induced adrenaline. The ultimate emotion. *Incredible!*

10

The rain sounded nasty, even threatening as it lashed at the window shutters in front of him. The sheets pounding in relentless waves down across the corrugated tin roof overhead held more menace than music, but he knew the sudden storm—a monsoon downpour common this time of year—was also washing the filth outside down deep, narrow gutters to the river. Nature's way of cleansing the streets of Saigon . . . or trying to.

Every few seconds her muffled screams would sound above the din of the heavy rain, and Collins would grasp the window frame harder, wishing he were an ocean away . . . wondering why there was no glass beyond the bamboo shutters, forgetting the reason for the grill-like shield.

He squeezed the chicken wire instead, putting pressure on his fingers slowly yet intensely, until the skin was lacerated and began to bleed, but the pain was minimal, and didn't serve to make June Wanda's sobs go away.

The rain was so heavy now that he could barely see the dim yellow street lights below. When a spiderweb of lightning bolts appeared through the shutters, everything outside seemed to vanish before his eyes. All that remained was an echo of nearby thunder and the crying.

"You're just wasting your time *and* my time," he heard Ross whisper down to her, and with the memory of her latest album cover still fresh in his mind's eye—Wanda, clad in peasant's garb, strumming a cheap guitar beneath a canopy of forest trees while in the background an elderly couple rowed a small boat across an amber pond at dusk—he turned to stare at them.

She was stripped to her undergarments and was tied to a chair tilted back on its rear legs. A wet towel was draped over her face from the nose down, and Chandler was slowly pouring a bucket of water across it.

The procedure produced a gagging sensation that felt identical to drowning.

Ross raised a hand slightly, and Chandler stopped.

"It's not like I was asking for the key to the city," Ross muttered, turning his back on her as he feigned hurt and insult.

God, Collins swallowed hard. Where was he coming up with all this crap? What had started out as a simple hit had escalated into a prisoner capture, and now a question-and-answer session with the failing grade death. Asking her about her true motives, her contacts stateside and Hanoi, who was really bankrolling her activities. . . .

Collins was sure Ross would soon bring up the bit about the cache again too.

"I know you've got a safe house hidden on this side

224

of town somewhere." *There he goes . . . right on schedule . . .* Chandler lifted the towel off and gently slapped first her left, then right cheek. ". . . And if you level with me, you *might* just see the sun rise over Saigon tomorrow."

Wanda choked, coughed, caught her breath, then produced her best Hollywood laugh, mocking the lot off them. "You think your little Chinese water torture trick can break me?" she flicked her chin at big Chad. "Why I've been through the hardest guerrilla courses—"

"—The clowns in Cuba have to offer," Ross interrupted. "Yes, yes . . . we know all about that."

"Okay honey." Chandler took his cue. "No more Mister Nice Guy." He took a washcloth from the bucket and wadded it up, smiling down at her the whole time.

"Why you worthless, two-bit cocksucker—" she lashed out at him, but Chandler grabbed her chin, jerked her mouth open as far as it would go, then forced the cloth in nearly to the throat. He then taped her lips shut and slapped her head back.

"You're as dumb as all the GIs suspect you of being," Sewell mumbled softly as big Chad, holding her head back by the wet-slick hair now, began funneling a trickle of water from the bucket down into her nostrils.

Wanda's face flushed crimson as she gagged against the searing pain. Thirty seconds slowly passed.

Finally she began kicking her feet against the ropes holding her ankles to the chair, and shaking her head back and forth.

"Enough," Rose sounded bored.

Big Chad, still grinning, kept pouring patiently, expertly.

"Okay, *Chandler*," the lieutenant touched his elbow, and the ex-mercenary, smile fading, (like a child teased with candy, only to have it jerked away in the end), moved back.

Sewell stepped forward and ripped the wide tape from Wanda's lips. "Do yourself a favor," his voice was firm, grim and unemotional. Totally unamused. "Answer the man's questions. This ain't no Hollywood gameshow, honey. And there ain't no two-bit revolutionary cause worth losin' your tits over." He jerked the washcloth out of her mouth, and Wanda began hacking mucus. She turned her head to the side and threw up water.

Chandler stepped back out of the way just in time and he curled his lips in disgust.

When Ross placed the needle under her fingernail and began slowly tapping it home with the butt of his pistol, Collins turned away and stared out the window again. He could hear the lieutenant saying, "How 'bout if we jerk the fillings from your teeth and dig around in your old cavities for a while, little Miss Heroine of our times—"

"A legend in her own mind," Chandler muttered.

But as he watched the rain falling like sheets of warm gauze beyond the shutters, he was hearing Amy gasp after they found her in the roadside gulley and tried to lift her limp body into the commandeered police jeep. One round had entered her upper right chest below the clavicle, missing the major bones until it exited out the center of the shoulder blade, leaving behind a nasty wound. But Amy would live. Ross had bandaged her up, filled her with antibiotics, and now she was sedated in an adjoining room.

They had been unable to locate Cory.

"This is getting us nowhere," Chandler complained.

Ross had tapped five pins into the fingers of Wanda's left hand. Blood trickled down onto the floor from the minute wounds. And from her bottom lip, which she had bitten through to keep from crying out.

June Wanda matched Ross's glare with a comparable scowl of contempt. "She's tough," the lieutenant conceded under his breath. "I'll give her credit for that."

"Schizo, if ya ask me," Sewell commented. "Hardcore one minute," he nodded down to her now, "and a wreck the next." He referred to the way she appeared to fall apart under fire.

Ross nodded to Chandler, and the giant of a man stepped forward again and slid his massive hand beneath the clasp of her bra, snapping it apart.

Her breasts sprang out loosely, glistening with sweat and spittle as they separated, full yet sagging heavily.

Sewell rushed over to a nearby table and swept the paper plates off with his forearm, clearing it completely.

"Get the det box," Ross instructed Collins.

Brent remained at the window, eyes glued to the heat lightning outside.

"Collins!" Ross raised his voice slightly. "Get the fucking dynamite detonator from the other room."

Brent did not want to move. He did not want to venture into the dark room and perhaps find Amy cold and lifeless, staring back at him.

Why did you abandon me loverboy? he could hear her accusations already, uttered from unmoving lips, spoken with the eyes, her face ghostly pale.

"Brent!"

Chandler and Sewell had cut Wanda's bonds and were dragging her over to the table.

They slammed her down on her back, spread-eagled, ripped her panties down her thighs and off the ankles as roughly as possible, then bound her limbs to the corners of the table, using twine that gouged her flesh, digging deeper into her skin the harder she struggled.

Collins turned and started for the door to the adjoining room.

Bully!

The word echoed between his ears like a shot from his past.

He stared straight ahead, but he could not help but see Wanda out of the corner of his eye when he passed her. Chandler was flicking the edges of her nipples with his fingernail—the way you would snap and sting someone during horseplay—trying to make the flat, brown swirls grow taut.

Bullies!

Collins rubbed at his temples. Big Chad was smiling. There was something wrong about that. They should not be enjoying it all so much. Did they strap Diem down a year ago and let Amy whack his pecker with the sharp edge of a ruler?

He was beginning to doubt why he was there. Why any of them were there. In Vietnam. And he was beginning to wonder if the team was comprised of such

astute professionals in their individual fields after all.
. . . They were all acting like a bunch of horny, sadistic soldiers of misfortune.

"Move it, Brent." Sewell pumped his elbow up and down.

"Time is tight," Chandler agreed. Whatever that meant.

The cool brass of the doorknob set off a chain reaction of memories that took him back to his old days on the force. *Brass*. Belt keepers, TCP whistle, the clip on his holster, the emblem on his cap, the department insignia and precinct numbers on his collar. . . .

Only his shield was non-brass. *Silver*. With gold numbers and letters inlaid.

The blood, sweat, and tears he had shed just to get through the academy. And they had nearly dinged him on the unannounced eye exam. But he had faked it, and proved to them 20/20 vision was fine and dandy but by no means mandatory for the job. Hadn't he maxed the combat shooting course, earned an expert rifleman's badge in the service, and scored so high on the p.d. monthly qualifications that the chief finally made him the SWAT team's sniper?

Four eyes my ass!

He entered the room with Amy lying on the bed, still thinking about the circumstances that had motivated him to seek a career in law enforcement in the first place.

All the wrong reasons.

Excuses that would have shown up on the fifteen hundred question shrink screen these days—but there had been no such extensive pre-employment obstacles back then. You proved your mental capabilities on the

street. The same place some cops ate their service revolvers and spilled their brains into the filthy gutter
from the open door of a souped-up squad car that had
been their office ten hours a day (or night) for the last
twenty years.

*Some pulled the pin and forgot to throw the gre-
nade. . . .*

He was nine years old when they robbed him. Walking three miles to church on Sunday morning, through
the projects, to keep his mother happy. Too stupid or
naive to ditch and spend the lousy hour at the Bowl-
O-Mat. Taking a short cut through the old stock car
race track that was now abandoned and overgrown
with weeds and sunflowers . . . would soon be leveled
into the dust for a shopping center that would also col-
lapse and fail—after he'd spent his teenage years
pumping gas there evenings . . . through the hot dry
summers and winter blizzards so he could buy the old
red Galaxy 500. Between the A&W and the Taco Bell
. . . *Toodles* would bring him a Pepsi, when she was
ringing bells for the Salvation Army at Gibson's up
the way. . . .

They were a year older than him. One black, one
Mexican. (Though he would never look at people by
race until he joined the marines and they'd become
spades and spics. As a cop, he'd have called the duo a
salt and pepper team). Appeared out of nowhere.
Confronted him right where the stands had used to
be. Punched him off his feet when he couldn't produce his money fast enough.

A lousy nickel.

Strong-armed robbery, he'd call it later. No knife,
no piece. Just fists. His father and Dave-down-the-

street had gone looking for the pair after he had mentioned the incident in passing—to explain the cut lip and torn pants knee—but he had felt no real fear. Just inconvenience, embarrassment at having not had more money in his pocket, and guilt at having missed mass. Mother said God would forgive him due to the circumstances, and that night she had made peadoehee for supper and served angel food cake with strawberries afterwards.

And when he advanced to junior high and saw them again. Hanging out in the halls, picking on the smaller kids. The wimps, they'd call 'em today. The frail geniuses. *The meek shall inherit the earth.* Twist their arms for their lunch money.

And he had never thought to tell his father he now knew who the boys were from that incident the year before. He never thought to confront the punks personally.

But hadn't he knifed their bicycle tires (probably stolen anyway) one rainy afternoon, and tossed a brick through their front picture windows by the light of the moon? *Don't get mad—Get even*: Patterson, his boyhood buddy and streetwise after-curfew adventurer, had taught him. And hadn't he looked the black dude up after he got out of the marine corps and wiped the streets with his face right in front of Bucky's Tavern?

The Mexican had run away from a juvenile detention center and died in a south L.A. gang fight at the age of 16. *So fuck him and his ghost and his lousy memory anyway!* Always picking on the wimps who retaliated in the only way they knew how: win first place in the science fairs.

The wimps.

Something about the way they were put on the earth to be intimidated, terrorized, and beat up on a weekly basis.

Someone had to protect them.

Even a skinny jerk like himself.

He had been threatened with suspension three times for picking fights with the bullies and throwing one of them through a sliding glass door in the school cafeteria.

The assistant principal always started off with his crew-cut, narrow-eyed scowl—*so small, yet constantly raising hell, boy!*—and ended up laughing at his ethnic jokes and tossing him out of the counselor's office with another warning.

He never looked at the police as protectors of wimps. They were the guys who pulled you over for speeding through stops signs on your 3-speed, or chased you and *The Pack* off the school rooftop at 3 a.m., *(Guiterrez jumped right off into a thirty foot deep stairwell, and Benny died from fright—guys who just didn't make it . . .),* or responded to traffic accidents on Friday night, or gave mother a ticket for letting Sonar tear off a dumb jogger's arm after he reached over the fence to pet the deceptively sluggish-looking St. Bernard.

Until Easter Sunday.

He and Tom had been catching black dragons on Washington Street when the drunk plowed into the road sign at the triple intersection. *Call the cops* his star twin had suggested, *and KDZA—win an album from the newsline!*

It had escalated into a 22 mile chase with shots fired, a grand finale right at the—believe it or not—

232

exact location where it had all started; and he had won the newstip-of-the-week prize: a June Wanda record, *The Pursuit*.

He would never forget how the five patrol cars had forced the hit-and-run suspect to the side of the road. Ten officers then stormed the vehicle on foot, filling every window with six-inch revolvers.

Outfuckinstanding! He'd never forget that scene. How they pulled the dude right out through the window, stomped his ass for taking them on a 110 mile-an-hour tour through town. The power of life and death at their trigger fingers. The electricity in the air. He could actually feel their adrenaline coursing through his veins.

And from that day on he knew his life would be on the street. With his brother cops. Life at high speed, governed by the threat or smell of gunsmoke, with maybe an inspector's funeral, the *grande finale*, at 22. . . .

He though about the wimps only two or three times while with the P.D. Dealing with the bullies of society on a daily basis had dulled him to the plight of the victims over the years, until he lost all memory of the reasons he initially became a protector in the first place.

Fuck it, a marine sharing his foxhole in Korea had said one night as they lay awake, watching the perimeter for sappers sneaking through the wire. He had tried to tell the man about right and wrong . . . how his sister had written that his best friend back in The World was in the hospital after being ganged up on by some thugs after his lunch money. *Fuck it*, the marine had looked up at the moon like nature was a nuisance.

233

Don't mean nothin'. And he had come to wonder if combat had turned both of them into the bullies he so despised.

Brent Collins reached down and untied the straps on the belly pack leaning against the bedpost. He pulled the dynamite detonator out, realizing the distance from the doorway to the bed was only ten feet yet his mind had travelled back years and years in a single slow-motion flashback. He became suddenly aware of the darkness all around him, and his own attempts at being quiet. For a moment, he became frightened, and sweat started to trickle down the small of his back.

Amy. . . .

He could detect her scent in the room. The perfume she dabbed on her throat even on the combat missions—Ross had yelled at her about that a couple times. Now he could smell blood in the room too.

He forced his eyes to look up at her, fighting the fear a ghoulish, white-faced vampire, thirsty for lost blood, would be staring back down at him.

She was still unconscious though. Hardly breathing. Head turned to one side. He should change the dressing on her wound . . . *somebody should!* They should get a doctor for her. Even a Vietnamese physician, or a Chinese herbalist.

But he retreated from the room after locating a ten foot length of wire in the bottom of the pack and pulling it out frantically with a resisting cemetery screech.

"Come to papa." Big Chad had his hands out when Collins re-entered the main room. Eyes locked on the detonator box, smaller than a car battery, Collins handed it over to him and returned to the window.

"Got one of those little hummers to stick up, anyway," he giggled, rushing back over to Wanda's side to flick at her nipples again.

As Ross busied himself attaching thin, nearly invisible wire to the oversized clamps on the side of the box, Chandler carefully wrapped the middle section of the wire around the edges of Wanda's temporarily erect nipples before they could fall flat again. He then tightened the wire loops so it would not fall off regardless, and handed Ross the free end. For the first time, the simple technique produced pain so intense that a scream escaped June Wanda's snarling lips.

The lieutenant attached the length of wire to the empty clamp and lifted the handle, pulling the shaft from the bowels of the o.d. green det box.

"Give her a taste of the juice," Chandler coaxed Ross on, but the lieutenant hesitated, glancing over at Collins.

"Brent," he said, smile falling like an unsuccessful cake in the oven.

The team's sniper remained at the window, ignoring them.

"Collins." Sewell raised his voice, pulling the other man from his trance. "The honor's all yours. . . ." Though they all wondered if there was really any honor involved in torturing a woman tied helplessly flat on her back, nude to their eyes. Even June Wanda.

But they were testing him, Collins sensed.

A few seconds later, his hand was on the handle. *Brent Collins has not gone soft*, his conscience spoke back to him forcefully. *Push the fucking idiot-stick, stupid!*

As though experimenting with the equipment's sensitivity, he hesitated, as Ross had done, then pressed the handle down a half inch.

The slight movement sent a surge of weak electricity through the wire running around her breasts that would not have detonated a blasting cap but threw Wanda's head back in extreme pain. She bit down on her lower lip, and tears rolled from the corners of her eyes, tumbling along the sides of her face.

"Push it all the way down!" Sewell coached him on. "Give her the full ride, Brent!"

"Slam it down!" Ross agreed, displaying an unusual shade of emotions.

"What a candy ass," Big Chad goaded him. "Let me show you how to do it, wimpo . . ."

Brent Collins rammed the handle home with all his weight and the body of the woman on the table seemed to rise inches off the cool metal as her lips curled back away from her teeth.

A long, drawn-out scream filled the room and Brent Collins's soul in reward, and before the echoes even began to fade, a giant of a soldier brandishing a Thompson machine gun crashed through the hotel room door in an explosion of splinters, and ordered them all flat on the floor.

11

"Well Brent-baby," the big man with the machine gun motioned toward the naked woman on the table-top with his weapon's muzzle, "didn't mean to be crashin' your party like this," and a wide toothy grin creased his features, "but you shoulda invited me in the first place."

Collins stared back at Hank O'Leary, the officer from Marine Intelligence, with a blank expression. The guy was decked out in full combat gear—helmet, flak jacket and all.

Keeping the Thompson trained on the two bigger men spread-eagled on the floor, O'Leary slowly moved sideways closer to the table.

"You let the guy follow us?" Chandler muttered over to Collins. "Don't you know how to lose a lousy tail?"

But Collins knew O'Leary had not been at the shoot-out on Le Van Duyet. No one could have kept up with the chase from the soccer field incident, and he doubted that—

"Don't blame my buddy Brent," O'Leary answered Chandler's accusation. "I've known about your safe house here for close to a week now—since you set me up with that cocktease at the outdoor theater." He glanced back at Collins. "Man, was *she* cold turkey! Got my ass blitzed like a pro then disappeared out the bathroom window . . . politely. Didn't even get to grease my dipstick, *pal*. But anyway, I caught sight of her lovely young tush beatin' feet down the street, and despite my slightly inebriated mental capacity, managed to follow her here.

"Been watchin' this joint ever since."

Ross found himself grinning mentally. O'Leary had said "*I've* known about your safe house here. . . ." and the keyword was "*I*." Why hadn't he said "We?" Could he be operating this little stakeout alone? Even though Collins appeared to be an acquaintance from somewhere back, the marine probably kept a log back at the office, or made sure an associate knew where he was and what he was up to.

"Can we get off the floor now?" Sewell looked up and sounded bored as he braced himself on his elbows.

"Not till I figure out what you clowns are doin' with this dame here. Last time I saw a table blessed with such a—" His words trailed off into silence when he recognized June Wanda's sweat-streaked, exhausted yet still defiant features. "Aw fuck." His weapon's barrel slowly sank as he let his eyes roam about the curves from throat to thighs. "I done walked over my head into a pile o' shit again," he muttered sadly.

"This is business, Hank," Collins revealed, ignoring the angry glare Ross directed at him. "Be a buddy: walk right back out that door and forget what you saw here tonight."

"Business?" O'Leary said incredulously. "*Whose* godforsaken business, *buddy*?" He turned back to face them just as Ross and Big Chad took the opportunity to leap at his blind side.

"Oh no you don't!" He whirled out of range, bringing the machine gun back up. "This sucks, Brentbaby . . . oh, this truly fucking sucks. I smell Agency antics here, pal. This is worse than any shenanigans we ever pulled in Pusan together." His expression was critical and disapproving . . . almost fatherly. "This bitch is big business! People gonna be turning this town upside-down looking for her young tits!" He was backing toward the door, careful to keep them all covered with a slow fanning motion of the Thompson.

He did not notice the door slowly opening behind him.

When Cory MacArthur, charcoal-blackened face streaked by rainwater with coveralls torn and tattered, silently entered the room behind O'Leary and wrapped his arms around the big man without warning, Ross and Chandler sprang forward and latched onto the weapon.

They wrenched it free without a shot being fired accidentally—or on purpose—and Sewell came flying through the air after them, knocking both O'Leary and Cory over backward with a stunning bodyblock.

"You know we're going to have to kill him," Ross told him later, after they had subdued the powerful marine with flexicuffs and rope, "no matter how close you guys were in Korea."

"If the squad's secret . . . its mere existence gets

out," Sewell agreed with Ross as they stood nose-to-nose with Collins, "then we've all had it."

"Y and his associates back at Puzzle Palace will have no alternative but to eliminate us rather than risk embarrassment to the country."

And so it went. Talk, talk, talk, and they had left O'Leary lying on the floor in the corner where he couldn't help but listen to them discuss his execution. No one was eager to terminate an American hero with four rows of combat ribbons already on his chest and a Congressional Medal of Honor recommendation to his credit.

Now Ross was back playing with his spasmodic bleach-blonde ragdoll on the tabletop. Chandler slammed the detonator handle up and down from time to time with unrestrained enthusiasm. Collins watched it all from his corner, silently, the warm night breeze through the window behind him causing the hairs on the back of his neck to dance about, mocking the whole session.

"I want to know the real reason you stopped off in Saigon," Ross repeated the same sentence monotonously for the fifth time, without changing his tone or voice level a fraction.

Wanda just forced another laugh, and Chandler slammed the T-shaped handle home. A strong current of electricity danced alone the valley between her breasts jutting straight up against the strain of breathing, and she arched her back and screamed.

Chandler smiled at the noise, and waited patiently for her to drop her spine back down against the tabletop. When it was almost flat, he gave her another burst, and again she strained against the bonds, catlike, chest heaving, face contorted, wires creasing her breasts down the middle, leaving red welts against the skin.

"Shove it where the sun don't shine, asshole!" she spat back at him against the uncontrollable tears cascading down over her cheeks. "I can take anything you . . . *amateurs* can throw at me."

Chandler snickered and, reading Ross's mind, set down the detonator box.

"Bring out the persuader," the lieutenant said softly. Big Chad disappeared into the dark room containing Amy, quickly reappeared after rummaging through the belly pack, his perpetual grin only slightly eroded, and produced the menacing-looking cattle prod in his hands.

"Fresh batteries?" Sewell laughed.

"Evereadies," Chandler gave the thumbs-up. The aluminum prod was about two feet long. And a good two inches in diameter.

Chandler moved around so that he was staring straight up Wanda's spread legs. He patted the prod gently like it was a favorite nightstick.

"You wouldn't," she hissed out at him.

"Honey, you done ventured across the dark frontier when you took on Uncle Sammy. Tripped over the invisible yet clearly defined line. Now you're in the land of dirty tricks, lover." He made a tight circle with his thumb and forefinger and slid the aluminum shaft in and out harshly. "And we all know all's fair in love and war."

"Kinky," giggled Sewell, bracing his hands on his hips in anticipation as he took up a good position from which to watch.

Chandler started toward her, still patting the cattle prod and switched it on. The room came alive with a sickening buzzsaw sound.

"All right, all right." Wanda's eyes lit up and locked onto the tool farmers used to shock their animals into moving a certain direction—usually diary cows toward the milking machines. "I'll tell you why I'm here, but it's not all that hot—you'll be disappointed."

"Let me be the judge of that," Ross snapped.

"A family back in the states has paid . . . has donated a generous contribution to my husband's political campaign recently. In return, I've promised to visit their POW son in Hanoi, and speak to the North Vietnamese more about releasing him."

Ross's smile returned.

"Additional funds were needed to pay off the right people."

"Good ole communism," Sewell said sarcastically.

"And I arranged to pick it up here since the wire services wouldn't dispatch it to Hanoi because of—"

"How much money we talking?" Chandler slapped the prod noisily now.

Wanda hesitated, then said, "Twenty thousand."

Every man in the room snorted, shifted about, and guffawed in disbelief. "Jam it *where the sun don't shine.*" Ross laughed at Chandler, and the ex-mercenary eagerly moved closer, like a trained gorilla. Collins got a vision of him cramming a banana into a garbage disposal.

"Okay, all right," Wanda never let her eyes stray from Chandler's hands. "Two hundred and fifty thousand." The room went suddenly silent. "To be delivered to the old abandoned French fort across from the

242

Anne-Marie traffic circle."

"Two hundred and fifty thousand," Ross repeated. "They originally must have paid quite a bit more."

"They are . . . *quite* wealthy. Oil. Houston, or Dallas. I don't remember now. The old man desperately wants his son out of a cage and the Air Force flight suit and into the executive offices of his Texan dynasty."

"Why should we believe her?" Sewell asked.

"Where is the Anne-Marie traffic circle?" Ross ignored his chopper pilot.

Wanda remained silent a few moments, then said, "What insurance do I have you won't just kill me after I give you the directions how to get there?"

Ross quickly lost all patience. "Suck it to her!" he told Chandler, shaking his head from side to side in resignation.

Big Chad clamped a meaty palm against the inside of Wanda's thigh and pushed the legs farther apart, then touched her slightly with the end of the prod.

The shock to her genitals nearly enabled her to break free of her bonds, but the twine held. "I don't know the location of the fort!" she screamed. "My driver was told how to get there, but you killed all my bodyguards!"

"Don't just give her a peck with it," Cory moved forward. "Jam the damn thing in there, bro! I wanna see her twist and shout!" and he did a little dance maneuver, twirling around on his heels as he snapped his fingers in the air over his head.

"Where's the safe house?" Chandler asked Ross's question again, but Wanda was still twitching out of control.

"I know where the French fort is at," a voice at their feet announced quietly. All eyes fell to Hank O'Leary's form, tied up against a wall. "And I'd wager she's got more than a lousy quarter million greenbacks waitin' for *us* there."

"So the old soldier of fortune deep in your soul shines through, eh my friend?" Collins spoke for the first time.

"I don't trust her *or* him," Cory said.

Ross was thinking about the POW sitting in his cage in Hanoi. Would what they were doing in Saigon, a world away, jeopardize his chances of survival in the North?

"I say take the jarhead along for laughs." Chandler frowned uneasily. Sewell clapped him on the back and seconded the motion.

"So let's kill this bitch then and get it over with," MacArthur was dead serious.

"Yah," Chandler's frown became a grin again, turning a little more from evil to demented with each breath as he flicked the prod off and placed it snugly against the outer folds of Wanda's vagina, sore but still sensitive.

Ross looked down at the woman. She was regaining some of her composure finally. "Tell my boys here why I can't let them kill you," he frowned, thinking back to the circumstances surrounding the Diem hit a year earlier, and how they almost didn't make it out of Saigon after that one. Old Man "Y" was playing games, it seemed. Perhaps all their near captures in the past weren't just coincidence. Perhaps it was time to start looking out for Number One . . . padding the pension a little with some freelance spoils of war. Perhaps it was time to say fuck loyalty and allegiance and honor. "Tell them why we need to spare your life so you can continue to parade around back and forth to the bungalows of Ho Chi Minh."

"Yah, tell us!" Chandler caught Ross off guard by plunging the aluminum shaft deep between Wanda's legs. The lieutenant rushed forward as she let out a painful gasp and began to throw up again.

"Turn the fucker on!" Cory shouted. "Both the damsel in distress and her dildo!" but Ross pushed Chandler aside and started to gently withdraw the cattle prod.

It was a model that was activated by twisting the handle slightly, and before he had completely withdrawn it, another hum of faint power filled the room, and as her insides heaved against the shocking jolt, June Wanda bit through the tip of her tongue, blacked out, and began choking on her own blood and vomit.

Ross rapidly tore through her bonds with a knife off his web belt and turned her onto her side, feeling nothing emotionally as her swollen breasts slapped against his wrists. Mentally, he was castigating himself for taking so long to recall the file photos he had reviewed long before any June Wanda had made her debut as a recording artist.

Just then a series of rocking explosions erupted in the street below, blowing out the shutters and upending a parked car down the block. Everyone, except the unconscious woman, dove to the floor, and after a series of secondary blasts sent the walls creaking, the electricity in the room flickered a few times, then went out altogether.

The men shuffled about on the floor cautiously,

taking up instinctive positions in the event they had to defend the room against a sudden attack through the door.

Slowly all fell silent, except for a few pieces of plaster still separating from the ceiling. A lone siren wailed in the distance. A frightened dog barked in a dark alley three floors below. Dust swirled about the room, settling on the Americans.

"So why *do* we gotta let her live?" Chad Chandler finally let out his little snicker as he broke the eerie calm.

The cloak of quiet returned to enshroud the tense bodies in the room, then their lieutenant spoke. "Because she is a U.S. government undercover agent," Ross cleared his throat of indecision, disgust, and the dust, "the first to successfully penetrate both the antiwar movement, the Black Panther party, and the bedrooms of the Hanoi politburo."

12

June Wanda clutched the abrasive shawl around her throat and tried to squeeze her legs tighter together, but the sedan was just too small: the large men on either side of her continued to press in on her as the Renault raced along the northern edge of Saigon, hitting every bump and pothole. She felt as if her consciousness, her mind and memories, her very identity was in danger of being jarred loose, but she dared not speak out again. They had been gracious enough to let her slip back into her clothes before taking her down into the night and tossing her into the rear seat of the small sedan.

She would never forget the words of the man on her right when she regained consciousness on the floor of the hotel room. A random VC terrorist attack had toppled power lines outside, and as sirens converged on the block and secondary explosions shook the building, she began yelling how she could take them all straight to the hidden fortune without further delay. The man on her right—Collins was his name?—had slapped her repeatedly, telling her to shut up . . . police and militiamen were soon swarming through the tenement in search of casualties, and additional blasts were sounding in housing projects all around as government troops mopped up the guerrillas responsible or raided suspected sympathizers' homes.

"Blast her ass!" the man on her left—Big Chad was it?—had insisted. *Use the clamor of sirens and rescue operations following the sapper attack to cover the sound of discharges.* "Use your head!" the man on her left had argued. "Jam the barrel down her throat if you want to—now *that* oughta serve as a makeshift silencer, ol' buddy!"

Their lieutenant sat in the front seat, and the kid with the charcoal black face drove in and out of the martial law roadblocks. The man they all referred to as a "poor excuse for a pilot" followed behind, "piloting" an identical gold Renault they had borrowed from the hotel staff with just the proper amount of persuasive scrip.

"Take a right here," the brute of a marine balanced over the stickshift in the floorboards motioned for the youth with the general's name to turn out of the maze of back alleys they had been traversing onto a wide, brightly lit boulevard.

"Le Van Duyet?" Ross glanced over at Hank O'Leary. The intelligence officer was still tightly bound with his wrists behind his back.

"That'll take us back out toward the airport," Cory said.

"Remember that torn-up pile of bricks we saw on our landing at the hot LZ, Justin?" Chandler asked the man crushed against the passenger door of the front seat. "When we had to walk a good ten miles into town?"

"Couldn't be," Ross glanced back over the headrest at Wanda.

"It's been a couple wars since the owner wasted any money on landscaping projects," she responded softly. The words held the usual tainted sarcasm, but little energy for argument.

"So now we know where we're headed," Cory said. "I say we off 'em both." O'Leary cast him an irritated look, and reverting to his schoolboy defenses, the kid chose what he thought was a humorous form of expounding. "Less bodies'll give us more mileage." Motor straining, gas pedal floored, the Renault was lucky to break fifty klicks on the speedometer. Nobody in the car laughed—they were too careful keeping track of the canh-sats sleeping at the numerous checkpoints. Any rifles fired to stop the Renault, or landrovers sent out in pursuit would require an alternate plan of action the group had already mapped out and briefly rehearsed before leaving the hotel courtyard. But the roadblocks remained dark.

Brent Collins found himself thinking about Amy the entire ride north toward Tan Son Nhut. She was in no condition to accompany them on this latest mission, and probably shouldn't even have been moved, but they had transferred her to another safe house prior to heading for the French fort. Ross had come up with two locals to watch over her, (More associates of Mr. Y? He hoped not), and the lieutenant had assured him they'd be able to purchase a permanent ticket to freedom if this, the ultimate war zone heist, panned out. Collins was out-voted, and out-gunned. He silently accompanied them, wondering if the Vietnamese watching over Amy were even then dismembering her body, spreading the evidence through the sewers of Saigon, and chucking her head out into the middle of the *Song Saigon* . . . With Ross, despite the sermons back at LZ London an eternity ago, you often wondered how far loyalty among team members really went.

"It's the same place," Chandler concluded, after they had raced along Le Van Duyet for fifteen minutes, turned down a dirt road southeast of Quoc Lo Soi, and coasted up to the edge of a cliff overlooking the sea of elephant grass that stretched out to the southern runways of the airfield. Headlights extinguished valleys before, they now watched by bright moonlight the activities of the men four hundred yards below them.

Half of the fort's outer perimeter wall had crumbled under mortar attacks a decade earlier, during skirmishes with the Viet Minh, and the two structures of red sandstone and stained brick left standing certainly appeared deserted. There were no lights anywhere, except for the dull, glowing embers that jumped about, only to float away on the warm evening breeze, when the men below sucked on their cigarettes.

Two patrol jeeps loaded down with American MPs had stopped to share a campfire coffeepot with a Vietnamese QC patrol. And they just happened to pick the shattered walls of the old landmark to shield their artificial flames from the wind.

"Christ," Ross muttered a half hour later, as he took his eyes from the binoculars and glanced at his watch: zero two hundred hours. The nametag on the sergeant leaning against one of the Hog-60s in the gunjeep blazed back at him, white on an o.d. green strip. "The same sonofabitch tripped us up when we first landed here," he hissed under his breath, so low the others didn't hear. "Fucker must work 24 hours a day . . ."

But Brent Collins had heard him. *A 24-hour cop*, he mused, watching the QCs slap the MPs on the back in playful farewell, and vice-versa as they broke up the informal chowhall and resumed routine patrol. *You don't ever wanna be a 24-hour cop*, his partner back in The World had warned him, *Else you'll take it all home with you and end up eatin' your piece, Brent . . .* God, how he'd gladly go back to the stress of the street and the badge—*As opposed to what?* the elf sitting on his shoulder mocked him silently. Collins slapped at the mosquito sucking blood from the back of his ear. "As opposed to all *this* crap," he grumbled, sweeping his arm out to encompass the endless waves of elephant grass shimmering below him to the black horizon. His eyes focused on the shadows moving about between the quonset hut-sized remnants of a once glorious and lively colonial outpost. *The new centurions were loading up.*

"They're moving out," Ross announced, his eyes carefully watching Collins. "We'll give 'em ten to leave noise range, then walk down to the fort."

"Looks like they're headed back to that compound Matt sent a blooper round into last week," Chandler, who had taken over the binoculars, observed, chuckling.

"And the Arvin MPs are beatin' feet back into the boonies," Cory stated, his own smaller, folding binoculars trained on the dark forms scurrying about below.

A string of thin, wispy clouds rolled in from the east, obscuring the moon, and when the silver glow disappeared from the land, Ross motioned for Collins to guard both Wanda and O'Leary as the entire group started down through the brush toward the base of the small, open-ended canyon.

Boobytraps. Sewell ground his teeth and shook his head bitterly as he assumed a point position fifty meters off to the right of the group. *Should be takin' it nice and easy, step by step.* He crashed through the reeds, Ithaca shotgun at port-arms so the wait-a-minute vines wouldn't snag it.

Ross held up his hand when they reached the bottom of the hillside, and directed Cory to move up and recon the edge of the fort as a precaution.

Halfway to the piles of former perimeter wall, the moon appeared like a silver beacon in the blanket of cloud cover suddenly, and he froze, a gray statue against a black backdrop. *A sentry would have spotted him long ago.* Ross felt uncomfortable. Either the elaborate defenses he had expected to encounter were non-existent, or guards were waiting to spring a pointblank ambush on them close up, and he doubted Wanda would willingly skip into the loving arms of Mister Death.

The moon darted in and out of the increasing clouds then vanished again as MacArthur disappeared between the leaning pillars that had once been the impressive gates of the fort. Five minutes of silence followed—Collins could picture the kid eating this shit up, scooping it in by the lungful as he low-crawled deeper into the structure's shadows. A deer barked somewhere beyond the treeline, and a short form, indistinguishable from the taller reeds at first, bounded back toward them out of the darkness.

"What about sentries?" Ross asked quickly.

"Past tense," Cory responded. "Them Army coppers weren't just on a coffee break, Justin. More like an after-action chat."

"Elaborate," the lieutenant demanded quickly, growing impatient. His .45 was out of its shoulder holster—he seldom carried a rifle anymore.

"I found two dinks lyin' just inside those archways, where the MPs had set up their campfire. Rounds through their foreheads, wearin' empty ammo pouches and them black pajamas."

"Weapons?"

"Missing."

"Man, it's black enough out there now to cut with a bayonet." Sewell had silently moved up from his position out on the point. For the most part, he was ignored just then.

"Either the QCs or the Americans came across the sentries before we got here," Ross decided. "Took 'em out in a brief firefight . . . or a one-sided exchange—"

"If they were sleeping on duty," Cory referred to the dead men.

"And didn't even call it in," the lieutenant concluded.

"Powder burns?" Collins asked softly.

"Negative. Shot from long range."

"Fuck the body count, anyway," Chandler agreed with Ross. "Means nothing but brass crawlin' all around, paperwork, and stuffin' stiffs into bodybags."

"Just a little shoot-em-up on the outskirts of good ole Saigontown," Ross grinned, suddenly developing a respect for the buck sergeant he had encountered twice now. "Log it as a shots-fired, no contact. Send the AKs home to hang above the fireplace mantel in snowswept Delaware or Denver."

"Thought they took out two genuine Victor Charlies," added Chandler, "but all they bagged were more o' Wanda's no-account bodyguards."

"You'd of done better with a rent-a-cop," added Cory, glancing back at the silent woman standing next to Collins. She ignored him though, concentrating instead on the sinister-looking walls of the fort, "or a guard dog."

"Let's go," Ross motioned them toward the structure. "And keep it spread out. They still might have a hold-out in there somewhere. I don't want him—"

"Or her," cut in Cory.

"—To get us all with one shot."

But they found no other sentries waiting in the misty gloom. Ross had positioned Wanda in front of himself and Collins, so that she'd take the brunt of any boobytraps, but after stepping over the bodies of the sentries with only the slightest groan of revulsion, she proceeded directly into the nearest of the two buildings that remained standing.

The door to the structure had been torn away years ago, and the first cubicle they entered—a storage room with thick, cinderblock type walls—was littered with debris: broken crates, used ration cans, and mats of vines clinging to it all through the open windows. The room was about fifty feet square, and except for an empty rice storage locker in one wall, appeared to have no other exits. *Looks smaller from the inside*, thought Ross as he scanned every foot from floor to ceiling.

"Tell me what I'm looking for," he whispered to Wanda, his pistol snugly against the nape of her neck as his eyes raced along the walls, inspecting every corner, crack and crevice. Strange the way they treated her, an acknowledged spy of the red, white and blue now, but even weirder was the lack of concern any of the team expressed about the caution Ross was exercising.

Collins expected to find a secret tunnel system similar to the elaborate set-up the government had invested in LZ London, back in the mountains of Colorado, but Wanda produced no such surprises. Instead, she went straight for the storage locker and punched in two dusty, wooden stakes that were set into the wall at shoulder height.

An imitation wood panel, thin as tapestry it now became evident, fell away and fluttered to the floor. She kicked it aside and invited Ross to push open what was obviously a hidden panel.

"Ladies first." Cory stepped in front of the lieutenant protectively, causing Sewell to shake his head in disbelief: such blind, misplaced loyalty, even after all of this . . . Could the team's integrity actually be saved?

Wanda shrugged her shoulders and stepped back to the panel. There was no hocus-pocus, or tapping of secret buttons. She merely pushed her weight against one side, and the narrow door sprang inward.

"Welcome to my villa," she said sarcastically, but even before Wanda finished her sentence, Ross and Cory had jumped past her through the doorway, into a room of comparable size.

"Mirrored room effect, Justin?" Cory was at a loss to explain where the space for the adjoining room had come from—out of thin air? *Chamber of horrors?* he wanted to add.

"No." Ross was still busy scanning the room for hostilities. "It's just a matter of architecture: building two rooms of comparable size, side by side in a larger frame and making it appear only one of them exists while hiding the other. The French had a particular fondness for it. I forget the term they used . . . glazing, or something. Whoever built this fort a hundred years ago certainly had a sense of humor."

It was hard to ignore the decorations in the room—the color of wall hangings and sparkle of fancy furniture was quite a contrast to the adjoining room cluttered with trash. It was furnished with rattan chairs holding plush European cushions, and a large brass bed with a lace canopy in one corner that gave the place that touch of class . . . a look of Paris-by-the-Seine buffet.

"Impressive," Collins admitted, "but why here, of all places . . . in this dump? Why all the glitter for just a safe house?"

"Oh this is nothing, compared to my flat on Nguyen Hue," she revealed, and Ross scratched down a mental note. "But when you spend half your life underground, it is nice to surround yourself with beauty whenever possible."

Ross locked eyes with Sewell and gestured toward the door. "Take Chad and scout the other building. You saw how they hid this room, so you know what you'll be looking for." They started out of the room. "And be careful," he added, unnecessarily.

"So show us this traitor's treasure you've been hoarding," a friendly Hank O'Leary spoke up.

Wanda, sensing some sort of condemned-man bond between them, smiled warmly and reached down to pick up a white ceramic elephant statue beside the coffee table. Ross thrust his .45 out at her, locking his elbow. "Slowly," he warned.

The "Buffy" was about a foot high, six inches wide, and boasted a brightly painted turban and glass jewel-adorned blanket and saddle. It was close to a work of art, by Saigon standards. The GIs loved them. And the room was aglow with them, Collins suddenly noticed. Buffies on the night stand beside the brass bed, in each corner, on shelves flanked by ivory dragons and jade Buddhas.

June Wanda smashed the heavy statue against the pointed edge of the teakwood coffee table, and the elephant's trunk collapsed in a shower of plaster splinters.

The dim room, illuminated by but a single Chinese lantern beneath the mirror in the ceiling over the bed, was suddenly alive with blinding sparkles as a virtual waterfall of diamonds flowed onto the bamboo floorboards, creating a glittering pile of silver ice.

"Now that's what I call international currency." Cory's eyes were wide with awe and disbelief, but Ross's had not strayed from Wanda's. This was when a woman was at her most dangerous. Or foolish.

Or both.

"The other statues are similarly rich in treasures of the Orient," she revealed as all eyes except Ross's scanned the other Buffies spread throughout the room. "Rubies, sapphires, gemstones of every taste and persuasion. Gold coins for a king's ransom in that one there," she pointed to the far corner, "and enough cocaine in that one by the bed to get an army higher than the Vietnamese Air Force."

Cory dropped his defenses as he raised his hands, palms up, and turned a slow circle, surveying all that was now theirs, to be divided up—he hoped and prayed—amongst the small team of self-proclaimed warriors. "This is a dream come true!"

"It is only wealth," June Wanda said sadly. "There are things in this world . . . in this land, much more valuable." She stared at Ross without blinking.

"Like ideals." His tone was of a man equally unimpressed.

"Yes."

"Hey, look what we found!" Chandler and Sewell had re-entered the room, and were holding up a delirious white woman dressed in a rice gunnysack. One eye was blackened shut, and her right arm appeared twisted as if it had been broken months earlier and never treated or allowed to heal properly.

"She says she's an Army CID agent," Sewell announced. "We found her in the other building, caged like an animal in an underground pit."

"Any more hidden rooms like this joint?" Ross compared the dazed agent's face with photos he had seen of the missing woman Y's people had shown him.

"No," answered Chad, "None."

The CID agent was coming to, and the men sat her down in a chair by the doorway. "Looks like we've located the investigator they sent in to break up the Bald Eagle's white slave racket," Sewell quickly put two and two together. "And all this time I honestly gave her up for dead."

"The stories she'll be able to tell—" Chandler started to say, but Cory was darting across the room, between them.

"Look out!" he yelled, as Wanda reached up and jerked down on the Chinese lantern's kite-like string.

Twin blasts of brilliant light erupted on either side of her as the anti-personnel mines built into the intricately carved walls exploded. Positioned directly under the lamp, she was inches out of the dual kill zones, between the expanding spray of a thousand beads of nine millimeter steel as they screamed forth from behind her, barely missing her arms, and tore into the people frozen ten feet away.

The brunt of the blast struck the female agent from the Criminal Investigations Division in the face, ripping her beauty away that quickly. In the time it took for the concussion to puncture her eardrums, a dedicated law enforcement officer had lost both her future and relieved smile.

Her mangled torso flopped back into a stunned Collins, protecting him from the hail of metal, though he felt something warm was dripping down his elbow now.

Young Cory, who had been rushing toward the blonde starlet with the suddenly sardonic grin across her face, had been catapulted backwards by the blast. His right arm now hung helplessly against his side as he sat between the unconscious forms of Sewell and Chandler.

The room had quickly filled with dense smoke after the boobytraps were set off, but Collins had not been deceived for long. Even now he could sense her form gliding toward him through the silver haze—the lantern, bobbing about and from side to side frantically, had survived the explosions and now sent shafts of light down through the dreamy nightclub setting of smoke.

Collins, on his knees now, brought his gun hand up and squeezed his trigger finger in, but he was clutching only space—his revolver had been slapped away by the rolling force of the concussion.

With his left hand he drew the commando knife from the sheath strapped to his calf, and sliced out at the muggy air with it.

He caught her full in the center of the thigh with the second blind whirl as June Wanda rushed for the exit, trying to vault over the lot of them, twisted elbows and assholes in the doorway. She screamed shock and outrage through her lungs, and as the blood sprayed down on him, Collins forced the blade in farther, to the hilt, then tore downward, splitting her leg open to the knee as he pulled her down on top of him.

She beat at his face with her fists—not like a helpless woman, but as a trained jungle cat patiently penned up in its circus cage somewhere only to taste sudden freedom when the trainer leaves the lock off. Pain immobilized his gun arm as she fell across his elbow wound, but he lunged forward, still blinded by thick smoke, and plunged the knife into Wanda's stomach, disemboweling her.

"Damn you, pig!" she screamed into his ears, refusing to die, her face inches from his own. "Damn you! Damn you!"

But he pushed the blade in deeper, yelling, "No!"

when Amy's face flashed before him.

"No!" He withdrew the knife and rammed it home again as Ross's face flashed before him. The lieutenant was standing on a misty riverbank, holding the head of a Viet Cong by the hair. The jungle all around him was alive with the chatter of animals screaming . . . *monkeys in the trees!*

"No!" Collins pulled the muscle in his arm, so hard did he shove the knife up into Wanda's ribcage. Chad and Matt and Cory were beating someone in his vision now, and as they turned to laugh at him and his predicament, his friend Hank O'Leary appeared beneath their flailing fists, reaching out for help, crying . . .

"Damn you! Damn you!" June Wanda was still screaming into his face as he jerked the blade about in her chest, trying to puncture the heart (where was it? *She had none!*) but tearing a lung instead. When he saw the bullies from his high school days tying Amy to a tree and forcing their cocks into her mouth, he ripped the knife out sideways, tearing the woman's chest open down the middle.

"No, damn you! No!" he screamed, slashing her throat once from ear to ear, nearly to the inner wall of the back of her neck.

But the final assault on the revolutionary from tinsel town was unnecessary. Her heart in Brent's hands, she would never make another Top-40 record, never another award-winning movie. And never broadcast another treasonous speech over Radio Hanoi.

June Wanda was dead as a Manchu legend. She had become part of the body count.

Justin Ross rose from one knee, breaking above the cloud of smoke that had settled to his beltline. Arms folded across his chest, he silently watched Collins for a few minutes as the ex-policeman slowly, methodically pulled the intestines from Wanda's belly; then the bloodied lieutenant stepped outside into the night.

He sucked in the hot sticky breeze, rubbed at his temples, and lit up a rare cigarette without glancing around for a change. Then he looked skyward, wondering if he would see a falling star.

13

The Vietnamese band was doing an excellent job of imitating one of June Wanda's current pop hits, but the GIs matching each lyric with vulgar obscenities did their best to shout down the song—making it hard to really hear the words—and the musicians finally melded the notes into a popular Johnny Cash medley of jailhouse blues.

Brent Collins smiled at the stripper dancing on the narrow stage above the band, (she had been trying to lock eyes with him during the last three ballads), toasted his drink to her bouncing chest, then returned his attention to the men sitting around the table in the Miramar nightclub.

Justin Ross, his cheek sporting a two inch horizontal gash, was working on his tenth beer and staring at the go go girls in their bamboo cages suspended amidst flashing multi-colored lights against the far wall. Chandler and Sewell also exhibited various superficial injuries, and were drinking their pain away with *ruou de* rice wine.

Cory, his arm in a cast and balancing a slender, top-heavy bargirl on his knee, smiled and raised his own glass clumsily, thinking Collins was toasting him.

Amy was on a hospital ship floating somewhere in the middle of the South China Sea, logged aboard as an Army nurse who had taken shrapnel in a VC rocket attack outside Pleiku. She would survive.

Hank O'Leary would not. In fact, he was already six feet under. *Better to be judged by six of my peers than to be carried to my grave by the same six pall bearers* . . . was Brent's favorite saying. Filling a plot in the cemetery of the Asian town he loved with all his heart. A sliver of lead the size of a pea had pierced that heart, toppling the big man forever.

At least the Marine Intelligence officer's death served to culminate a touchy situation. Ross didn't have to kill him after all.

A search of the secret room in the old French fort south of Tan Son Nhut had revealed a treasure trove of documents. Ross and Collins had spent the next two days sifting through the evidence.

Yes, June Wanda had been a senior agent in the National Security Agency. *Serving her country honorably*, Justin Ross wanted to fart in honor of her memory as he thought about the documents uncovered in one of the Buffy elephant statues. Highly confidential strategy reports smuggled from the War Rooms at the Pentagon and Saigon's own MACV installation. Papers the woman was about to pass to the communists on this latest foray to Hanoi.

For June Wanda was a double agent. And her greater loyalties—if she possessed any at all—rested with the men in Moscow. To the death.

"Made the front page," Collins announced as he thumbed through a recent copy of the *Stars & Stripes*.

" 'ACTRESS AND POP SINGER JUNE WANDA MURDERED BY KGB AGENTS ON OUTSKIRTS OF SAIGON,' " he quoted the headline. "Says here ol' Wanda got caught in the middle trying to pit the Chinese in Peking against the fat cats in Hanoi, only to have the Ruskies—*with a little help from us*, he mused—cancel her ticket. Nothing here about the NSA . . ." Damned if they hadn't arranged the evidence so things would look like a complicated communist conspiracy before they sent an anonymous tip to the canh sats.

"And nothing about the treasure we . . . liberated from Traitor June," grumbled a cranky big Chad with a drunken slur.

"So aptly put," belched Sewell. The team had set the fortune in stones aside to build an orphanage in a desolate slum of downtown Saigon—where the bleeding hearts rarely strayed. Some of the ice would, of course, be stashed away for a rainy day—*God knows the monsoon lingers over Viet Nam forever*, Cory MacArthur lamented.

A subtitled sidebar on the front page told about a Cambodian princess being terrorized by heroin-running renegades from the countryside, headed by a colorful Robin Hood-type bandit leader. Collins furrowed his brows as he concentrated on the story. Perhaps the team could journey there on their own to rectify the situation and rescue the damsel in distress before their next assignment.

Naw . . .

EPILOGUE

Prisoners of War Kenneth Southe and Sean McKane were eventually released by the communists after the farce of a peace treaty that followed the cease-fire in 1973.

The young American pilot Wanda had been paid to help free escaped on his own from the Hanoi Hilton in 1969, only to be recaptured by the Pathet Lao in the rain forests outside Sop Hao two months later. Captain McKane reported seeing the man returned to North Vietnamese custody in mid-June 1970, alive and uninjured. However in 1982, after lengthy negotiations, his remains were turned over to the U.S. government's Joint Casualty Resolution Center in Bangkok with no explanation for his death provided by his captors.

June Wanda's husband, Black Panther activist-turned-pacifist politician, part-time preacher and now somber widower, Tyrone Mohammed-Abdul, was elected democratic senator from New York.

Nine days after the election he was assassinated by a lone sharpshooter while leaving a bank. A large quantity of laundered money was found on his body. The assassin, described as a military-type with a scoped rifle, was never apprehended. . . .

THE SAIGON COMMANDOS SERIES
by Jonathan Cain

NEW ADVENTURES FROM ZEBRA

THE BLACK EAGLES
by John Lansing

#1: HANOI HELLGROUND (1249, $2.95)

They're the best jungle fighters the United States has to offer, and no matter where Charlie is hiding, they'll find him. They're the greatest unsung heroes of the dirtiest, most challenging war of all time. They're THE BLACK EAGLES.

#2: MEKONG MASSACRE (1294, $2.50)

Falconi and his Black Eagle combat team are about to stake a claim on Colonel Nguyen Chi Roi—and give the Commie his due. But American intelligence wants the colonel alive, making this the Black Eagles' toughest assignment ever!

#3: NIGHTMARE IN LAOS (1341, $2.50)

There's a hot rumor that Russians in Laos are secretly building a nuclear reactor. And the American command isn't overreacting when they order it knocked out—quietly—and fast!

#4: PUNGI PATROL (1389, $2.50)

A team of specially trained East German agents—disguised as U.S. soldiers—is slaughtering helpless Vietnamese villagers to discredit America. The Black Eagles, the elite jungle fighters, have been ordered to stop the butchers before our own allies turn against us!

#5: SAIGON SLAUGHTER (1476, $2.50)

Pulled off active operations after having been decimated by the NVA, the Eagles fight their own private war of survival in the streets of Saigon—battling the enemy assassins who've been sent to finish them off!

#6: AK-47 FIREFIGHT (1542, $2.50)

Sent to stop the deadly flow of AK-47s and ammunition down the Ho Chi Minh trail, the Black Eagles find the North Vietnamese convoys so heavily guarded it seems a suicide mission. But the men believe in their leader Falconi, and if he says they can do it, by God they'll do it!